The strange lockdown life of Alice Henry

Ann Oakley

¶

Published by Linen Press, London 2022
8 Maltings Lodge
Corney Reach Way
London W4 2TT
www.linen-press.com

Cover art: Colourbox.com
Typeset by Zebedee
Printed and bound by Lightning Source
ISBN 978-1-9196248-4-6

By Ann Oakley

Fiction

Overheads (1999). London: HarperCollins.

A Proper Holiday (1996). London: HarperCollins.

Where the bee sucks (1995). In: (eds) Jones RG, Williams AS. *The Penguin Book of Erotic Stories by Women*. London: Penguin Books.

Death in the egg (1995). In: (eds) Williams AS, Jones RG. *The Penguin Book of Modern Fantasy by Women*. London: Penguin Books.

Scenes Originating in the Garden of Eden (1993). London: HarperCollins.

The Secret Lives of Eleanor Jenkinson (1992). London: HarperCollins.

Matilda's Mistake (1991). London: Virago.

Only Angels Forget (1990). London: Virago (under the name Rosamund Clay).

The Men's Room (1988). London: Virago.

Selected Non-fiction

Forgotten Wives: How women get written out of history (2021). Bristol: Policy Press.

Women, Peace and Welfare: A suppressed history of social reform, 1880-1920 (2018). Bristol: Policy Press.

Father and Daughter: Patriarchy, gender and social science (2014). Bristol: Policy Press.

A Critical Woman: Barbara Wootton, social science and public policy in the twentieth century (2011). London: Bloomsbury Academic.

Fracture: Adventures of a broken body (2007). Bristol: Policy Press.

Gender on Planet Earth (2002). Cambridge: Polity Press.

Experiments in Knowing: Gender and method in the social sciences (2000). Cambridge: Polity Press.

Man and Wife: Richard and Kay Titmuss, my parents' early years (1996). London: HarperCollins.

Essays on Women, Medicine and Health (1993). Edinburgh: Edinburgh University Press.

Social Support and Motherhood: The natural history of a research project (1992). Oxford: Basil Blackwell (reprinted with new introduction, Policy Press, 2019).

Taking it Like a Woman (1984). London: Jonathan Cape.

The Captured Womb: A history of the medical care of pregnant women (1984). Oxford: Basil Blackwell.

Women Confined: Towards a sociology of childbirth (1980). Oxford: Martin Robertson.

Becoming a Mother (1979). Oxford: Martin Robertson (reprinted with new introduction under the title *From Here to Maternity: Becoming a mother,* Policy Press, 2019).

The Sociology of Housework (1974). London: Martin Robertson (reprinted with new introduction, Policy Press, 2019).

Housewife (1974). London: Allen Lane.

Sex, Gender and Society (1972). London: Temple Smith (reprinted with new introduction, Ashgate, 2015).

About Ann Oakley

Photo by Reuben Oakley-Brown

Ann Oakley is a writer and a sociologist. In a distinguished career lasting nearly sixty years she has produced many trail-blazing publications that span the fiction – non-fiction divide. Her first published novel, *The Men's Room*, was serialised by the BBC in 1991. This was followed by six more novels reflecting her interest in women's lives, the family, pregnancy and birth, and university life. *The strange lockdown life of Alice Henry* is her first novel after a break of more than twenty years.

Ann's non-fiction writings include pioneering books about sex and gender, housework, women's studies, reproductive health, social policy and research methods. She has also published biography and autobiography including the acclaimed *Taking it Like a Women* in 1984. Most recently, *Forgotten Wives*, and *Women, Peace and Welfare* celebrate buried histories of women's intellectual and domestic work, and their world-shaping activities as reformers and policy activists.

Ann divides her time between London and a rural retreat in the Midlands, and between writing, research, swimming, gardening and an active role in the lives of her three children and five grandchildren.

Reviews of Ann Oakley's previous novels

A Proper Holiday:

'Ann Oakley...has a sound literary reputation for the tart examination of domestic frailty....*A Proper Holiday* makes you think a little and smile a lot, which qualifies it for proper holiday reading.'

– Penny Perrick in *The Times,* 1996

Scenes Originating in the Garden of Eden:

'Don't be put off by the long-winded title, this is written by the woman who brought us the sex and sociology saga *The Men's Room* and is just as enjoyable...Oakley has a piercing eye for contemporary mores and the story rattles along. A rural romp which could make you glad to live in town.'

– Liz Page in *The Northern Echo,* 1993

'Worth reading for its old-fashioned integrity and for what Oakley has to say about men and women and the way we live our lives.'

– Jennifer Potter in *The Independent on Sunday,* 1993

The Secret Lives of Eleanor Jenkinson:
'Oakley continues to write with insight and wit about the themes at which she excels – the strengths of women, the weaknesses of men...Oakley's voice is not a shrill one. Rather, she writes about men and women with a humanity that works its own subtle propaganda. Her story of one woman's lot is candid, celebratory, funny and philosophical.'

– Sophie Johnson in *The Sunday Telegraph*, 1992

'*The Secret Lives of Eleanor Jenkinson* is an intelligent honest exploration of women and women's writing over the last 30 years.'

– *The Oxford Times*, 1992

Matilda's Mistake:
'...a delicious comedy set in the post-post-feminist, apres-Thatcher future...The social observation is detailed and generous...This is a gloriously witty fantasy written with irresistible elan.'

– *She*, 1990

'Oakley is irreverently funny about things we suppose we aren't allowed to laugh at. A savagely amusing book, the satire nifty and lightfooted, although inclined to put you in a very thoughtful mood long after you have finished reading it.'

– Penny Perrick in *The Sunday Times*, 1990

1 Alice wonders what to do with the rest of her life

It can happen to anyone at any time. The out-of-place pain, shooting fireworks in the skull, smoky vision, a labouring chest, paralysis in the foot department. Death.

I wrote my obituary early this morning when the sun had only streaked the sky with pink. 'Alice Henry, aged seventy-four, a woman of rabid determination and minor talent, died today of undisclosed causes.' Of course I knew what they were but it was too late to pass on the information. 'Her legacy includes a few books that were reasonably insightful in their grasp of significant social issues, and earned her pitiably small amounts of money. She should have been a dentist instead – people always need help with their teeth. Alice did not die peacefully, and she was not surrounded by a loving family who will remember her fondly and forever because they were all somewhere else at the time, and their memories of her will be awfully mixed. She left two sons: Jack, who is a newspaper editor, and Nathan, who leads a private life.' This last bit is a euphemism for 'we haven't been able to find out anything about him'. Anyway, I didn't leave them, they left me. That's what children do.

Most obituaries are completely fatuous. No-one can know what it's like to die except for the person who does it. It's really extraordinary how many people die peacefully. In the last edition of *The Times*, which I found on a bench in the park, fifteen out of seventeen did so. One died suddenly and one without any adverb at all. I don't suppose many of those whose lives were squandered in care homes during the Covid-19 pandemic felt very peaceful as they took their last breaths alone and completely unventilated.

The obituary was the start to a very weird day. I woke at seven to windows dripping with winter condensation. There was a message on my mobile phone purporting to be from the tax-avoiding online retailer Amazon with a story about my last order not being deliverable due to my billing address and my real address not matching. I ponder on that concept, a 'billing address'. What does it say about the tone of our civilisation? The Amazon order was for a book on rural sociology, a new consignment of zinc tablets, and a shocking yellow kettle to cheer me up. Contrary to the message, these items had all been delivered, in fact dumped on my doorstep by a delivery person who ran away speedily, as they all do now.

This episode was followed by a phone call from a person with a female voice who informed me that my electricity meter was coming to the end of its life.

'So am I,' I said.

'It needs to be replaced,' she said.

'So do I.'

She read from a routine script. 'Mrs Henry, Alice, can I call you Alice?'

'No, and anyway it should be *may* not *can*.'

She ignored this with a short, sharp silence. 'We need

to gain access to your property in order to install a smart meter. We have already sent you a number of communications about this. I would be grateful if you could please arrange with us a date for installation to take place.'

No bloody chance. We both know, I told her, that smart meters are anything but smart, and moreover they aren't a legal requirement. I had seen this one coming and had done my research. The only response that halted her flow of saccharine pleas was my refusal to allow anyone covered in unknown viruses to enter my property in the foreseeable future, given the current awful circumstances of the Covid-19, hereafter known as the BV, the Bloody Virus, pandemic.

Later on, I went to have my feet done. I'd been troubled for a while by a selection of curling yellow toenails and one bent toe. I found the place, called *Nice Feet* on Google and, with considerably more difficulty, above a station car park in Tottenham. There was a note taped to the door: *Please park to the left of the drainpipe. Stay in your car, the therapist will fetch you for your appointment.* Having come by bus, I loitered by the drainpipe. The therapist, when she descended the stairs, was dressed entirely in orange. Bright orange hospital scrubs, orange-laced trainers, orange hair ornaments, orange mask. A bright orange manner. The room was windowless, but she left the door open in the interests of viral circulation. It was nice to lie on a couch and have my feet rubbed. It was, I realised, the first bodily contact I'd had with anyone for a long time. She dug away at my feet earnestly with a mixture of files and clippers and then asked me to walk up and down so she would see how my feet actually behaved in practice. It cost £80.

When I left *Nice Feet*, my watch said I had only just arrived. We were just a few days before the annual rigmarole of the clocks going back, so I thought it possible that time had got entirely screwed up. Maybe we were all going backwards, under the influence perhaps of the aliens who were the real source of the virus, not as previously thought the animals in the Wuhan food market, nor the secretive Chinese scientists. We were all being returned to our original moments.

*

For me it was the day when I burst upon the world, bloody and screaming, or pale blue and floppy as a mute rag doll. I'm not sure which because my mother had been notoriously vague about biological detail. We are all born, but only some of us are lucky enough to inherit a birth story. Mine came from my older sister, Susie, who was seven when I was born.

'Dad brought me into the hospital,' she enjoyed telling me, 'and you had just done the most ginormous poo. It was all black and sticky and it went all over the nurse's uniform!'

I have always felt that the introduction of two sisters to one another could have been better arranged.

When I was born, I knew who I was. The alveoli of my lungs, those tiny sacs that fill with oxygen, breathed in the disinfected hospital air, and the shock of those first inhalations forced a cry out of me, a sharp existential yell such that no-one could miss the fact that I had a voice of my own. It's easy for babies. They cry when they need to. They insist that their needs should be met. Of course

14

we're all extensions of our mothers at first, and neither we nor they can tell where one body begins and the other ends. This is a problematic that has swelled the coffers of countless psychotherapists and other practitioners of black magic for absolutely ages.

When I was five, I fell off a wall and skewered my knee on a jagged paving stone. My mother stuck a plaster clumsily on the cut and told me not to be such a baby. Susie, who was entering puberty and was therefore experiencing her own unwelcome encounters with blood, was quite unsympathetic too. I recall the effect of this incident on my consciousness of self. With that unplanned descent to the hostile ground, I was stunned to discover the intense, unalterable vulnerability of the human body. Even at five, it dawned on me that the body was clearly not something to be counted on. It might let you down at any time.

Later I learnt that you could forget about the body for perhaps years or even decades, aside from the odd headache or twisted ankle or encounter with a non-fatal virus, but then there it would be again, insisting you give it some attention. Listen to me. You can't do without me. You need to look after me.

＊

Birth, death, and the bit in between, where we are all stuck now. Susie lives on her own in a small terraced house in the backstreets of Sheffield, behind the station. She's quite bent over, as befits an eighty-one-year-old who's never been fond of exercise and whose favoured occupation is lying on the sofa watching a huge TV purchased by one of her many daughters. You can see it from the street. Susie leaves it on to deter the burglars even while she's in the back making tea.

The day after my visit to the bright orange podiatrist I decided to take a small trip out of London and my usual routine. In England we were now some days into what would become known as the first lockdown but for the moment it was the only one. Quite a lot of politicians were invisibly lathered in the virus which appeared with regularity and its little signature red spikes on our television screens. The prime minister's chief adviser was spotted two hundred and fifty miles from London where he argued he was testing his eyesight. My own modest excursion was beyond the rules, but at least I wasn't going to lie about it.

So here I am in the grounds of a stately home, a place as layered in history as the world now apparently is in the BV. The sixteenth-century turrets of this grand house rise picturesquely against a silken blue sky. Carpets of fallen yellow-gold leaves stretch along paths under trees which have seen centuries of births and deaths and epidemics of this and that. These trees have looked down on families enriched by slavery and other historic ways of misappropriating the labours of others. They have watched over the discovery of parliamentary democracy, railways, old age pensions and women's rights. Now they hang over me as I pick my way across the soaking grass. If trees could think, what might their minds be doing now? Who is this woman, short with cropped grey hair like a field mushroom, a little on the rotund side, with shoes that let the water in, and an attitude of fixed attention to the movement of her body through space? She is deep in thought, her brain buzzing with electrical activity as people pass by. Her face is wet from leaky eyes which respond to the cold even as they search the landscape for interesting objects to occupy her mind. She walks fast, perhaps trying to deny the force of ageing. Her hands, folded in the deep pockets of a shabby green coat, are decorated with arthritic nodes and do not carry the conventional mark of a wedding ring. If you look really closely you can see that there might have been one there once. The skin on that finger is slightly grooved, where it once capitulated to the pressure of heavy metal.

I take myself for coffee in a small enclosed garden given over to lavender and English roses exhausted by all that summer blooming. I'm acutely conscious of the fact that I really shouldn't be here, breathing in the ghosts of summers past, lost in admiration of Elizabethan turrets ranged across a sparkling sky. The table where I sit has a big notice on it saying it has been sanitised and to please turn the notice over when you leave. I put my paper cup of coffee on it – the BV has banished china ones. The sun filters through the towering trees and tries to warm my cheeks. The cold air changes the temperature of the coffee. There's nobody else here, it's as though I'm entirely alone in a decimated universe, alone, afraid, discombobulated. And old.

I must work out what to do with the rest of my life. This is a project more usually attributed to twenty-year-olds, but that's because nobody has thought to ask us, the old ones. We're just supposed to languish at home waiting for death. 'Shielding' is what the politicians call it. What they really mean is locking us up at home. The supermarkets will charter extra delivery vans piloted by poorly-Englished drivers who will dump crates of supplies on our doorsteps for us to sanitise. Every object is a potential source of contagion, and shopping will never be the same again. It reminds me of what they told women when the Yorkshire Ripper was rampaging the streets in the 1970s – just stay at home and nothing will happen to you. Lock up the victims. So here we are again, being handed the same message. You can only see us oldies as numbers or lines in tables and graphs purporting to show the progress of the BV. I don't like being represented as a number. My personhood stands outside the statistics, waving its own cheery flag. What are the old shielding from, and why? There are worse deaths to be had than from the red-spiked virus. Collisions, bombings, burnings, paralysis, murder.

*

When I was doing French A-level a long time ago, I started to read Marcel Proust's *A la Recherche du Temps Perdu* in French, with its striking first sentence which is translated in English as 'For a long time I used to go to bed early'. This isn't a book for insomniacs. It'll do an excellent job of keeping you awake. For Proust, going to bed at any time of the day or night was a lengthy and laborious process, punctuated by many wakings, changes in position, noises, dreams, visions and memories. The title of this masterpiece, I've always thought, was mistranslated as *Remembrance of Things Past*. 'A la Recherche' is an active process, a deliberate decision to initiate a general rummaging around in the backrooms and attics of the past. Research is something you choose to do, not something that's foisted on you by a trick of the brain cells. So that's one thing I could do to pass the time – finish the whole three volumes in French. I still have them. They stare at me from the bookcase opposite my bed every night and every morning. It has the advantage of being something I could do at home now that outside options are countermanded by the BV.

Ageing prompts pandemics of mental excursions into the past. Memories appear in your head quite uninvited, when you're doing something else, paying a bill or cleaning shoes, or even working, which I still do, contrary to the political version of the over-seventies as idle, finished creatures. What's so destabilising about these memories is that they arrive laden with all the original emotion, and more. Meteoric fragments that shoot their flashing colours suddenly through your head.

*

I see myself again as a child in my parents' home, watching with an enduring feeling of safety my mother in the tiny kitchen making custard, yellow and overpoweringly sweet. I watch myself watching Susie parading around far too proudly in her first pair of heels in the narrow hall before going out to meet some boy or other, and the same flood of mixed envy and distaste possesses me. I want to be both like her and never like her.

Scraps of conversation from sixty or more years ago levitate among my brain cells. My grandmother and my mother arguing about how I was being brought up. 'You should be stricter with the child, she twists you round her little finger. And she doesn't wash her hands properly.' A bit of wisdom that haunts me a lot these days.

The fear of that first day back at school after the long escape of the summer flows over me, the smell of the wooden floor in the hall on which we had to sit to say our prayers.

My first love, a bossy girl called Janet who bullied me, although we didn't have the language for it then. The desire for her eyes to alight on my face, the veritable scent of her haughtiness.

The first man to enter me, considerately as it happens, although I had nothing to compare it with then. Afterwards I wished that I had loved him more.

The clothes I was wearing when I met Alan, a red flowered skirt and a blue linen blouse, like a garden in summer.

Feelings. Great rushes of love. Alan, the babies.

And volcanoes of irritation and anger. Alan, the babies, my mother, my father, practically my whole family, and certainly the professor of sociology at the Midlands university I went to who was an experienced misogynist. I remember him telling me how he fucked his PhD students on the standard issue scratchy brown desk, and I remember looking at it and thinking they probably got splinters in their bottoms. But if that was all they got, they were lucky. Not me, though. He never went for me. I think he could tell I was a resister at heart.

The far-off memories are the most vivid, as though we are growing back into ourselves. Growing down, rather than up. I remember Jack as a small child telling me how babies become grown-ups and then they become babies again. I remember him, with all the ingenuousness of children, asking me to tell him why people die. He wanted, as he made clear in repeated petulant assertions, not a peroration on the journey of the soul, nor a description of demography, but a precise account of what happens physically to the body at the moment of death. He wanted to know the mechanisms that cause it to cease being alive and become dead instead. Once I had tuned into this, and given him such an account, he asked me to buy him an ice-cream from the Mr Whippy van in the park.

*

I don't think Proust will do as an end-of-life project. He was a horrid little man, vain, self-absorbed, narcissistic in the extreme, with unpleasant habits such as killing rats in order to achieve sexual satisfaction. He lived in and for himself. His volumes of memories and/or researches were just explorations of his own psyche. I must find a worthier subject to occupy my remaining years and get me through this dreadfully occupying pandemic. The politicians might want to hang 'do not resuscitate' notices above our beds, but they forget our human right and burning need to have living projects of our own.

2 Woman decapitated at Kensington

From my London sitting-room window I watch the diurnal life of the neighbourhood. BBV (Before the Bloody Virus) people used to pass in an unfailingly regular pattern: parents and children kitted out with rucksacks and lunch boxes on their way to and from school; dog-walkers by the dozen, peaking around 11 a.m. when it was coffee time in the park; the runners, of course, bright-eyed at the beginning and sweat-dripping at the end of their repetitive mini-marathons; couples, alternatively amorous or argumentative; at the weekends whole families with a preponderance of dads on Sundays sent out while mums cooked the kinds of lunches that call for yet more walks.

I live in Stoke Newington, in the London Borough of Hackney. Grazebrook Road borders on one of the entrances to Clissold Park, an area of swampy greenness in an eye-wearying built terrain. The park announces itself defiantly as a multifaceted resource – playgrounds and a paddling pool, tennis courts, a skate park, a rundown bowling green/education centre, an aviary, the remains of a river and two quite splendid lakes decorated with floating white swans. At the end of my road, the gates and the railings are festooned with admonitory red and white notices: *Help us to keep Hackney safe for everyone. If the park looks full, please come back another time or go to another park.* There's a separate banner of commandments for the runners which exhorts them to keep to the left, stay two metres apart, run on their own without overtaking, and refrain from spitting. Not many runners seem to read the notice. The BV has caused them to multiply like the virus itself, and it has quite banished the regular school comings and goings.

Since I split with Alan, or he split from me, to be more accurate, thirty years ago, I've lived on my own, mostly. It's easier only having yourself to argue with. I bought this flat seven years ago with money from a small university pension. The house is three stories and I have the bottom two: a big sitting-dining room and kitchen on the ground floor, two bedrooms and a bathroom in the basement. There's a square garden full of weeds which is theoretically mine, but I regard it as foreign territory. Upstairs live an exceptionally noisy young couple who otherwise do their best to be good neighbours. It's a pleasing house to look at, solid, with imposing steps, a portico-ed blue front door, just the right kind of house to accommodate the habitual seething of a seventies' radical like me.

This is an area that has housed many protesters and non-conformists over the years and is now known for its multiculturalism, in other words as a place where the white British middle-class can boast about their politically correct life-style and enjoy lots of ethnic restaurants. Walk down Stoke Newington High Street and Church Street today and you'll see lots of such places, shutters down, mourning the enforced pause, and perhaps sadly the permanent end, of all their owners' dreams.

The bay window next to the blue front door of the

house in Grazebrook Road is where I spend most of my time. Up here I'm perched above the crowd like an umpire at a tennis match. I occupy the position of a detached observer. I work at a grubby old pine table, and when I need to think about what I'm doing, I cast my eyes beyond the page or the screen out of the window and onto the pavement that carries so much mundane life. 'Mundane' is an appalling word, it devalues what ought to be sacred – our daily life in the world.

I'm working on two things at the moment, neither of which fulfil the requirement of being a meaningful end-of-life project. The first is a manuscript about nationalism and identity by an Eastern European academic called Professor Jannsen Pluss. Even allowing for English being his second language, the text is mind-numbingly ponderous. It ought to be rewritten in simpler language, although this would run the risk of revealing the complete absence of anything interesting within it. I'm only the copy-editor, a job I do freelance to make money, and because I'm a bit obsessed with words and grammar and that sort of thing. I've had the misfortune all my life, and all the time, to think in, and about, words. Thoughts take shape in my head in words, neatly typed in an appropriate font – Calibri and Arial 12 are popular – and they run past my mind's eye like old-fashioned tele-prompts, a bit jerkily at times, occasionally sticking together, and periodically embellished with small asterisks, like dazzling fireworks. My own books, three on schooling, consumerism and my favourite premonitionary one on the environment and climate change, took ages to write because I agonised about absolutely every word and every punctuation mark. As a copy-editor I'm paid to agonise. But Professor Pluss's prose is simply too painful. Every page has at least one verbless sentence on it despite the presence of a verb being a defining feature of a sentence. Capitalisation is used entirely randomly and he seems never to have heard of the semi-colon, let alone the colon. His understanding of apostrophes is completely lacking. He puts them anywhere or nowhere. It was a very sad day, in my view, when the Apostrophe Protection Society closed down, its progenitor being ninety-six and thoroughly depressed by what people had done to it. I'm quite near the end of the tedious task of correcting Professor Pluss, and hopefully The Publisher will give me something more congenial to work on next.

The second object of my attention, when I can shove Pluss to one side and avoid looking out of the window, is an article for one of the glossies about the myths and realities of rural living. People have become more interested in this recently given how much time they spend at home. The scenery of nature has some kind of anti-rational nostalgic appeal. I don't know much about country living myself, having never tried it because my sister and I were brought up in Pinner which only pretended to be a village. Well, half of it pretended to be a village, with a few devitalised Tudor houses and a winding road called Chapel Lane where we met our boyfriends, and the rest was what they called 'garden estates' constructed in the 1920s and 1930s in a mood of post-war cosiness. Our family inhabited a redbrick semi in the un-aptly named Meadow Lane. Susie and I went to Pinner Wood Primary School in the company of Elton John, who was then called Reggie Dwight. Neither of us remember him at all.

For my magazine article on country life today I've already combed the landscape of Jilly Cooper novels about women in green wellies with shaggy dogs and marauding lovers. I've interviewed a few people, including my friend Elsa, an anthropologist who lives in a moist village in the middle of England and who is exceptionally analytic on the subject. Then I decided to take a little expedition into rural sociology in the hope of finding something more engaging to write about. Hence that book, nestling beside the yellow kettle in my Amazon delivery parcel. It proved to be a good buy, introducing me speedily to something that sounded quite promising – the report of research into life in an English village published in 1909 by a woman called Maud Davies. Her book is referred to as a classic, one of the first studies to probe the mundanities of country life among working people, so much so that the people whose village she wrote about tried to stop her publishing it. Unusually for the time, says my newly-delivered sociology book, Maud Davies's research combined acute personal observation with the collection of numerical data and the interrogation of documents such as maps and parish records. She was one of a group of women researchers who pioneered the systematic study of ordinary social life at a time when men were more given to armchair theorising about it. With a background at the London School of Economics and with Beatrice Webb, both highly esteemed institutions, Maud had equipped herself for a promising career in British social science. Her future looked bright. She was an interesting woman, I thought.

The Saturday after I discovered Maud Davies I went to do my weekend stint, another income-supplementing pastime, at a bookshop called *Another Chapter* in the High Street. The BV was threatening bookshops with closure so they were teetering on the edge. It was raining and there were only two people inside the shop, a man in a wet grey mask and a woman of about my age in a purple flowery one. Her glasses were misted up and she was having trouble reading anything. When I arrived, Sally Dixon, the bookshop owner, was busy renewing the 'Please remember social distancing' signs and she seemed somewhat preoccupied, I thought by the general challenge of staying financially afloat in a pandemic, but in fact, as she informed me, by an infestation of fleas that had landed on her cat.

'Do we have a copy of Maud Davies's *Life in an English Village*?' I asked Sally.

'Never heard of it,' she said unhelpfully.

'Well, perhaps we could order it?'

'Why do you want it?'

'You don't ask other customers that,' I pointed out.

'You're not a customer.'

'Actually I am, at this precise moment.'

I was five minutes early for my shift, and I am an extremely pedantic person. This helps when it comes to grammar, syntax and punctuation, but I can see that otherwise it may be annoying.

The man was lurking in the architecture section and was in the process of taking off his wet grey mask. Sally went over and rebuked him. He turned a pair of amazingly blue eyes on her and I heard her exclaim, 'Oh, it's Stephen Dearlove, isn't it? I'm sorry, I didn't recognise you.'

'No, it's quite difficult, isn't it, with all these disguises we have to wear now.' His voice was a low tenor, almost operatic in tone, quite captivating at a time when there was little to be captivated by.

I watched him as he picked first one and then another

tome off the shelves. I noted how he seemed always to turn to the index first (indices, by the way, which are the often-ignored plural of index, bear surprisingly little relation to the text in many cases), and how careful he was to return every book to the exact same place on the shelf.

'You do know who he is, don't you?' Sally whispered loudly when we were both back behind the till.

'Not a clue.'

'Honestly, Alice, can't you remember anything?'

I remember a lot, as we've already established, but not necessarily everything. There wouldn't be enough room in my head for that. Stephen Dearlove was apparently a poet. Sally later directed me to a shelf-load of his books. He'd given a talk in the bookshop about a year ago, which is how she knew what he looked like without his mask. She said I'd been there too, and, now she mentioned it, I did faintly recall the lack-lustre evening, poorly attended by the locals who couldn't drum up much enthusiasm for modern poetry or for the wine in limp plastic cups, a dreadful Chardonnay Sally had got on sale or return from Aldi.

Today Stephen Dearlove carried a hefty, illustrated book about trees over to the till. 'It's for my nephew,' he explained, then asked us if we had sanitised it.

'No, we can't spray alcohol on our books, it rots them,' Sally replied, frowning rather.

He paid with a credit card after carefully wiping the card reader with something he whipped out of his pocket, and then asked us to order a copy of the latest enormous biography of Sylvia Plath. He clearly had a preference for big books.

Sally left me in charge while she went for an eye test at

Scrivens. I used the time to do a little random internet searching about Maud Frances Davies. I was rapidly becoming rather hooked. And what I found immediately was a string of references concerning, not her life, but her death. Maud Davies was found dead on the Metropolitan Railway in London between High Street Kensington and Notting Hill Gate on Sunday, February 2nd, 1913, at 2 o'clock in the morning. A railway worker called William Clark discovered her body. *Maud Frances Davies, aged thirty-seven, an authoress, and a woman of independent means.* She had been decapitated and a number of small puncture wounds were found over her heart, one of which had penetrated it. A broken hatpin was found in it. The last train had passed an hour and a quarter before William Clark found her, but her watch had stopped at 4.50 p.m. the previous day, so that was probably when she died. The watch, a cheque drawn on Child's Bank, and her hair, were used by her brother to identify her. As far as I could see, the mystery of her death had never been solved. Accident, murder or suicide? The inquest recorded an open verdict. Remarks were made during the proceedings about a recent love affair and Maud's involvement in an investigation of something called The White Slave Trade. It was suggested that some 'ruthless element' in the said trade might have been responsible for her death. This untimely end to her brilliant career made her even more intriguing.

'I've got Elschnig's pearls in my left eye,' said Sally triumphantly on her return from Scrivens.

'Is that something to be proud of?' I inquired, still immersed in Maud and paying insufficient attention to Sally's optical news.

'Well no, but it's quite rare.'

'So is being decapitated by a train,' I said.

She looked at me curiously. 'Are you feeling alright, Alice?'

It was still raining when I walked home from *Another Chapter* past all the locked down non-essential shops selling mobile phones and reconditioned washing machines and then the posh bit of the High Street decorated with organic vegetables and vegan delicatessens – yes, this is the plural of delicatessen, even though it seems wrong. Most of the shops have stayed open in our area with assorted pavement signs and notices instructing us to stay apart, using flexible definitions of what staying apart means. Wearing a lavender silk mask made by my fifth niece, Crystal, I bought a piece of haddock for my supper. The last of Susie's children, Crystal, is the most mentally healthy, in my opinion, due mainly to having been benignly neglected as an afterthought child.

After I'd cooked my haddock – nothing complicated, just baked in foil with lemon, olive oil, garlic and parsley – and watched the news – more deaths, more directives about how to lead our lives delivered by men in suits and women imitating them – I settled down with a glass of Sauvignon Blanc Val de Loire to pursue my enquiries into the life and death of the mysterious Maud Davies. I ought to be working on the piece about living in the country, or finishing Pluss, or phoning my sister, or WhatsApp-ing my sons, or laying mouse traps for the scurrying that quite possibly isn't only in my head. The rubbish needs emptying, and the flat could do with a good clean. But Maud calls me with the high-pitched, desperate voice of someone who is trapped in the past.

*

Maud Davies is lucky to have found me since I'm quite a dab hand at negotiating my way round statistical and genealogy sites, having put in some practice a few years ago helping a computer-phobic historian with his research. He should have acknowledged me as a joint author of his paper because he really couldn't have written what he did without me, but I think he regarded me as a secretary. Maud's first appearance in the Census was in 1881 as a little girl of five living with her family in Surrey in a grand, originally seventeenth-century, house called Mitchen Hall with a gabled roof and multiple chimneys. There were four children and four servants. The other children were called Cecil, Byam and Warburton. I assumed Cecil was a boy but his middle name was Charlotte so he wasn't. The servants were Emma (a housemaid), two Elizabeths (a cook and a nurse) and Annie (a nursery maid). Maud's father was described as a 'Barrister at law not in practice and Local government inspector of schools'. Her mother, like most wives at the time, wasn't credited with an occupation at all. She came from a family called Conant, one of those multi-branched moneyed clans who inhabited swathes of middle England for centuries. So there is little Maud, encapsulated in this bubble of upper-classness, with just thirty-two years of her life yet to run. By poking around further in the family tree I can see that this was nevertheless more than her sister, Cecil Charlotte, or her brother, Byam. Cecil died aged fifteen in 1892 and Byam as a soldier in the Boer War in 1902. Maud would have carried the grief of these losses with her to her own death in the railway tunnel in 1913.

My researches are interrupted by Mick and Angie clattering down the stairs. I watch them going out of the front gate. She goes first with a white knitted hat on her dark flowing hair, not a good choice for the rain – she's a very impractical young woman – and then him, in huge dark glasses, carrying a Tesco bag. They aren't wearing masks. I must buy some more. It's probably a fiction that the masked will outlive the BV, but such fictions are handy at times like this. A police car insinuates its sapphire warnings into the darkness. The BV has turned our street into a thoroughfare for flashing-light vehicles. An ambulance outside a neighbour's house doesn't raise the pulse rate as much as it normally would, but I still find it very destabilising.

*

A long time ago the boys were young and we were living in the much less multicultural Crouch End. Jack was a very wise seven and Nathan a very boisterous four who was given to throwing himself at and off everything. Once a week I went to an evening class on illness and literature, just an excuse to escape the house really. We had a dog at the time, some kind of woolly grey mongrel, rather unpredictably behaved. I was never in favour of getting a dog but Alan and the boys insisted. As I walked back one evening after discussing Elizabeth Barrett Browning and her mysterious illness on the sofa from which Robert rescued her, I saw an ambulance outside our house. I ran to see my darling rumbustious Nathan being loaded into it, having been badly bitten by the unpredictable woolly dog. He (the dog) was put down. An interesting term, why not put up? Nathan enjoyed the attention of the ambulance crew and the nervous young doctor who sewed him up. Alan got off fairly lightly with a few broken plates hurled at him and stern warnings about his accelerating deficiencies as a father.

The Decennial Census of England and Wales, Scotland and Northern Ireland is conducted every ten years, which is why it's called decennial, a neat word most people wouldn't know. The first ever Census had the ignoble purpose of counting the taxable population or the number of men who could be sent to their deaths in war. It takes 100 years for Census data to be released for public consumption, so 2022 will be an exciting year for Census-plunderers, but 2032 won't be, as the entire 1931 Census for England and Wales went up in flames in a Middlesex storeroom a week before Christmas in 1942. Six fire watchers were employed to prevent this happening but it's thought that one of them chucked a lighted cigarette at the piles of schedules and enumeration books, which was inordinately careless. Why didn't the other five put the fire out, especially given the liberal quantity of fire hydrants with which the office was apparently supplied?

Asking questions of history only generates more questions. That's why ultimately the answers can only be supplied by the imagination.

I can see from the 1891 Census that Maud and her family have moved from prosperous Surrey to the even more prosperous Broughton Grange estate in Oxfordshire. The ghosts of the Bloomsbury set walk here, in gardens and meadows seven times the size of Clissold Park: the writer Lytton Strachey, with his long red beard and his delicate white hands painted so carefully by Dora Carrington, his suicidal lover; that querulous, philosophizing conqueror of women, Bertrand Russell and so many others, all under the direction of the extraordinary Ottoline Morrell whose family owned the place for two hundred years. Virginia Woolf called Ottoline Morrell 'garish as a strumpet', and said she walked 'like a cockatoo with bad claws'. I do love the Bloomsberries, they were so determined to have fun, however awful life was.

Maud is fifteen when the Davies family rent Broughton Grange. Another brother, Claude Martin, had appeared, born like his siblings in St George's Square, Pimlico, so the family was wealthy enough to have two houses. On Census night in 1891 they were in Broughton where they were enumerated along with another family, the Vandeleurs: Frank, a clerk in the War Office, and his no-occupation wife Emily, and two daughters, Evelyn and Sheila. It takes a little more fiddling around in Ancestry public member trees to work out the link: Emily Vandeleur was Maud Davies's aunt, her mother's sister. In 1891 the number of servants has gone up to five to accommodate the increase in household size. Instead of a nurserymaid there's a schoolroom maid, and a coachman has been added. The cousins Maud and Evelyn were the same age and would have roamed the Broughton estate together.

How did the Davies family end up in rural Bloomsbury? Cecil Charlotte's death in 1892 was registered in Banbury, Oxfordshire, so she probably died at Broughton Grange. I'm tempted to order a copy of her death certificate but that would be carrying all this too far.

Like Maud Davies's heart in the Metropolitan Railway tunnel, my night was punctuated by dreams. Disconnected pictures of the past rearranged themselves like a badly done jigsaw puzzle: a small girl, perhaps one of Susie's or perhaps Maud herself, being hoisted in the air by a tall man standing beside an empty aquamarine swimming pool; a train rattling over some obstruction on the tracks; a band of children in Edwardian clothes playing in sun-splattered parkland riddled with peacocks who had hatpins growing out of their heads. Although I wasn't personally attacked in these dreams, I certainly felt attacked when I surfaced in the morning. A thick fog claimed my head. It needed the kind of light relief the custodians of the BV pandemic had deprived us of ('of which the BV pandemic had deprived us' would definitely be better): a gathering and a gossiping over a meal and a bottle of wine, sharing a gross of popcorn in front of an awful film, perusing clothes in unlikely shops with friends and without any intention of buying. I badly needed a new coat, but there was nothing to be done about that so I put the old one on and went to the park. Walking is the only fog-relieving pursuit left to us.

The bushes and the trees were nearly bare now. Shrivelled blackberries thrust themselves into my line of vision, but I had to focus my attention on the slippery leaf-strewn path. I walked round in the shadow of the two churches, the old and the new, past the playground with its reduced sprinkling of children, and round to the north (I'm told it's the north but I was born entirely without spatial skills). Opposite Clissold House a lone deer grazed morosely. Attributing emotion to an animal is an ism we're not supposed to commit these days, but the lack of human company changes all our perspectives. Our brains as well as our bodies are locked down.

The deer in this park are the non-breeding sort, and, after a decade or so of being gawped at, the old ones are carted off to a deer retirement home in Devon, and replaced with new models. A few years back, shortly after I came to the area, a campaign was launched to free Clissold Park's wildlife. On a very hot weekend even further back, Alan and I took Jack and Nathan, who were both by then fully committed to the sultry part of adolescence, to the London Zoo where a new exhibit was advertised – a human in a cage. We saw him rise from his bed, dress for the office, go to work, eat, go home and back to bed again, all in one unbroken series of motions. We didn't see him excrete or copulate but the animals did that. That's what it feels like, this lockdown. We're caged and observed, a condition that condemns us to continuous self-observation – watching, noticing, criticising, evaluating, analysing. The boundaries between the self as subject and the self as object melt and disappear. Politicians play games with the truth, and then we launch our own games, trapped in the tangle of fact and fiction.

3 Going to the hospital
about my ankle

A Tuesday in November and I'm going to the hospital about my ankle. This is a yearly event and is normally of no consequence except this year, being that of the great pandemic, it's the only assignation in my diary for the whole week, and is thus a happening of some significance. Instead of rushing, and getting to the hospital at the last minute, and forgetting my appointment letter, and having a brain hopelessly stuck in whatever it last focused on, I am up early debating what kind of socks to wear. Mr Abraham, the consultant, is a dashing New Zealander with streaky blonde hair. When he stands up, he's much shorter than I expect, probably because the status we assign to doctors, or rather that they require us to assign, always makes them seem bigger than they really are. The socks are important because Mr Abraham will want to rest his clinical gaze on my ankle which has never been the same since it was bent in a collision with a pavement outside a bar in Lanzarote seven years ago. It goes numb sometimes, and is prone to give way without warning on walks in Clissold Park, and then it will swell alarmingly and I'll waste a lot of time studying it.

The sun is shining for a change, and on the walk from the bus stop to the hospital I promise myself a treat in the patisserie after my appointment, except that it's no longer there. The blinds are down, all signs of life gone. It was a place with long tables where you were invited to be friendly while trying not to drop crumbs everywhere – altogether too Covid-friendly an environment to survive.

Outside the revolving plate glass doors of the hospital a man in a mask barks out something interrogatory to me. It's directed at my right ear which is a little deficient on the aural front, so I try the other one. Yes, I do have an appointment. And yes (fumbling for my phone) I can prove it. The signage in this building has always been up the creek so it takes me a while to reach my destination – the clinic on the fourth floor which deals with bones. Three women in masks sit behind a curved clear plastic shield. They're glued to their computer screens, so they don't notice me standing there. The usual strategy of staring hard at them, coughing loudly and shifting from one (damaged) foot to the other doesn't work, especially not the coughing which provokes hostile looks from the people in the queue behind me because I could be emanating the BV.

I go to sit down in the waiting area. Out of the window, the flat grey landscape is interrupted by a few naked trees and tall buildings in the distance. I've been in this hospital several times as what they call an inpatient, a term it's hard not to hear as impatient. On one of those occasions, I had the good fortune to be allotted a bed by the window. I was in a ward high up, higher up than I am now, and I was delighted to discover that at night the window by my bed became a theatre of many-coloured lights: a whole syncopated scintillation of reminders that life goes on however ill or quietly decomposing you are. Every night I asked the nursing staff to leave the blinds on the window up, so I could fall asleep watching the play. It's not a widely known fact, but it is a matter of common sense, that sick people get better faster if they've got something nice to look at.

I wait forty minutes outside the door that has Mr Abraham's name on it. Since the door doesn't open and shut at all during this time, I assume that the patient in there must have some desperately extensive complaint that involves thorough examination of many bones. Perhaps not just the foot and the knee and the hips and the pelvis but the entire spine and all that branches off it. Eventually I ask the three women at the reception desk what might be taking Mr Abraham so long, and they exchange knowing glances and say it's quite usual for Mr Abraham to take his time. Then one of them gets up rather slowly and reluctantly and knocks on his door. I hear her give him the information that he has a patient waiting. He closes the door and then a few minutes later opens it quite nonchalantly, as though absolutely no delay has happened, and calls my name. Inside the room I can't see any evidence of what he might have been up to all that time. There's no pile of hospital notes he might have been perusing – and anyway real hospital notes hardly exist any more. There's no disarray or dishevelment in the room such as might suggest some other medical or non-medical pastime. I want to ask him what he's been doing but I don't quite dare. I look him squarely in the eye as far as I can, given the mask situation. The eyes do carry traces of the expressions that decorate faces lower down, but only traces. He's perfectly polite to me, and after taking a quick look at my foot and asking me to wiggle it around and stand on it, he tells me to continue with the exercises he'd given me last time, which I've forgotten, and come back in a year. So the consultation is a complete waste of time. I don't think Mr Abraham even notices my socks, which are a particularly fetching pair of blue Marimekko ones I bought on impulse at an airport in Finland.

'It's just one example of body housework,' I complain to my friend Elsa on the phone later. 'If it isn't my ankle it's my teeth and if it isn't my teeth it's that mole under my left breast and if...'

'I know, Alice,' Elsa interrupts. 'It happens to all of us. You need something else to think about.'

'I do know that,' I say.

4 A week in the country

Elsa and I met at university decades ago when we were insouciant young things and much less worldly-wise than we pretended to be. She wore contact lenses, which I thought very mature, and I was already an aunt, which she considered amusing. My sister Susie had rushed into marriage with a pet-shop owner, resulting in a miscellany of cats, dogs, parrots, fish and babies. Elsa had grown up in Croatia and came to England for education at the instigation of a cousin who mistakenly thought this part of Europe was a good idea. We were both the first people in our families to go to university, so we didn't really understand what it was all about.

I think I thought it was about having fun for three years and, most importantly, finding out about sex and other non-academic pastimes. Elsa was much more serious. She was frighteningly work-focused right from the start and talked about the essays she was writing or the group discussion papers she was preparing or her quest for hard-to-get volumes in the library on all the foggy walks we took that first term. It was a horrible winter and smoking fuel hadn't yet been banned. We walked endlessly across the campus of East Midlands University from one building to another and back again. The buildings were more or less indistinguishable one from another, apart from the colours of their windows and doors and their labels. The architect had cataracts in his eyes like Monet, but blurred images of bricks were really no help in designing a new university. East Midlands University, known as EMU, used to be Motley Poly until it was repackaged as a higher grade institution, but it was still in Motley, a medium-sized Midlands town with a reputation for epidemic rates of teenage pregnancy.

Elsa and I met because we were assigned beds in the same pre-packaged room housed in a block called Longfellow, with blue windows. All the blocks were named after male writers, but nobody noticed that mistake then. Elsa and I clung together through all the traumas and exhilarations of student life, except that she spent more time in the library, painted green and called Shakespeare, of course, and I spent more time in bed with young men, sequentially not simultaneously. Elsa was studying anthropology and knew she wanted to be an academic, though she never explained why. I was doing a sociology and English literature degree, and just planned to do well enough for my mother not to complain that all that penny-pinching had been a waste of time. She liked to exaggerate, my mother, especially about the sacrifices of motherhood. She was still doing that when she died, though at one point she did grasp my hand with hers which was exceptionally cold, and utter the mysterious words, 'Don't believe any of it, Alice, I made it all up'.

The EMU days welded Elsa Posavac and Alice Henry together in that kind of friendship that weaves its resilient way through changes of jobs, relationships, homes, body size, hair colour and income, through accidents, illnesses, driving fines, burglaries and broken freezers, and past all those periods of minor mental collapse that seem to dog women's lives. Now, years later, we go on holiday together and to the theatre sometimes, though not at the moment, of course, and we speak to each other once or twice a week, or more often if we think we have something of consequence to report.

Women our age commonly spend a lot of time thinking about their children and grandchildren. Elsa doesn't have any, her career-focused life having left no space for motherhood. So, with respect to my need for a new engaging project, she's very unlikely to point me in the direction of more nurturance.

I am very fond of my boys but I don't understand them. Jack lives in a village called Steeple Claydon in Buckinghamshire with Patti who runs an eco-cosmetic business from their marble-topped kitchen. It's quite a dull village, the nearest tourist attraction being a grand country house where Florence Nightingale wrote some of her notes on nursing. Jack edits a local newspaper and has been writing a novel for a very long time. We aren't allowed to mention it. The prospect of his finishing it is almost as worrying as the possibility that he never will. Jack and Patti have twins, Sam and Sara, who are obviously not identical since they are of different sexes, a point many people miss. Patti gave birth to them at home which concerned me but was all part of her mission to be an earth mother. My other boy, Nathan, has red hair like his Scottish father and he does something in the music industry from a canal boat in Leiden in the Netherlands. At least, when I last heard from him that's where he was. I'd be happy to visit him there or wherever he currently is, but of course the BV has stopped all that.

43

Not that Jack and Nathan want me to mother them. Even as children, I felt they accepted my mothering with slight disdain. When I was good, I was good enough, but when I was bad, they didn't really notice. I do sometimes think I'd like to be an involved granny for Sam and Sara and from time to time I have them to stay for a night or two in Stoke Newington, and take them on day trips to the Zoo, the Science Museum and Legoland. But I don't think they like London very much. Now that they're nearly teenagers they have incomprehensibly absorbing social lives of their own, of course.

In other words, I don't think motherhood or grandmotherhood will solve the problem of how to spend the rest of my life.

'I can't come and stay with you,' I said when Elsa rang up yesterday to suggest this. 'Remember we're in the middle of a pandemic and we have to stick to the rules and regulations about bubbles and so forth.'

'Oh phooey,' said Elsa, 'you haven't got Covid, have you? No. Well, neither have I. You can't catch anything here because there are almost no people and it's very sterile. You can wear a mask and gloves if you like. I've put a one-litre bottle of sanitising fluid in the spare room.'

She met me at the station, a thin, alert creature in a tailored cinnamon raincoat, and drove me to her village which isn't far from our Alma Mater, a Latin term meaning 'nourishing mother' that by no stretch of the imagination describes the institution we attended. Elsa's cottage is very pokey with rooms leading out of other rooms and corridors where you least expect them. It was dark when we got there. She'd left a single light shining by the front door that created a small circle of brilliance in an otherwise entirely black world. The light illuminated a selection of plastic plants in hanging baskets by the front door. The garden is also full of plastic flowers because Elsa doesn't like gardening any more than I do. I waited behind her while she searched in her bag for her keys and I took the opportunity to inhale the wet earthy smell of the countryside. Then I was ready to inhale the smell of her house – the ashes of a wood fire, the fragrance of an old fried egg, and an odd scent of maybe tea and lavender. She noticed me sniffing and explained that she'd bought a new room spray.

'Now, Alice,' she said firmly, 'at six o'clock when the church clock strikes the hour, I will make us a cocktail. At seven o'clock I will make dinner. We're having a brodetta, that's fish stew to you. You will make the salad. I have a nice ginger cheesecake for dessert from the new Waitrose. We can watch the news if you like.'

Personally, I'm not in favour of watching the news any more because there really isn't any. Just more about the BV and graphs with rising lines and dreadful stories about old bodies in care homes and displays of men in suits who can't make up their minds what to do and others who are much given to temper tantrums.

Elsa's plan was fine by me. The fish stew sounded enticing. We sat in front of her real wood fire, not one of the two fake electric ones she has for convenience. We ate the brodetta in front of the real fire at the appointed hour. There was absolute silence all around us except for the odd owl in the trees on the crest of the hill above the cottage, and the odd dog depositing its faeces in the village undergrowth.

'Don't you get lonely here?' I asked. The contrast with

my own flat in Stoke Newington was tremendous, something that always struck me when I visited her. Here there was simply nothing to watch out of the window, absolutely nothing.

'I am content,' she said. 'We are old women now, Alice. The days of wine and roses have departed.' Elsa's Croatian accent, which lingers despite all her years in England, gives her speech an authoritative crispness. Anything she says sounds so indisputably true.

I found myself quoting:

You are old, Father William, the young man said,
And your hair has become very white,
And yet you incessantly stand on your head,
Do you think, at your age, it is right?

'*Alice in Wonderland*, Chapter Three, Advice from a Caterpillar.' Because of my name, I know the text well, and those cocktails of Elsa's were very strong.

'It's far too soon to give up, Elsa. We must go on standing on our heads.' Of course, talking of heads made me think of Maud Davies and her severed one, so I told Elsa all about it. She was most intrigued. But her reaction was rather too analytic. She immediately moved on to how concepts of accidental death have changed over time. I just saw poor divided Maud spread out on the railway tracks, a life brutally halted far too soon.

*

The next morning, after porridge and an interrupted night due to the church clock, Elsa told me she'd been ruminating on Maud's story and she had a few thoughts about it. We went for a walk round the village in the rain. All you could hear was the dripping – rain falling off and onto every available surface including the jumbled roofs and gables and the dry stone walls that weren't dry at all. Cutting through the middle of the village, the tiny river rushed past with unusual size and vigour. The rain presented a serious challenge to my London footwear. I was thinking I should buy myself some flash new wellingtons when Elsa broke into my waterlogged thoughts.

'Have you considered that mention in the inquest reports of the white slave trade? It was not uncommon for philanthropic young women at that time to concern themselves with the capture and sale of females for prostitution and domestic work. Mind you,' she went on reflectively, sidestepping a pile of dog shit hidden in the mud, 'according to some feminists the two are the same. Women who live with men and do the housework and have the sex are no different from prostitutes. It is a respectable theoretical position.'

Elsa had an annoying habit of going off on academic tangents. We turned the corner by a ruby red cotoneaster bush and saw fat cows chewing wetly in the field on the other side of the road. The rain intensified, hitting our backs with renewed virulence.

'This Maud,' Elsa persisted, 'when she met her unfortunate death, where had she been and was she involved in that campaign to stop trafficking? I have some papers upstairs on the National Vigilance Association if you're interested. Whiteness,' she continued, obscurely. 'Purity. Virginity. The unblemished nation. The body politic. In the early twentieth century the topic of young

British women stolen into sexual slavery was very much in vogue. It is most interesting, but some of it is quite farfetched. There was a novel by that woman, the American actress who did Hedda Gabler, what was her name... Elizabeth something? She also wrote a play, very ahead of its time, about a mother who strangled her handicapped child.' Elsa rubbed her hands together distractedly. 'Robins, that's it: Elizabeth Robins. And the book about the white slaves, that was called *Where Are You Going To?*'

'A question for our time,' I said.

'What?'

'The BV. Being stopped and interrogated.'

'Oh yes. And in fact there were associations of ladies that sent volunteers out to railway stations and parks to question young women about their destinations.'

'In case an evil man was luring them somewhere for immoral purposes?'

'Just so. The imagery was very striking. Those who made a study of this trade were extremely fixated on ideas about the contamination of the pure unsexed body. Women's bodies. Only virgins possessed pure bodies. It was all very sexist and also racist. Nations had to be pure and white and so did bodies.' Elsa shook her head with twenty-first century disbelief.

'But was it true?' I asked. 'Did it really happen that large quantities of virgins were trafficked into prostitution? And, if so, how did they do it and which routes did they use and who were they, anyway?'

'The definition of white slavery,' enunciated Elsa carefully, 'was the procurement by force, deceit or drugs of a white woman or girl against her will for prostitution. As I said, *white* here is a metaphor, not a literal description.'

I was by now keen to believe that Maud was onto something of considerable importance when she met her dreadful death. No complicated theories about suicide or accidents were needed to account for it, just a simple narrative about bad men and good women.

'I can't remember all that much about the white slave material,' said Elsa. 'I taught a module on The Empire once at the University of East Anglia and I found the white slave industry a useful way of introducing students to the idea of the female body as a site of nationalistic desire. If you're interested, which you obviously are, I'll go into the attic and see if I can find the box with the UEA material in it.'

When we were safe from the rain inside the cottage, I got out my notes, which I had thought to bring with me, as I knew Elsa wouldn't be able to resist a good story involving the human body. Her specialty was medical anthropology. She'd written a few books about it and a ream of articles and was generally known as an expert on the cultural framing of physiology and disease – how different cultures come up with different ideas about how the body works. Her last book was about the meaning(s) of hair. *The Culture of Hair* did well after a farsighted marketing person at Elsa's publisher came up with the idea of promotional leaflets offering discounts which she got distributed to smart hairdressers.

I had taken a look, courtesy of my expensive Ancestry subscription and during another quiet spell in *Another Chapter*, at Maud Davies's travelling habits. The shipping companies keep handwritten lists of people's names and occupations which have been digitalised. It really is terribly exciting to see these scrawled records of journeys across the oceans of the world. Maud had sailed from Southampton to Kingston, Jamaica, on a ship called *The Arcadian* in December 1912. En route, it stopped at Madeira, Bermuda and Trinidad. Then she left Jamaica for New York on 16th January 1913 on a German vessel, *The SS Prinz August Wilhelm*. Two weeks later she travelled to Liverpool from New York on *The Baltic*, and six days later she was dead.

All of which generates many questions. How usual was it then for a single British woman in her thirties to go on such voyages? What was it like on those ships? The crossing would have taken many days. It was winter and big ocean liners didn't have stabilisers, so Maud would probably have been seasick. And, most important of all, what did she actually do in Jamaica and in New York? Was it, in fact, anything to do with stopping the white slave trade?

'Well,' said Elsa matter-of-factly, 'this is obviously your project, Alice. This will see you through the pandemic and stop you wittering on about ageing and all your medical appointments. You must write a book about Maud Davies.' She folded her hands in her lap and smiled coquettishly at me, she, the author of dozens of academic books, all with masses of footnotes. She knows how much I hate footnotes. They are the bane of my existence as a copy-editor. Missing footnotes, misaligned footnotes, mis-numbered footnotes, footnotes that go on for pages, and footnotes that make no sense to anybody, and not even the author can remember why they were written in the first place. A book about Maud Davies would need footnotes. No thank you.

The spare room in Elsa's cottage is tucked away under

the eaves. There's a big white wooden bed and a crimson velvet chair and not much else apart from the litre bottle of sanitising fluid. As the light dimmed in the late afternoon I lay on the bed and regarded through the window the vast open sky. Over the nude black treetops a few birds hovered uncertainly, trying, like the rest of us, to make up their minds about the advisability of travel. A partial moon rose in the sky, shockingly white and brazen, its light splashed over everything – gardens, cottages, fields, paths, dustbins, the glaring yellow container of salt just down the road. Elsa's next door neighbour, a taciturn fellow in his eighties clothed in an over-worn duffle coat, came out of his house with a letter in his hand, startlingly white in the moonlight. I was standing by the window unashamedly spying. I felt that perhaps, all things considered, I was becoming a spy, some kind of blunderbuss amateur detective, or as Marcel Proust would have much more elegantly put it, a researcher in pursuit of the past.

*

There are researchers and there are the researched. The next day I changed positions while Elsa was occupied with a Zoom meeting involving several of her Croatian cousins who'd bought fluffy puppies at the same time. I guessed that the conversation was about doggie haircuts and continence training. Elsa hated dogs, so she probably muted herself and carried on with her latest book about feet and the shoe industry.

My own phone rang while she was still occupied with this canine nonsense. Since mobile phone reception in Elsa's village is rubbish, the ringing of the phone was an extraordinary event. Its screen showed one of those disturbing 'private number' alerts. Having established that I was Alice Henry, the private number woman explained she was calling about a study on memory which I joined in an absent moment a few years ago. I've long forgotten its purpose, but I fill in my online questionnaire dutifully every week and report absolutely no changes of any kind, except for once when I got cross about the lack of feedback and fed it a tissue of lies about malignant lymph nodes in my elbow and searing pains in my nose. There was still no feedback. Every two years the researchers in this study want us to answer a lot more questions in a telephone interview. How on earth did they manage to get through to me here? The woman – she said she was called Jill but she didn't have a surname – asked me if I could remember my name. When was I born? And so on. Did I mind if she asked me some personal questions about sensitive issues? Was I incontinent, could I still wipe my own bottom, was I capable of washing myself and shifting myself upstairs? There was a long section on teeth. Had I ever lost one? Were any of the ones I still had crowned or root-canaled? Which ones? How many teeth did I actually have? I stuck a finger in my mouth and made a rough guess.

It went from bad to worse. There was the predictable question about the names of the current prime minister and that fabled creature, the first female one. When Jill asked me who the President of the United States was I asked her if that was a trick question. We were in that curious interregnum between Donald Trump and Joe Biden in which videos of Trump being dragged screaming out of the White House were circulating furiously. So the answer to the question depended very much on your point of view.

The questions on mental health were particularly dreadful. Was I satisfied with my life? Of course not. Who, living in the middle of a disastrously managed pandemic in a violent, decomposing world run by crazy and/or stupid politicians, could possibly be? Did I ever feel anxious or depressed? Ditto. These questions, I told Jill, actually create dis-ease. If I wasn't depressed and disoriented before she got on the phone to me, I certainly was now. But I got my own back when it came to the memory test.

'I am going to read you a list of words,' said Jill, 'and I want you to try to remember as many as you can and repeat them back to me in any order you can manage.' I reached for a pen and paper and wrote them down as she enunciated them extra carefully in case I was deaf on top of everything else. 'Cabin, pipe, elephant, test, silk, theatre, watch, whip, pillow, giant'. I fed the words back to her in a different random order, ticking each one off as I said it.

'Amazing!' pronounced Jill. 'That's absolutely marvellous. Do you know, you're the only person who's got them all right!'

Later in her barrage of questions she returned to this topic and asked me if I could still remember any of the words. I consulted my list and decided to remember, in order to be convincing, only nine of them. I found it quite remarkable that none of the researchers in this study had anticipated the possibility that old people could actually be quick-witted enough to write the words down.

'I don't know why you bother,' said Elsa when I recounted this episode to her over tea later. She frowned. 'If you agree to take part in some research, you must take it seriously. If you don't, you could be directly responsible for invalid results.'

*

Both the pubs in Elsa's village were shut due to the BV and the entertainment facilities were otherwise non-existent so we went for an awful lot of walks during the week I stayed with her. One night there was a frost, the first frost of the season, and the fields were layered with white. The grass the next morning made a satisfying crunching noise like cornflakes under our feet. The sky was a smoothly ironed blue and the sun warmed our backs as we stepped carefully over the patches of ice on the road. Was Maud's village, Corsley in Wiltshire, anything like this one? Was it boring, but peopled by villagers who did say 'good morning' and 'good afternoon' as you passed them on the narrow frosted roads and footpaths, before they returned to cottages that looked as though they'd grown like vegetables out of the earth? Appearances deceive. What looks ordinary and peaceable on the surface may well hide abominable crimes against humanity. It was even possible, I said to Elsa, to move her on from her absorption in the ethics of my having cheated with my memory test, that someone in Maud's village had got it in for her because of what she wrote about them in her *Life in an English Village*. Maud didn't share the status of those she researched, so cross-class crime might be implicated. Her family lived in a grand mansion, Corsley House. They first rented it in 1894 and in 1897 they bought it for £6,000. The price included sixty acres of land and a cottage. I looked it up on a website called *The Move Market* which lists it as the poshest home in the area, now worth £4.023 million. So there might be motives for a Corsleyite hunting Maud down with a hatpin in the tunnel outside High Street Kensington Station.

The last walk we did before Elsa drove me to the station involved one of those Christmas-card villages with a duck pond. Elsa said it was a duck pond, but the ducks had gone somewhere else. The pond was overlooked by a pub with a raised terrace and extremely shuttered windows. England had now been re-arranged into a series of areas called tiers according to where the politicians thought samples of the BV had most congregated. Tier 3 meant a hard confinement of people to their own homes and so-called support bubbles, which often were not, as the pandemic was witnessing a huge surge in domestic violence. Men had more time to hit women and women had nowhere else to go. It was probably happening even now in the bedrooms and kitchens of these desirable limestone dwellings with their flawlessly painted front doors, their mathematically arranged log stores, and their exquisite views over the water meadows.

Elsa took me down a path that led away from the duckless pond. Church Lane it was called. Every village must have a Church Lane, and therefore a church. This one had a dazzling location looking out over the valley in three directions with expansive grounds for its peacefully-passed-away incumbents. Their gravestones leant dangerously (why do gravestones lean – is someone pushing them?) and were clothed in vivid green moss and yellow lichen. We tried to read the names on some of them but were defeated by the effects of age (not our own). It was then that organ music began to float out from the church. The moment became one of those surreal, out-of-time ones that overcome you completely by reaching forgotten memories of fully experienced moments – locations and people of great personal and existential significance. I entered a temporary state of rapture, feeling a deep longing for the person I had once been, a person with long, fully functioning limbs and brightly coloured hair, a person with unbridled ambition, no debts or credit cards, and only a few books, a person who didn't keep estimating the length of time she might have left on this virally troubled earth.

'What are you thinking about, Alice?' Elsa inquired, poking my arm. 'I've been round the churchyard twice while you've been standing there dreaming. I've even had a pee behind that yew tree.'

We lifted the heavy metal latch on the church door and went in. A very complicated sign directed us to yet another bottle of hand-sanitiser and a pile of post-it notes the colour of the lichen on the graves that another note instructed us to stick on any pews we used so they could be deep-cleaned afterwards. Opposite the heavy church door and under a luminescent window was a keyboard behind which crouched a small shrivelled-looking man. A cream-coloured woollen scarf lay curled untidily on a chair beside him and beneath it reposed a pair of freshly polished smart brown leather shoes. He looked up at us briefly and without interest. Elsa, who talks to everyone she meets, of this or that and often nothing much, went over and said 'good morning' to him.

'You from round here?' he shouted above the noise he was making and without taking his eyes off the keyboard. 'It's digital,' he announced, not waiting for a reply to his question. 'But it makes all the right noises.' He wasn't wearing a mask so we could see his smile. To drive the point home, his gnarled fingers took off on a symphony of chords and glissandos interspersed with snatches of tunes. There was a bit of *O God our help in ages past*, a smattering of W*e plough the fields and scatter*, and a seasonal dose of *In the bleak midwinter*. I went round to stand behind him. Instead of the usual stops of a standard organ, there were rows of square buttons, some illuminated, some not, and all bearing detailed descriptions of the sound they would make. The actual notes that issued forth appeared to come from large mesh panels high up on the wall above the organ, at right angles to the rather splendid old window, which is how the music had managed to get out into the churchyard and alter my mental state. Elsa asked him if he played for the services in the church. 'When I feel like it,' he chuckled. 'It's digital, you know. But it makes all the right noises.' We nodded. 'I do it all from memory,' he added, unaware of the contradiction.

When he stood up and put his shoes on, we realised that he really was quite old, in a different league from ourselves, perhaps in his early nineties. He must live in this village, maybe in one of the squashed cottages on Church Lane. Every day he put on his smart shoes and his cream muffler and he walked down the path to the church. He would have a key to the door and another to release the seductive digital possibilities of the organ. He didn't need an audience, it was enough to be there making and listening to his own music in a space he could fill with his own thoughts. After playing, he would wend his way home where his wife, or some other useful carer, would be stirring soup on the stove for lunch. After slurping this appreciatively with a chunk of bread, he would retire to his bed for a nap, while the tunes from the morning galloped happily through his head.

What it would be to have a simple life. A life free from conflicting obligations and conscientious musings on how to fill the future. On the train back to London I found myself able to make some decisions. They varied in scale and importance. I would locate my old Will and remake it, write out a list of instructions about what to do with me and my material possessions when I died, and then forget all about death. I would stop watching the news altogether. I would simplify my wardrobe by giving to charity anything I hadn't worn in the last two years. I'd try harder with the grandchildren, even if it did mean further encounters with their witch of a mother in Buckinghamshire. I'd make renewed attempts to locate Nathan, whether in Leiden or anywhere else.

Hopefully tidying up these ends would help me to focus on sensible plans for the future. Alternatively, and as Elsa had urged, I might pursue the mystery of Maud Davies's unfortunate death until its bitter end, even if I had to make that up myself.

However, control was wrested from me by what happened next.

5 Matters of fact

It's the first day of the next lockdown. Mick and Angie upstairs have the BV. They WhatsApp-ed to tell me. I asked them if they needed anything and they said, only to get out of this fucking country. Mick is from New Zealand, a place where the BV is having a much more difficult time because of a considerably more competent government than the one we have here. I imagine Mick is imagining all the volcanoes, fumaroles and vineyards, and all those wonderful beaches where hot water bubbles up through spotless sand and dolphins frolic in the fjords. But what are the rest of us imagining? More of the same, more wet grey skies, more political mismanagement, more BV. Boris's Brexit has finally got done, but there's very little sign of any border control which is what the whole thing was supposed to be about. The aeroplanes keep flying and dumping more loads of BV into our virally polluted air.

I'm having trouble with the last pages of Professor Pluss's manuscript. He says he's proposing a new analytic framework for the sociological study of nationalism and that it's made up of eight propositions but I can only find six of them, and two of those appear to be identical. Does Professor Pluss not read what he's written before he sends it to The Publisher? Does The Publisher not read it before he sends it to me? Does or will anybody read the book anyway? I rang The Publisher to discuss it.

'We had it peer reviewed,' he said, defensively.

'Two or three of the author's chums giving his text a quick once over is hardly a guarantee of quality, is it?' I said, sharply. 'What is a "primordial-constructivist approach", anyway?'

'I don't think I'm familiar with that phrase,' he responded weakly.

'Precisely,' I said. 'It's a central tenet of Pluss's thesis so we need to know what it is.' I went on to note that it isn't the job of a copy-editor to work out what an author is saying, merely to tidy it up so that it resembles a book.

The week after I got back from Elsa's I did my stint at *Another Chapter* and Sally handed me the copy of Maud Davies's *Life in an English Village* which had come in while I was away. Its glossy cover featured a grey stone Norman-towered church like the one Elsa and I had recently visited, and a woman in the foreground writing in a book. She was wearing full Edwardian costume, a long dress, boots and a large black hat that blended with the dark cypress trees behind her, an unfortunate compilation suggesting that women grow out of trees. On the back cover was a photo of Maud herself, a pinched, rather serious face, slightly prominent ears, dark hair drawn back off the face, a determined gaze, parted lips and a broadly striped high-necked blouse that looked as though it might be throttling her, perhaps in anticipation of what would later happen to her neck. This was definitely the face of a woman who knew what she was about, and who ought to have had many more years to do it in.

'Not your usual reading material, is it?' remarked Sally. *Life in an English Village* was a heavy book, 317 pages, including a map of the area and dozens of tables detailing the social and economic conditions of Corsley inhabitants. Holding the book and envisaging many happy locked-down hours reading it took me back to my early days at EMU when I'd been pleasantly overcome by the dryness and matter-of-factness of sociology compared with the flights of fancy taught in my Pinner girls' school. The careful computation of such topics as social class, industrial organisation and family types was a relief from the irrelevant genealogies of kings and queens. Because I was doing a combined sociology and English literature degree, fiction was never far from my mind. Later, I came to see that most sociology was equally fanciful and this was certainly true of Professor Pluss's manuscript.

And so, in the evening, as darkness enveloped the limited view of the world I had through my front window, I started on Chapter 1, *The Parish under Cley Hill*. This proved to be a lyrical description of the parish with the quantitative detail mostly confined to small-font footnotes, such as Corsley occupying 3,056 acres in 1891. Unlike many authors, Maud appeared to have a good grasp of what belongs in footnotes and what doesn't. She clearly loved her parish: its precipitous position on a plateau hung between the high chalk Downs and the sea; its rich and fertile soil cut by many nourishing streams; the queerly distributed village, hamlets made up of two or three dwellings each, with no real village centre. Standing on the hill above Corsley, said Maud, you won't see anything at all resembling a village. Here she advised her readers to consult the map she'd included in order to understand where everything is. I was turning the book this way and that to work this out when the doorbell rang.

A young woman stood there with a baby in her arms. My first thought was that she was begging. There'd been a rather racist article in the local paper recently about traveller people moving in on the moneyed classes of Hackney.

'I'm sorry to disturb you,' she said, with a faint European accent. Her face, unlined and pink-cheeked under the glare of my outside porch light, contained a pair of misty and anxious green eyes. Strands of chestnut hair straggled down the front of her worn leather coat, well within the grasp of the infant she held who was wrapped tightly in a multi-coloured blanket.

'My name is Mila,' the woman said tremulously. 'Your son, Nathan, gave me your address. There is something I should like to talk to you about. May it be possible for me to come into your home for a little while?'

My instant reaction was to wonder what Nathan had done now. 'Is he ok?' I asked both anxiously and crossly.

'Yes, I think he is fine,' she said, 'although I have not heard from him recently. That is not why I am here.'

Well, obviously Mila had to come in. She had a very commodious backpack which she relocated to my hall floor while shifting the baby bundle efficiently from one arm to the other. I moved Maud off the sofa so they had somewhere to sit. She unwrapped the blanket at this point and displayed a child a few months old asleep in a fluffy blue suit. 'This is Ed,' she announced.

I peered at him politely. He had amazing long black lashes splayed out like a Spanish mantilla fan on the unblemished porcelain cheeks possessed only by absolutely new entrants to this world.

'You are probably wondering why we are here.'

Yes, I probably was. I felt bound to offer her a drink. It was ten past six and Elsa, in her otherwise silent village, would have heard the church clock strike and made herself a poisonous cocktail by now. I poured two glasses of Pino Grigio and found a packet of parsnip crisps at the back of a kitchen cupboard. Mila drank almost all of her wine in noisy gulps. The baby stirred, momentarily opening his abundantly-lashed eyes, then closing them again. 'Edward is a nice old-fashioned name,' I said, to make conversation.

'It is not Edward, it is Ed,' she replied.

'Just Ed?'

'Yes.'

That seemed a little mean. Surely after all the effort it takes to get born, we deserve more than two letters? 'Does he have another name?'

'Yes, Kuiper. That is my name. Ed Kuiper is his name. This child,' continued Mila slowly, her green eyes locked indelibly on mine, 'is your grandson.'

No, I thought, I've already got one of those, he lives in Steeple Claydon with his parents and his twin sister. Sam, alias Samuel Josiah Alexander, a string of names that's a whole lot more generous and respectful than Ed. I stared at the new grandson-contender. He wriggled under my gaze and waved an arm in my direction. This isn't fair, I thought. I used to say that to my mother, whose retort always was, 'Life isn't fair'. It wasn't fair that as a child I never had any new clothes, only Susie's hand-me-downs or that I had to eat my mother's sticky over-sweet puddings. It wasn't fair that I went to a fourth-rate university in an unlovely industrial area, or that I'd been left to rear two adolescent boys after their father discontinued his relationship with me.

'If this is Nathan's child, he's never said anything about him to me,' I objected. 'How do I know you're telling the truth?'

Mila had thought of this. She scrabbled around in her backpack and brought forth a creased clump of papers which she unfolded and held out to me. The first two pages were in Dutch. The second two asserted that, according to a DNA Worldwide Paternity Test examining 25 short tandem repeat markers, the probability that Nathan Henry was the father of Ed Kuiper was 98.6%. The test was done three months ago, I noted, when Ed was less than a month old. Mila must have known where Nathan was then in order to pick up this additional sample of his genetic material.

It was typical of Nathan to become a father and not tell his mother, by which I mean that it was entirely in character for him to lead a mystery life away from prying parental eyes. He'd been doing that since he was about fourteen when we discovered he'd started a smoking club behind the bike shed at school. But why had the mother of his child come to tell me? The story of how Ed got here unfolded as Mila got through two more glasses of wine and dropped bits of parsnip crisps all over him. She lived in Amsterdam, in a little street between the Singel and Herengracht canals, and had been in a lesbian relationship with a woman called Tessi who ran a wool shop there, hence perhaps the variegated blanket. Tessi and Mila had decided to have a baby. Mila was keener than Tessi on the business of pregnancy and childbirth.

In fact, Tessi, it would turn out, was less than keen on the whole idea. At a nightclub in Amsterdam, one evening approximately fourteen months ago, the two women had encountered my son. Nathan was there on one of his multifarious musical businesses. Tessi and Mila, after engaging Nathan in conversation, had put in an unusual request, not for more drinks, nor for some of the reputedly free-flowing Dutch cannabis, nor for an entrée to one of Nathan's more lucrative musical enterprises, but for some of his sperm. He may have his faults, but my Nathan is a very pretty boy. Now I understood why I'd been immediately taken by Ed's eyelashes. They were exactly like Nathan's thirty-eight years ago. Nathan's sperm hadn't been delivered to Mila's uterus in the normal manner but via a turkey-baster, an implement which Mila informed me is now appearing in Dutch pharmacies for just this purpose. I imagined it laid out on highly organised Dutch shelves adjacent to displays of condoms, and perhaps what used to be called Dutch caps – contra- and pro-ception both in the category of consumer goods.

'I'm not sure I need this degree of detail,' I thought, and said. Mila replied that, on the contrary, I did need it because, as Ed's grandmother, I had to understand his provenance and how he had got here to this recumbent position on my sofa.

I picked him up as he stirred from sleep. It was that soft warm heaviness I remembered, the sense of holding something both breakable and precious, the remote mixed fragrance of soap, sour milk and shit. Ed looked at me with dark blue eyes in a wondering sort of way. I looked back, also wonderingly.

'I just thought you ought to know this child exists,' said Mila with disarming simplicity.

That's very considerate of you, I could have said, but I still wanted to know why they were both here.

The story unravelled further as I cooked us both pasta and made a quick pepper and anchovy sauce and Mila changed Ed's nappy using the wherewithal from her enormous backpack, and fitted in a few fast conversations in Dutch on her mobile. What about her own mother, I wondered, watching her through the gently rising steam of the linguine. The steam rose next to my lovely new yellow kettle, a real mood-improver, especially at times like this.

Mila's tale was sad. Her Dutch mother and English father had been killed in a Turkish Airlines disaster when she was ten. They'd been taking a short holiday, leaving her with a friend. There were apparently no relatives waiting to take Mila on, so she was brought up by the Dutch care system. Although this was better than ours, it was far from ideal, delivering Mila into the world as a confused young person of sixteen with an appetite for new experiences but insufficient resources for distinguishing the risky from the safe. She had trained and worked as a hairdresser, with a sideline as a tattoo artist. She showed me a small reptile on her upper arm and I feared for baby Ed's perfect skin. Mila and Tessi got together when Mila was only twenty, and Tessi ten years older. 'It was not an equal relationship,' she stated. After the episode with the turkey-baster it became less so. Tessi wasn't interested in the baby who disturbed her days and her nights. Her goal was to become a human rights lawyer, and Ed and his human rights were too much of a distraction.

Nathan wasn't interested in his son either because that wasn't part of the deal. He wasn't reneging on anything here because Mila and Tessi only wanted Nathan's genetic material, not his fathering. The situation underwent a dramatic change when Tessi de-lesbianised and entered a cloying heterosexual relationship with an American neuroscientist. She sold the wool shop and registered at the University of Maastricht for a law conversion course. Alone in their tiny flat in the Oude Leliestraat, Mila had felt isolated and depressed. A few solitary weeks of feeding and cleaning and holding and watching baby Ed made her think seriously about biological inheritance. She also mentioned the not unsalient fact that she'd run out of money. Tessi gave her the occasional handout, as did the woman who ran the hair salon where Mila had worked. Following Mila's prescience in arranging the DNA test, all attempts to contact Nathan had been futile. Nathan had deserted his Leiden houseboat and was not to be found. Messages left on his mobile went unanswered. She'd tried a couple of people in the music business but they had been unhelpfully cagey in their responses. Nathan's elusiveness, which I knew only too well, bore the stamp of truth.

'You can stay here tonight,' I said. 'But tomorrow we'll have to think of something else. I've got my own life to lead, you know.' This was said more for my benefit than hers. I had quickly begun to fear the scenario of Mila and Ed taking up permanent residence in my private space, my home or my head, or both. I found clean sheets and prepared the spare room/office for them by moving all the files and papers into a corner. The room was quite dusty and there was a pronounced mouse smell, but Mila was too preoccupied to notice.

I looked in on them before I went to bed. She'd left her clothes in a pile on the floor. A wet nappy was curled up under the window. Ed slept on his back, his arms outstretched like an angel, and she was on her side facing him. The moonlight delineated their postures, suffusing the room with a clarity that was otherwise missing from this situation.

I lay awake for a long time. Nothing in women's education prepares you for these modern dilemmas, like what you're supposed to do when an unknown woman presents you with an unknown grandson, like how to keep the lines of communication open with a young man who isn't so young any more and who doesn't want to be communicated with, like how to ensure you don't catch the BV from your infected upstairs neighbours, like how to persuade people that life isn't over just because you've become what they call a pensioner. About two o'clock I turned on the light to look up the level of infection in Dutch cities. There was quite a lot of the BV in the Netherlands, so much that they were about to go into a firm five-week lockdown which would include the closure of hairdressers and tattooists. Did babies transmit the BV? Why hadn't Mila been wearing a mask? And, while we're on the subject, when are seventy-four-year-olds like me going to get our vaccinations?

Exhausted by the effort of trying to decide what to worry about the most, I finally fell asleep just as the Stoke Newington dust people began their weekly racket with our wheelie-bins.

6 The sociology of family life

The birth of this child in Amsterdam had created an uncle, an aunt, two cousins and two grandparents. In Corsley, Wiltshire, Maud Davies calculated that 742 children had been born in 195 households in 1905, and 660 of them were still alive four years later. This wasn't a bad record for the time. Maud worried about the health of poor children in Corsley, but decided that, on the whole, rural children benefited from their families' practice of growing food in gardens and allotments: *The produce of the garden furnishes a large proportion of the food of the people. Potatoes, onions, greens, and other vegetables figure largely in the menu of the poorest households especially those with many children.* One labourer's family with four children ate potatoes, parsnips and bread for lunch on Saturday and potatoes with cabbage or onions on all the other days of the week. There was a surfeit of bread, dripping and cocoa in the diets.

At this point in my reading, the morning after the night before, Mila came into my bedroom carrying Ed, naked except for a nappy, so I had to put *Life in an English Village* down.

'Is it OK if I give him a banana?' she asked, indicating the fruit bowl whose contents would have been a rare phenomenon in Corsley. I took the opportunity to suggest that she wear a mask since we were in the middle of a pandemic.

'Oh yes,' she said, 'I do have one they gave me at the airport.'

'I've been thinking,' I said, 'and I think it'd be a good idea if you took Ed to meet Nathan's brother and his cousins. He might enjoy meeting his English family. Perhaps they might help you decide what to do next.' I felt a little gleeful at landing this challenge on Patti. Jack would probably just go to the office as usual.

Mila looked a bit disappointed at the hint that she might move on. Had she been hoping to stay here indefinitely? And do what, precisely? I didn't know what to do about finances. A cynic would say that Mila had only descended on me because she wanted money, but I preferred to think there was a more charitable explanation – her motive being to seek a human connection. 'I'm still working, you know,' I commented in self-defence. 'I have to earn an income.' She looked as though she understood, but that could be wishful thinking. What did our leaving Europe mean for a person like Mila with a biological claim on a British man? Could she establish herself here? Is that what she wanted to do?

I went out to the nearest ATM and withdrew £500. Then I visited Olly the fishmonger. Sprats and bloaters featured quite often in the Corsley diets so I had fish on the brain and I bought some fresh sardines for lunch which I grilled lightly in olive oil and lemon juice.

'Oh, Mrs Alice Henry, this is very kind of you,' declared Mila, her hungry green eyes alighting hungrily on the plate.

With her hair newly washed and Ed now at her breast in the fishy air having demolished his banana, she looked the picture of happy motherhood. I took him from her after lunch and he grinned engagingly at me. In the afternoon I rang Nathan's mobile although she told me there was no point. I left a message explaining that a young woman had descended on me with a baby she said was his. I added that the baby did look like him. I asked him to call me. Urgently.

I phoned Jack to tell him the news but he didn't sound terribly surprised to hear that his brother had spawned an offspring without notifying anyone. I said I was too old to be running round after a baby and that I thought the whole Steeple Claydon family should be introduced to their new relatives. Jack was worried that the arrival of a baby might make Patti broody.

'She must be menopausal by now,' I said, trying to be helpful.

He agreed to a short visit because Sam and Sara were off school again after a dinner lady had tested positive for the BV, and the baby would provide a diversion.

I could hear Ed crying in the next room. I had a headache from insufficient sleep, and, to cap it all, Mila said she was going out for a walk. She didn't ask me if I minded, she just announced it. Was she angry with me for not being more accommodating? But what, really, could she expect? The front door slammed. Perhaps that was it, she was never coming back.

I picked Ed up, took him into the kitchen and moved him from arm to arm while I made a cup of tea. The whole place still smelt very fishy. I reviewed the plan I'd made with Jack. Mila, Ed and I would take the train to

St Albans and Jack would meet us at the station. This meant that Mila and Ed had to spend another night with me.

When she came back from her walk, without saying very much about it or even where exactly she had been, we watched *Masterchef*. A very fat woman made a towering mound of a dessert from everything creamy and sugary in the studio while an earnest young Asian man with a half-shaved head did something innovative with eels which he had to kill first. Mila wasn't as shocked by this as I was. She told me smoked eels are a Dutch delicacy and they have a ritual known as 'stomping the eels' in which people trample them in buckets before slicing them open.

The following day I got an Uber to take us to the station. We bought nappies in Boots in St Pancras and coffees from Pret. People weren't doing a lot of social distancing and the masks created an air of menace. You could easily imagine full-blown intentions to burglarise or terrorise lurking there.

At St Albans, Jack was parked where the taxis wait with his engine running and Sara on the seat beside him. She seemed disgruntled and barely looked at the baby. Jack, on the other hand, grasped his new nephew with both hands. He was nice to Mila too. There wasn't any other hugging because of the BV. Our conversation was quite brief because I had timed the journey for a quick turnaround and my train back was nearly due.

A policeman at the barrier stopped me. 'Excuse me, Madam, but may I ask you why you're travelling today? Only essential travel is permitted.' At least he got the verb right but it was troublesome having your motives questioned. I told him my travel was essential, I had to visit an important site for my work as a writer. I thought the story about the handing over of a previously undiscovered grandson might be too complicated. He let me go just as the London train was pulling in. If not, what might have happened? *Alice Henry sadly died from Covid-19 after she caught it in St Albans police station where she was being questioned about breaking government regulations. It was later disclosed that cleaning of the station had been contracted out to a private firm who did a dodgy deal involving fake sanitising fluid from Vietnam.* It would be a more likely death than Maud Davies's on that railway line. I was finding it hard not to think about Maud. My mind was utterly over-awed by the image of her lying there in two parts as a consequence of hatpin and train injuries, both of which were the proximate, not the ultimate, cause of her death.

I've been ruminating quite a lot on causes of death. What people die of isn't necessarily the cause of their demise. If a teenage boy dives off a cliff, he doesn't die from drowning but from a kind of toxic risk-taking. A middle-aged woman who's crushed by a car while crossing the road goes down as a vehicular death but the real cause was her anxiety about her anorexic daughter which stopped her looking both ways. The BV deaths we hear about may be technically due to the virus, but why do some people get it, and get it badly, while others don't? Men get it more than women and men don't wash their hands as much as women, so there you go. My mother died at ninety-six but her death certificate doesn't say that she died of old age, which she did. Our cells are dying all the time and this cellular mortality eventually overtakes our will to live, pushing us into the crematorium or the soggy earth.

My meditations on mortality were helped on their way by the new manuscript The Publisher had sent me to replace the nonsensical Professor Pluss one. 'I think you'll find this more to your liking,' he'd said, laughing awkwardly. Its subject was certainly promising: *The Female Sleuth in Modern Crime Fiction*. It had a subtitle, as these things always do, that was rather less promising: *Gender and the feminist turn*. I imagined Edwardian women with suffragette banners keeling over in droves as in 'a turn for the worse'. But its author, Dr Esmeralda Ahmad-Wicks, had something else in mind. I tuned into some aspects of her subject since I had read voraciously in those realms of modern crime literature over which she had cast her analytic eye. I was familiar with such key personnel as the gun-carrying, whisky-swigging V. I. Warshawski of Sara Paretsky's novels and the much smoother, but also whisky-swigging, Dr Kay Scarpetta of the Patricia Cornwell ones. I admired them both, but had never puzzled over their feminist credentials. Both, I remember, were excellent Italian cooks. The loose ends of cases whirled around V. I. Warshawski's head 'like trails of fettucine', and Dr Scarpetta even made her own pizza dough. *The Female Sleuth* was a manuscript at least parts of which I could hope to understand.

Remembering what Elsa had suggested, female sleuth-like, about the white slave trade and Maud Davies's death, and feeling a need to tell her about recent developments in my life, on the train back I got my phone out to call her, but as I did so it started ringing.

'Alice,' the voice shouted, 'is that you, Alice? Can you

hear me?' It was Alan, my ex, who had reached a stage of only partial understanding of many things, including how mobile phones work. He frequently rang mine by mistake because as an 'A' I'm at the top of his contacts list. No conversation was complete without him observing how much he hated machines and asking why this one engaged in such appalling acts as storing text messages for several days and then delivering them all at once.

Alan was ten years older than me. When we'd been together for twenty years and our sons were teenagers, he left me for a much younger prototype. Kerry was a teaching assistant at the boys' school. She had strawberry blonde hair and strawberry lips and we saw her quite regularly because of Nathan's dyslexia. They both liked her – Nathan and his father – but his father took it to extremes. I was picking Nathan up from school one day to drive him to a football match. It was spring, and randomly-spaced daffodils wiggled their lemon heads at me as I walked down Park Road in Crouch End. I was feeling quite happy and thinking about a rather fascinating manuscript I was working on about women married to famous men and how the wives never got credit for all that washing and cooking and transportation of ideas into masculine heads. Joining the huddle of parents by the school gates I bumped into (those were the pre-BV days when you did bump into people) Jackie, the myopic mother of a girl in Nathan's class.

'Oh Alice, it's you,' she said, enthusiastically. 'I've been hoping to see you, but I must have missed you last week.'

We talked about the latest news in the Fred and Rosemary West murder case, and then Jackie said, 'Alice, I think there's something you ought to know. Well, maybe you know already but I'd be neglecting my duty as a good neighbour if I didn't mention it, slip it into the conversation somehow. It's about Alan and that teaching assistant, you know the one with coloured hair. On Wednesday last week I was early because I'd been to see my mother in Enfield and the bus back was faster than usual so I was standing there eating a sausage roll from Tesco's when she came out of school. Alan was picking Nathan up and he'd arrived early too, and he and that girl, well woman, I suppose, went straight off round the corner together. Out of sight. I couldn't hear what they were saying, but they passed quite close to me, which is how I saw them, and then when they thought they were out of sight, he put his arm round her. I don't think he noticed me. I think Alan only had eyes for her, if you know what I mean.'

So that was the beginning of the end of my marriage. I cried, of course I cried, and I screamed at Alan, and he looked appropriately belittled by his behaviour, but nothing could apparently be done in the face of his completely irrational and damaging passion for Miss Pink Hair. She was twenty and he was fifty-four. After a spell of the usual hyper-dramatic episodes in which I screamed even more and Alan sobbed about love (or lust) in that mournful controlled way men have, and she came round and shrieked at both of us, and Alan changed his mind three times about leaving, and I almost left as well, they went off into the sunset together, into a ground floor flat on Ealing Common.

In his phone call to me on the train, Alan described himself as miserable. He wanted me to go and see him, something I tried to avoid because it made me miserable too. I had got used to living without him in all the years since Jackie's blurted report, and it really was a relief. But at the same time, being reminded of what had happened did tend to bring back the anger. I asked Alan if he was self-isolating, but he thought I said suffocating, which he denied.

'How is Kerry?' I asked, politely.

'Gone,' he said. 'Buggered off. With a nurse from the hospital.'

I found that quite hard to take in. Eighty-four was a bit old to be deserted. On the other hand, that's what's liable to happen when you fall for a young thing. But a *nurse*? 'I didn't realise Kerry was a lesbian,' I said.

'Good God, no,' replied Alan. 'He's a nurse called Jonathan. Good at his job, actually. Kerry met him when he came to dress my leg. I've got some sort of nasty ulcer on it. It's red round the edges but a bit yellow and full of pus in the middle. I can smell it from here. I quite liked him until I found out what he was up to.'

I didn't feel sorry for Alan. I gave that up when he walked out on me. But I agreed to go for a visit. Only one, I warned him. All this family stuff was getting in the way of my generating an income, not to mention my irresistible lurkings in the life of Maud Davies. There were other assignations too, body housework I called them. I had to fit in another before I went to see Alan in Dagenham.

7 Are you on any tablets at the moment, Mrs Henry?

The optician had sent a reminder text observing that it was at least a year since anyone had inspected my eyes. I thought I'd noticed some blurring in the left upper quadrant of the right one but that could be a result of too much Maud Davies-ing, or filthy glasses. Alan, when I was married to him, was adept at spectacle-cleaning. I used to take them off, hand them to him without a word, and he would pull a clean hankie out of somewhere and restore their pristine clarity. Perhaps he performed this useful service for other women, but I don't recall Miss Pink Hair wearing glasses.

And so I made an optical appointment. There was a red 'Do not enter' sign on the door. Another sign, one you might expect Mr Barrow and Son, Optician, to get right, was so small it was practically invisible. A large man in a white coat opened the door. The usual BV questions emerged blurred from behind his white mask, including one about whether I'd recently been abroad, magnificently thoughtless in the circumstances. The interior of the shop gleamed white with a hospital scent. Two more large sanitised men in white coats circulated around two white desks. My one took me into a side room and asked me to sit on a chair covered in a sheet of plastic. He put my coat and bag on another similarly dressed. Many decades of eye tests had made the routine familiar, although it was more technologically advanced than it used to be. With my chin and forehead pressed into an eye-evaluating contraption, fast-moving displays of lights challenged my eyes either to behave or misbehave. I took my mask off to do this because I thought the claustrophobic feeling induced by mask-wearing might affect the results, but he told me to put it back on. Afterwards, in one corner of the tiny room, he sat at a computer whose screen displayed maps of my eyes which were visible even to me. He tapped away busily. His very large feet stuck out sideways. His hands were small so he really was quite out of proportion. His hair was greasy and long, curling over the collar of his white coat.

Waiting to see the Son part of Mr Barrow and Son I noticed two other customers, both white-haired men in black coats with black masks. They made the optical environment even more alien. One of them was selecting a new pair of glasses from those ranged round the room in illuminated, labelled rows: 'Child, Free-£20,' 'Women, £39-£59', 'Women, £85-£99', 'Women, £129,' 'Women, £185'. There was apparently nothing available between £59 and £85. All the glasses looked pretty much the same to me, but then I didn't have mine on. Purple signs promised the exciting but unlikely prospects of 'total satisfaction' and 'free unlimited after-sales service'.

The young Mr Barrow who'd been doing my eyes for about twenty years looked older above his mask, his eyes more lined. These lines crinkled when he smiled, or rather the crinkling made me guess that there was a smile lower down in response to something I'd said.

Pointing to a large container of sanitising fluid I commented, 'You must get through gallons of that stuff every day.'

'You have no idea,' he replied, crinkling.

He began with the usual questions about headaches and general health.

'Are you on any tablets at the moment, Mrs Henry?'

A curious word that, *tablet*, from the Latin, *tabula*, a table. The more usual *pill* is peculiarly British but pills were surely never flat like tables. And I've given up explaining that I'm not Mrs Henry. Elsa always says I should have done a PhD like she did so I could restyle myself Doctor, though she did warn me that this can elicit unpleasant recitations of bodily symptoms from complete strangers.

The young Mr Barrow didn't look attractive in his white plastic apron but with his legs neatly crossed while he studied my ocular history on his screen, he was so much smaller than his three assistants that he could have been another species. I reported to him the periodic presence in my vision of items that resembled upside-down question marks.

'Floaters,' he said, 'nothing to worry about.'

'I'm not worried about them,' I said, 'I just don't like them.'

He turned his head towards me, indicating that he was prepared to give the topic the more serious attention I seemed to want. 'Caused by degenerative changes in the vitreous humour, the gel that fills the eyeball,' he told me.

'I don't know why that isn't something to worry about,' I said.

He ignored the remark.

We proceeded through the usual stuff reading lines of letters which I used to memorise in order to show off, until I realised this was counterproductive since it resulted in lenses that didn't work. When we got to the bit where a huge frame is balanced on your nose and lots of different lenses are inserted in it, with a request to report 'better, worse or the same as the first', I got the feeling that the young Mr Barrow knew what I was going to say, and my job was to guess what it was. My eyes were visited by tears and he asked if I had dry eye syndrome. Unwarranted moistening is quite inexplicably a symptom of this. Yes, I could claim that disorder. I even had some drops for it in my bag. And so we progressed, until Mr Barrow opened the door of the little windowless room and asked me what I could see in the distance with two different lenses. Were the customers choosing expensive Armani frames and the large-footed optical assistant fuzzier with the first or the second?

All this I studied with interest. Had it been an ordinary non-BV day in my ordinary non-BV life I would have been itching to get out and making lists in my head of urgent things to do. But, now, having my eyes checked was an entertainment, a diverting theatrical performance. I realised I was keen to engage the young Mr Barrow in conversation as a change from talking to myself but I guessed he was used to this in his customers, and he had to get on. Besides, after each one of us he had to wipe down every surface of the room from the chin rest to the lenses to the glossy card with text in different-sized fonts.

The text used to be Dickens but now it was something unappealingly modern. I was pretty sure that, had I been able to see it properly, I would have spotted quite a few syntactical mistakes.

There were small changes to the astigmatism in both my eyes but I didn't have Elschnig's pearls like Sally from *Another Chapter*. I was disappointingly normal and my eyes were disappointingly ageing like the rest of me. The new lenses would cost £236.46. No, I didn't want to choose a new frame, Armani or otherwise.

All those flashing dots and fuzzy images had given me a headache and I needed a coffee. I stopped outside my favourite café in Church Street and tried to push open the door but it wouldn't budge.

'You need some help breaking in, love?' inquired a man from the bread queue next door.

The shop was closed. I took my custom to another, where coffees were served through a hatch in the side wall. I asked for a croissant and a flat white.

'I've just sold the last one, but I've got one from yesterday, it's a bit hard at the end, but I won't charge you for it,' came the reply through the wall.

I found a seat by the cemetery gate where I could eat and drink, but I failed to notice the water on it and when I got up, the back of my coat was soaking.

Why do so many people wear glasses anyway? When I got home, I googled this question. Apparently, it's just another symptom of our unhealthy civilisation with too much time spent indoors looking at screens. So the lockdown will be good for opticians. There'll be an explosion of expensive spectacle-wearing. As I read about ageing and eyes, mine stumbled on this unpleasant sentence in one paper: *As organisms age, all their biological systems should be expected to break down and fail with increasing regularity, and eyes are no exception.*

8 Visiting Dagenham

It took him a long time to open the door. When he did, I could understand why. He was walking on crutches. He looked like a really old man, curled over the crutches, knotted fingers gripping them, wizened face, eyes a foggy blue and cream. He'd brushed his remaining hair carefully over the top of his head, all traces of red having departed. The house smelt musty and decidedly under-cleaned.

'Alice, Alice, Oh Alice,' exclaimed my ex-husband in heartrending tones as he reached out for my hands.

We sat at the kitchen table which was heaped with used crockery and torn utility bills. How long had Kerry been gone? In his disorganised kitchen I made tea, much needed after a punishing journey on two buses and two trains from my house to his. The number 149 bus to Dalston Junction, then the Overground to Whitechapel, then the District Line to Becontree, then the number 62 to Alan's road. About half the people on half the buses and trains had been wearing their face masks either slung like hammocks under their chins or pushed up against, not over, their nostrils. I wore my butterfly mask and a pair of black cotton gloves. It would have been easier to get to the Ealing Common flat where Alan and Kerry had set up their first love-nest, but Kerry's family came from

Dagenham, mostly from the Ford factory, and she wanted to get back there.

'We should be sitting two metres apart,' I reminded Alan.

'Have a biscuit,' he said. 'I think there are some custard creams somewhere.' He looked around but the custard creams didn't reveal themselves. His fondness for teeth-rotting biscuits had been one source of dissension in our marriage.

A memory came back to me of our first meeting. It was in the student bookshop on the EMU campus, a dispiriting, half-empty place. Alan was in the history section and I was next door in sociology, looking for a copy of Emile Durkheim's *The Rules of Sociological Method*, which I didn't want to read, but had been told I had to. The light in Alan's eyes drew me to him, and then I fell for the correctness of his speech which was delivered in full sentences with verbs and correctly placed subordinate clauses. But time had passed and that Alan bore little resemblance to this one in the cluttered ex-council house with the wind turbines turning on the horizon. His hands, and the mug of tea, were shaking as he regaled me with the story of Kerry's desertion one Monday afternoon following a visit from Jonathan the Nurse.

'I had this sore on my knee,' he told me for the second time. 'It had gone all yellow. I rang the doctor but they weren't seeing anyone because of Covid. How can you be a doctor and not examine anyone? It beggars belief.' He sighed. 'They said I had to send a photo. Well, of course I don't know how to do that though I do have a new mobile phone.' He fished around in his felted gilet and produced a phone in a pink case. 'It was Kerry's, she left

it for me when she went. She bought a new one, an, an...
what do you call them?'

'IPhone,' I supplied. That was typical of Kerry, always
wanting the good things in life.

So an odiferous knee had initiated Kerry's romance with
Jonathan the Nurse. 'She was just doing what you did,
exchanging her partner for a younger version,' I pointed
out. 'He *is* younger, isn't he?'

'Forty-one to her fifty,' said Alan gloomily. 'Mind you,
she's always looked after her appearance. They wanted to
go to Fuerteventura, but they couldn't because of all this
silly virus business, so they went to the Holiday Inn near
Heathrow instead. Kerry said it's got triple-glazed windows.
She's very sensitive to noise.'

After an appropriate silence, we exchanged disjointed
news about children, ours and theirs. Alan had inveigled
a daughter called Evangeline out of Kerry. He wasn't very
clear about what had happened to Vangie, though he
claimed she'd become a trapeze artist. And then the
grandchildren. I told him what I knew about what was
going on in Sam and Sara's lives, and then I decided to
tell him about Mila and Ed. I don't think he fully
comprehended the mechanism of Ed's conception.

'That's very peculiar,' he said. 'How can you bring up
a baby safely on a houseboat? I wouldn't like to do that.
It might fall in.'

I tried to explain that there was no living on a houseboat
involved for baby Ed and his mother, and that they were
at this very moment ensconced with Jack and his family
in Steeple Claydon.

'When I was a boy,' said Alan, his eyes acquiring an
extra layer of mist, 'I wandered into a stream one day.

We lived in a big house with a meadow and a stream running through it. They fished me out just in time.'

Actually, Alan grew up in a Glasgow tenement, in unimaginably impoverished circumstances.

'Now, what was I saying, Alice? Oh yes, you see, Kerry isn't coming back. I'm all on my own now.' He put on an immensely sorrowful expression.

There was a loud bang behind us and a large black cat sidled in, mewing. I bent to stroke it while it arched its back enthusiastically.

'The cat's Kerry's as well. She's coming back to fetch it when she's settled.'

'That seems rather unfair. It's company for you.'

'I don't like it. Bloody animal. Wakes me up at night with all its noises. So does my bladder. Prostrate, you know.'

'Prostate,' I corrected automatically. A surprising number of men I knew had mispronounced prostate problems. It was difficult for them to come to terms with the sudden horribleness of an organ they didn't know they had. Not being able to pronounce it must be part of the disassociation.

I did a quick survey of the rest of Alan's house. It was an abysmal mess – papers and books and unopened mail and newspapers with torn corners, dishes with dried cat food ready to trip up a person on crutches, open tins of baked beans and Campbell's Cream of Tomato Soup on the sideboard, a mile of greasy plates and caked-up saucepans in the sink.

'You're letting yourself go,' I told him firmly. 'You're only eighty-four and you've only got the beginnings of dementia. Your clothes smell and your housekeeping skills haven't improved over the years.'

'Only eighty-four,' he repeated. 'Only eighty-four. But that *is* old, Alice.'

To move the conversation in the opposite direction, I showed him a photo of Ed on my phone taken the morning after Mila landed on my doorstep. 'This is your new grandson. This is why we have to keep ourselves going.'

He peered at the image, and I stretched it out with my thumb and forefinger so those wonderful lashes came into view. Alan was more impressed by this manoeuvre than by the baby. He wanted to know how I did it and whether he could do the same with Kerry's pink phone. 'You could teach me, Alice. You've always been good at things like that. I hate machines. You're on your own, too, aren't you now? What happened to that French chap? Did he die? Where do you live now? Hampstead, is it? Or Willesden? I'd come and see you, but I can't walk far with these things.' He kicked one of the crutches which was leaning against the table. It fell on the cat which shrieked loudly and ran away. 'You know what you should do, Alice, you should come and live with me. There's plenty of room. You wouldn't have to share my bed if you didn't want to. There wouldn't be much point in that anyway, not with my prostrate problems.' He lapsed into a morbid silence.

I cast around for something more cheerful to discuss than the prospect of the two of us crammed into this small dirty house. It was December, so the weather wasn't a promising subject. And it might lead to climate change and the prospect of the world and all living things as we know them disappearing. More immediately there wasn't a great deal to look forward to – no parties or fancy Christmas celebrations or trips to Lapland to see Santa or trips to the Canary Islands to see the sun, as Kerry and her new paramour had discovered. The constant news of thousands dying with the BV had recently been enriched with the looming total collapse of Brexit negotiations which was causing miles of stationary lorries, hugely expensive food, mountains of paperwork, hundreds of ruined businesses and the inability to take your pets abroad ever again. In the USA, President Trump was celebrating the end of his reign by ordering five executions. There he was, sitting in the White House as gloomily as Alan in Dagenham, eating his hamburgers and figuring out what extra awful mischiefs he could inflict on the world before finally giving into the democratic will of the people.

I did think of mentioning Maud as a change of subject, but that wasn't an uplifting story either. I was now spending increasing amounts of time imagining various possible versions of what might have happened to her, but it was all fiction. And Alan would find such a tale about a forgotten woman he'd never heard of cognitively challenging. Maud deserved more than a blank stare.

So I tidied his kitchen, although I wasn't brave or foolish enough to take on the rest of the house. I told him I would find him a cleaner who would wear a mask. I wondered out loud why Kerry had abandoned all responsibilities towards him.

'We had thirty happy years together,' he remarked in her defence.

'So this is love,' I said, indicating the state of the house. 'An excuse for abandonment.' I meant both of them – Alan leaving me for her, and her leaving him for Jonathan the Nurse.

I left Alan sitting in the kitchen with a bowl of tinned

ham and pea soup. The cat returned as I was leaving and settled on the clean tea towel I'd put out. Alan still had that yearning look, but even in his cognitively impaired state I think he had the glimmer of an understanding that I was resolved to do something more with the rest of my life than return to the role of man-carer.

I did love Alan once, oh yes I did. I loved the young Alan with the firm straight body and the clear eyes and the lush ginger hair and the passion for medieval history, especially the Ottoman invasion of Greece in the fifteenth century. I loved the Alan who made me feel like a woman and onto whose manly chest I could rest my bewildered female head each night. I think we were both bewildered by what parenthood did to us. I became a yawning soggy caricature of my own housewife-mother, a person devoted to the smaller things of life, like the price of nappies and the nits, oh god the nits. He descended into an inchoately dissatisfied version of masculinity, a man who had it all but who really didn't enjoy it.

We played the gendered couple game, Alan and I, in those far-off days in Crouch End. It was a routine that included dinner parties. We'd invite couples we scarcely knew but had met at the school gates or in the local health food shop – always couples because we were extremely heterosexist then. They were to come to our house at seven o'clock, by which time we had to get Jack and Nathan into bed and ideally asleep, or at least promisingly quiet, and I'd been cooking all day and was completely exhausted, and all I wanted to do was go to bed as well.

The worst was moussaka. It was one of Alan's favourites because of its origins in the Middle East, an Arab dish dating from the thirteenth century. All the aubergine slices had to be fried first which used enormous quantities of olive oil. Then the mince had to be combined with tomatoes and onions and spices and a liberal dose of cheap red wine and simmered for ages and stirred throughout. Then everything had to be amalgamated in layers with the final torment of the béchamel sauce which was another disaster waiting to happen – a roux with butter, flour and milk which requires the utmost vigilance not to burn or turn into lumps.

It makes me sick to remember those dinner parties now. The doorbell always rang at 7.10 because it was polite to be a little late. Alan made everyone drinks, usually G and Ts. We had wine with dinner and then brandy and After Eights with coffee. The other couples went home just before midnight when the hourly rate for babysitters doubled and Alan and I were left with all the clearing up. He wanted to leave it until the morning but I couldn't tolerate the thought of those greasy aubergine-d plates at breakfast. One thing led to another and we usually had a flaming row which escalated beyond the washing up. On one renowned occasion I threw a cast-iron frying pan at him. Our arguments woke the children. I couldn't sleep when we finally got to bed in the small hours. And Alan wanted to have make-up sex, which he considered the best kind, while I had a headache from all the cooking and the alcohol and caffeine and the fatuous talk about schools and what type of car to buy. Oh yes, I did love him. Once.

9 The insanity of women

Maud Davies was thirty-seven and not obviously connected to a man when she died. This was unusual in an age when women were supposed to marry in their twenties. At the inquest into her death, her brother Captain (Claude) Martin Davies said that Maud had recently emerged from a love affair having decided not to marry. There was a suggestion that this unrequited man was stalking her and was sufficiently angered by her rebuttal to puncture her heart and throw her off the train. The newspapers at the time reported the case with forensic excitement: *Social worker's strange death. Underground puzzle. Tunnel mystery*, and so forth. Elsa, who had a British Newspaper Archive account, had kindly printed out these columns for me.

One of the reporters at the time had clearly shared my growing obsession and Elsa had marked this report in bright green highlighter. It was in *The Globe* newspaper for 6 February 1913 and it detailed the investigations carried out by the reporter – a 'representative' – of the newspaper, who tracked down Maud's address to a London County Council flat within two turnings of Euston Station. Euston is where the boat train arrived at two o'clock on the afternoon she died. Why hadn't she gone to her flat round the corner instead of to High Street Kensington? She'd apparently left her luggage from her round the world trip – which must have been a lot – on the platform. The newspaper representative went to Maud's flat. It was a mean habitation for a 'refined lady', just two rooms rented for seven shillings a week in one of the dingier streets off the Euston Road with a squalid entrance filled with costers' barrows. The representative knocked on the door of an adjacent flat and was told Maud had been away for weeks and probably hadn't returned to England yet, though she had left money with another neighbour for the cleaning of her doorstep and door knocker. When informed of Maud's death, the woman was quite dismayed. 'She was a remarkably nice lady...In fact, she was so superior and obviously with means, so I could never understand her living here.'

The newspaper reports played with the idea of suicide as the inquest had despite it being highly improbable that any rational person would stab herself in the heart with a hatpin fifteen times as a method of choice. There are much easier ways – drugs, gas, carbon monoxide, all readily available then, even jumping into a river or sea. In any case, the police surgeon who gave evidence affirmed that the cause of Maud's death wasn't the hatpin wounds, but the decapitation. Did she actually want to kill herself? Perhaps as a result of the failed love affair? Or exhaustion due to overwork, which she had given to friends and family as a reason for her travels abroad? Is this perhaps the essential insanity of women, allowing things to happen rather than choosing what we want to happen? I was particularly intrigued by the report in *The Globe* of Maud's dinner with a man called James Joseph Mallon, three or four days before she sailed on *The Baltic*. Mallon was secretary of an outfit called the Anti-Sweating League, one of the reform organisations to which Maud belonged, which campaigned on behalf of the most poorly paid and ill-treated workers for an improvement in their conditions. At her dinner with Mallon, Maud had discussed her scheme for gathering waitresses into trade unions and had apparently told him that she was looking forward to returning to this work 'with renewed zest' after her travels. This didn't sound like the words of someone contemplating suicide.

I'd started to keep a little notebook in my bag in which I jotted down things that occurred to me concerning Maud Davies. Jimmy Mallon went in there. By now I felt I had a fairly good sense of her personality; it had been examined with some thoroughness at the inquest. The registrar from the London School of Economics, a Miss Christian Mactaggart, who had known Maud for fourteen years, described her as 'a sane, sedate, clear-brained, level-headed' woman who 'preferred philanthropy and the study of social conditions to the easy life of luxury'. Miss Mactaggart definitely ruled out suicide. So did Maud's brother and her friends. One of these, a stained-glass artist called Caroline Townshend, declared that Maud's death was definitely an accident.

The first inquest was adjourned, and the second returned the opinion that no evidence had been uncovered suggesting murder. Again, it was suggested that Maud had murdered herself because she was mentally ill. On *The Baltic*, she'd seen the ship's doctor who diagnosed the early stages of pneumonia which can cause delusions, he said, a view with which I didn't agree, having had it twice quite badly

94

myself and having remained sane throughout. On the boat, Maud had befriended another woman with the same surname, a Mrs Margaret Henrietta Davies of Palmers Green, who gave evidence. She quoted Maud as saying to her the day before *The Baltic* landed at Liverpool, 'What does this mean? The boat is full of spies. Haven't you seen them?' Maud Davies had asked Margaret Davies if she could go with her on the boat train from Liverpool to Euston. As they passed Pinner Station, Maud said, 'We are getting near London now,' slipped off her coat and left the carriage. Neither Margaret Davies nor her coat ever saw her again. At Euston, Maud bought a ticket to High Street Kensington where she had friends. At High Street Kensington she purchased a further ticket to Notting Hill Gate, one stop back on the Metropolitan Railway. And that was her last ticket and her last train journey, if, indeed, she did get on the train. One improbable theory, expounded with some seriousness at the inquest, was that Maud had gone into the waiting room at High Street Kensington Station, stabbed herself fifteen times, and then gone down to the tunnel where she was hit by a train.

The BV is giving us all the time in the world to play around, but the problem is that we play halfheartedly, enmeshed in clouds of ungrammatical public health commands: *Stay home, Save the NHS, Save lives.* I am not staying home. I'm going to High Street Kensington Station to see for myself the site of Maud Davies's unexplained death. I asked Elsa to go with me, but she refused on the grounds that she doesn't like London. The real reason is that she's very caught up in a particularly vital chapter of her book on feet, including a section on their biology. Did I know that one in 50,000 people are born without toenails? So of course she can't see the point of going to look at the tunnel at High Street Kensington. For me the point is obvious. I might learn something from actually being there that the books and the newspaper articles won't tell me.

It takes me three buses to get to the scene of whatever crime it was. In 1913, on the day Maud was there, it was wet and mild, whereas today I'm fighting my way through flurries of snowflakes. The flakes are mostly small, melting on impact with the flattened face masks on the pavement. My hands are a lot colder than hers would have been, at least until her body reached its last resting place on the railway tracks just before this station, en route to Notting Hill Gate. Remember, too, that she'd left her coat behind on the boat train.

The station buildings are new since Maud was here, but the signs down to the platforms have kept the old London Underground format, an arrow through a circle, a bull's eye. She would have seen them, indeed looked out for them, to guide her to the correct platform, exactly as I'm doing now. There are thirty-one steps from the ticket hall down to the platform. Today is a Sunday and that, combined with the bad weather and the BV, means that there are few people around, just solitary passengers in woolly hats and masks shifting their eyes between the screens of their phones and the moving letters of the electronic train arrivals board. A train is due in eight minutes. I walk up and down the platform trying to imagine what it looked like in Maud's time. I had investigated the history of the station before I came and found that it had been rebuilt in 1906, although the ceiling has the same design in the early photographs as it does now. But I don't think Maud would have been up to noticing her surroundings, given that she was either being pursued by someone who wanted to murder her, or was in the throes of her own wish to do so.

It was odd – that buying a ticket for just one stop. Was she in a hurry when she bought it, perhaps out of her own breath and with the breath of her pursuer hot on her slim Edwardian neck? Was she actually aiming to get off the train in the tunnel, lie down between the tracks and die? Above me, the station stretches its brick arches and vaulted crescent ceiling, and the pale snow-light falls out along the platforms that shine with the damp from travellers' shoes. From the station roof hang quite beautiful globe lights, like something out of *Habitat* in its heyday, the sort of thing today's chattering classes would be pleased to accommodate for their dinner parties. (I wonder, does the going rate for babysitting still double after midnight?)

At one end of the platform is the dark hole of the tunnel, flanked with London Transport danger signs. There's a door next to the tunnel entrance. I wonder where it leads. The platform edge is painted with two lines, a warning bright yellow line, and then a white line where the platform really ends. A series of round blue circles are recent additions stuck onto the platform, and under the words *Stay Safe Leave a Space* are the stylised figures of two men and one woman two metres apart with arrow signs between.

A train rumbles in. I see at once that it's almost empty. As I step on, it feels clean, colourful and efficient. Maud's carriage wouldn't have been like this. It would have been made of wood with properly upholstered seats. Most importantly, its sliding doors would have opened and closed manually.

The train's going into the tunnel now so that outside is instantly black. You can see nothing unless you put your face close to the glass and then you can decipher the outlines of pipes and cables clamped to the tunnel wall and the dark iron tracks on the other side. When two trains pass, there is little room for anything else. But Maud's body was here, just here, some seventy yards into the tunnel on the up-line, and it was here that William Clark, the ganger, found it very early in the morning the next day, after it had been lying there for some nine hours. During that time many trains would have travelled over or by it.

I notice two small openings in the tunnel as my train reverberates through it on its way to Notting Hill Gate Station. White light flashes in through these openings and then is gone. I get out when the train stops, conscious that whatever I'm now seeing – the renewed tessellation of the curved ceiling and the built arches, the bold red, blue and white station signs, the screaming red batons of the fire extinguishers, the posters advertising this and that – were not here then, that the air in this station was never air that Maud Davies breathed, because she never reached her destination.

I cross over to the other platform and take a second train back through the tunnel to High Street Kensington. There I linger, loath to relinquish my tenuous grasp on the territory of this peculiar, irresistible death. I go back to the tunnel end of the platform, peer into it, attempt to read its secrets. I don't understand how someone could open the train door and jump out so quickly after leaving the station, nor why they would. If they meant to die under a train, then why not just walk into the tunnel and not bother getting on the train at all? Perhaps that's what she did. But then there's the matter of the fifteen puncture wounds in her body. She was already damaged when she arrived on the train tracks. Was she assaulted on the train or before?

Two fat purple-grey pigeons block my path as I turn to go back down the platform and find the way out. You wouldn't normally need to step around a London pigeon – they take off a second before you reach them. But these two don't. Something is the matter. One of them is crouched low on the platform, its undercarriage squashed, its plump body spread on the ground, and it isn't moving. The other one, a couple of feet away, is taking a few steps this way and that, but displaying no intention of actually leaving the scene. On the contrary, it seems very much confined to the spot, as though unwilling to desert its moribund companion who now turns its head slightly, fixing one tiny glassy eye, I fancy reprovingly, on me. I walk on, feeling uncomfortable, as though I've just witnessed something I wasn't meant to see.

At ground level, just before the ticket barrier, I'm stopped by a man in an orange jacket.

'We've been watching you on the CCTV, Madam. Are you alright?'

I must have looked odd, poking my nose into the tunnel, and taking photos with my phone of the signs and walls and ceiling so as to remember them better. I tell him about Maud Davies – well, not her name, but the general outline of her story. I tell him I'm a writer. He nods with interest.

'You have to do your research then. Must get it right.'

He advises me that the London Transport Museum in Covent Garden might be able to help me. Because it would break company policy (which company? what policy?) he's unable to tell me much about these disturbing incidents, but he can promise me that they happen a lot, not every day, but with unceremonial regularity. Sometimes it's a drunk lad wandering into the tunnel for a laugh. Sometimes it's much sadder and more calculated. It's quite possible that these deaths go unnoticed at the time and are only found later, because a human body is nothing compared to the weight of a 200 ton train. Drivers don't even feel the impact of the train going over them.

So if she was murdered, was it by the rejected lover? Or by some organiser of the international traffic in young women fearful of the facts Maud had uncovered in Jamaica or New York? Or did some random stranger commit the evil deed? If the murder had been planned by someone who had come with her on the boat from New York, why hadn't she been killed on *The Baltic* when it surely would have been child's play to chuck her body overboard with no need for all these shenanigans involving hatpins and railway tracks?

10 One day in the park

The more the BV and the weather constrained ordinary life, the more immersed I became in the Maud story. Its narrative strength pulled me back to a past that has absolutely nothing to do with the present, apart from the vulnerability of women to trafficking and a diagnosis of insanity which are still with us.

In ordinary life we were approaching Christmas. The UK government had put thirty-four million people into an advanced state of lockdown. All the pubs and restaurants and other 'non-essential' businesses that reopened two weeks ago had closed again. Making life even more science-fiction like, the papers carried headlines about how a 'mutant' version of the BV was taking over. In the US, Joe Biden was finally taking over from the deluded Donald Trump and the White House was subject to a thorough sanitising operation involving the replacement of all its curtains and doorknobs. In China, air crew were advised to wear nappies so they wouldn't risk being infected when they used the toilets on aeroplanes.

And then one day in Stoke Newington, on one of my many perambulations round the park thinking about Maud Davies, and what could possibly explain her life and her death, I came across the poet from *Another*

Chapter with a fondness for large books sitting at a bench outside the café. I'd been for a very muddy walk circumventing the two lakes several times, and I was looking forward to a sit down and my flat white. I looked at Stephen Dearlove from a distance and I thought he looked quite nice, a welcoming figure sitting there quietly with his hands cradling a cardboard cup for warmth. We were all feeling starved of company, and here was some openly on offer. I went over and introduced myself, and reminded him where we'd met before. I said if he was writing poetry in his head, which is what I would be doing if I were him, a poet on my own in a park marooned in a pandemic, I'd be happy to leave him alone.

Oh no, he seemed quite eager to talk. It was, indeed, very pleasant sitting there with another cardboard cup of coffee warming my hands and my feet resting in muddy water, talking to another human being face-to-face without masks, which was permissible as we were drinking coffee. The sun came out, casting pallid lemon rays on Stephen Dearlove's lined, intelligent face. His eyes were quite as blue as I remembered and they matched the sky. He had a decent head of hair for a man his age, though I didn't actually know what this was. But I did know mine: you're seventy-four, Alice, I told myself firmly, so fantasies are completely off the agenda.

The lasciviousness of the old is hidden in sentimental myths of the *Brief Encounter* type – Trevor Howard and Celia Johnson in that wonderful 1940s movie, sipping cups of tea from chipped white china cups in a railway station where clouds of steam serendipitously deposit a piece of grit into her eye, and he, with all the magisterial authority of doctors and screen heroes, fishes it out with the corner of a crisp white handkerchief. We are allowed to be romantic but not earthy. We may admire the sly looks of love the elderly throw at one another but genital passion is a foreign country. We have surely given up all thought of how undressed skin feels in the warmth and moisture of the under-duvet world, of how bodies meet and rearrange each other, of protuberances that enlarge and explode. I wonder where such desires are supposed to go. Do they fly elsewhere in a kind of dancing pattern with the wrinkles on our skins, each wrinkle a departed lust? Those two, in *Brief Encounter*, eschew it anyway, and the allure of the film is precisely in their failed consummation, the might-have-been, the nearly-was – so very different from that messy tangle of limbs that leaves nothing to the imagination.

When we were young, we talked about sex with our girlfriends. First of all, it was, have you had it or not, then it was, well that wasn't anything to write home about was it? Not, of course, that one would. And then we entered the mature phase of comparing garish detail. Now we don't talk about it at all. Each of us holds within her a memory of what happened and how it was in that completely other world of the past.

I remembered sex with Alan as a very distant thing, friendly but not very entertaining. After Alan there had been various others, men who inserted themselves into my life and body for a time and then moved on, generally after a polite shove from me. On reflection, maybe I wanted the sex, not the man in my life, and certainly not according to that repetitive formula of let's move in together, get a mortgage together, do the shopping together, go on holiday together, get old together, die together. A total welding of lives. The last man in my life, a photographer called Marcus with very curly pubic hair and a Maserati sports car, came and went about ten years ago. So that's a decade of sex that lives on only in the mind.

On the bench in the park with Stephen Dearlove, the paper coffee cups were empty. I was looking at the clouds, the variegated grey-blues of the layers as the wind moved them in the space above the trees.

'It's really good talking to you, Alice,' he said with some earnestness.

I cast around for the mist of engine steam that ought to be encircling us à la *Brief Encounter*, but there was none, only the squelchy mud beneath our feet and the far-off cries of boys playing football.

Stephen started talking about vaccines. He listed the names of all those the government had bought to stem the tide of the BV pandemic: Oxford/AstraZeneca, Pfizer/Biontech, Moderna, Novavax, Valneva, Janssen, GSK/Sanofi. Enough, apparently for 218.5 million people, or more than three times the entire UK population. Stephen appeared quite heartened by this, while to me it sounded like greedy over-ordering. He began to explain the different techniques used to create the vaccines: how some smuggle the virus into our bodies to get the antibodies going while others tag it on to some other genetic material.

'There is poetry in chemistry,' he said. He talked about the vaccine trials to which many thousands of people were contributing, offering their arms in blind faith that this will do the world, but only a minority of those living in it, some good.

'I don't think I'd be brave enough,' he admitted.

Idly I wondered, because I was getting ahead of the

story here, whether I was brave enough to get immersed in a new liaison of the sexual type. I was fast-forwarding into a future that might never materialise, and wasn't supposed to at my age. In any case, there wasn't any possibility of Stephen Dearlove and I working out our destiny in a series of gentle would-be dates – drinks or lunches or dinners – in any of the pleasant hostelries that line this part of London. Takeaways, which were permissible, aren't any good when there's no obvious place to take them to. A paper bag soggy with fish and chips or butternut squash risotto – particularly badly adapted to a paper bag life – is an emblem of failed desire.

Stephen, it transpired, has coeliac disease, which shrinks the possibilities even further.

'Looking back,' he told me, confidingly, 'it's been a problem all my life, but it wasn't properly diagnosed until a few years ago. My wife Diane was fed up with the smell, you see. People with coeliac disease,' he added, reading the confusion on my face, 'tend to have very offensive bowel movements, and they fart a lot. She made me see a specialist.'

'And how are you now?' I asked, caught between the mysteries of coeliac disease and the mention of 'my wife Diane', and feeling rather romantically deflated by both.

'Absolutely fine so long as I stick strictly to the diet.' He paused, hopefully. 'You don't need to be put off, you know. There are lots of us walking around. Perhaps as many as one per cent of the population. That may not sound a lot, but it's six hundred and eighty-three thousand people.'

It was beginning to rain, my feet were cold, and I was feeling impatient, wanting to move on. Heartened by his use of statistics, I said, 'I'm seventy-four, which is quite old. I was married once but he went off with a strawberry blonde bimbo. He's got dementia now. We had – have – two sons who have three children between them.' Or possibly more, I suddenly thought, in the light of the free rein Nathan allowed his sperm. 'There've been a few other men in my life since then. I quite like men,' I added, trying to be positive, but thinking that I prefer them to be fully healthy if at all possible.

'Suffering is good for the imagination,' remarked Stephen, as though reading my mind. 'It's an old line, but it's true. Look at those last poems of Sylvia Plath's, the ones she left in a folder on her desk when she taped her children's door up and put her head in the gas oven.'

'You've been reading that new biography we ordered for you, haven't you?' I asserted. 'What about Diane? What does she think?'

'Diane was killed in a car accident,' he said. 'She was crossing the Holloway Road when a mad young driver crashed through the lights. Her neck was broken. Have you read any of my poetry? I couldn't write for a long time after Diane died, but then it came to me that I had to. Write myself out of that obsession with her death, you know. It's called *Traffic Lights*. There are twenty-seven poems divided into three sections, red, amber and green.

'That's a bit pedestrian, isn't it?' I said, cleverly, I thought.

'You mustn't make fun of death,' he said sternly. 'The point I'm making is that death can be creative. The ending of life makes us work at its meaning.'

I wanted to tell him about Maud Davies, but it didn't seem like the right moment to launch into a story that might take a bit of time to tell. 'My feet are soaking,' I said instead. 'I think it's time to go home.'

I had a small umbrella in my pocket which Stephen held over both of us. He was like a beanpole beside me, tall and sinewy, and the touch of his body beyond the grey raincoat nearly dissolved my concern about his bowel disability. He saw me to my front door, like a proper gentleman.

Later Jack phoned me from Steeple Claydon to report that Patti was surprisingly taken with Mila, whom she was treating as a potential assistant in her environmental cosmetic business, but the family was finding Ed's night-time screaming quite difficult. Sara had expressed a desire to come and stay with me and do some Christmas shopping in whatever essential shops might still be found. He could put her on the train at the end of the week and could I please meet her at Marylebone Station. 'It was entirely her idea, Mum,' he said, 'you should take it as a compliment.'

This gave me four days to get on with Dr Ahmad-Wicks and pursue the trail of Jimmy Mallon and other possible destroyers of Maud Davies's promising sociological life.

11 Zooming with Sara

'Zoom, zoom, zoom to the moon,' sings Sara. 'You really must learn how to do it, Granny! It's not difficult, I'll show you.'

It was, though, due to my computer not having a camera. So we set out for The Everything Shop – it's not called that but it does sell nearly everything from its dark, crammed cave of shelves. It's on the corner near the cemetery and Mr Shabir was sitting in the doorway behind a table where a BV notice explained that we couldn't go in but that he could fetch anything we wanted.

'My granny,' said young Sara, 'can't do Zoom because her PC which is absolutely ancient hasn't got a built-in camera. So what we need is a HD webcam with a microphone.' 'No problem, dear.' Mr Shabir smiled, rose from his Covid station and rummaged around at the back for a few minutes. 'Here you are, dear,' he said, handing Sara a box.

She examined it carefully, turning it round in her hands. 'I think this will do. It's got auto light correction. And face enhancement technology.'

'That sounds like a good idea,' I said.

'If it isn't right, please to bring it back,' he said, 'and I will refund money.'

Sara was overcome by the sheer number of shops in Stoke Newington after the consumer desert of Steeple Claydon, but worried by so many of them being open with long, non-socially-distanced queues outside. I thought she seemed rather over-sensitive to the possible ubiquity of the BV. I offered her a walk round the historic Abney Park Cemetery before realising that this was rather under-sensitive of me. She really didn't need to be paraded round rows of neglected graves. She wanted to go home, get the camera working, and watch some more episodes of *Dinnerladies*. It's one of my own favourites, but I was surprised to find that she liked it too. Maybe she found its total lack of violence and proneness to politically incorrect remarks quite relaxing.

Jack had been adamant that this little visit – only two nights – needed to happen because they all had cabin fever in Steeple Claydon with Sara the most badly affected. Her mother's online eco-cosmetic business was thriving due to the BV and people stuck at home vainly casting around for new ways to spend money on improbable strategies for improving themselves. Patti's new organic coconut teeth whitening powder was apparently selling like hot cakes. Mila and she were spending many hours either concocting things in the black marble kitchen or wrapping them up and taking loads of Paypal money for them. And so Sara was constantly being called on to mind baby Ed which interrupted her online schooling, and she wasn't fond of either activity.

'Why does this happen?' she protested. 'Why don't they ask Sam? We don't live in the dark ages any more. I don't even *like* babies. My mother isn't a feminist, Granny,' she went on to inform me in a bit of a hushed tone. 'She thinks female people are naturally maternal. She says women are part of the earth and men aren't and that's why women know how to deal with illness using natural things like she does. She says women are witches and she's one and witches used to be called wise women. So apparently when I grow up, I shall be a wise woman too. I think it's all rubbish, I don't mean the things Mum makes, I'm sure they do you good, I mean the stuff about females looking after babies. What do you think, Granny?'

'I think you're already quite wise, Sara.' She was making me smile, and I didn't want to laugh, because I knew she was being extra serious, so I decided to move the conversation on. 'So what is your brother doing at the moment?'

'Oh, he's so nerdy,' said Sara. 'He's doing an online course in quantum physics. He says he wants to be an experimental physicist and work in Silicon Valley and earn lots of money.'

Back in my house, she got Zoom working and soon we were looking at the face of nerdy Sam in Steeple Claydon. Sara has long straight red hair and Sam's is brown and curly and now well past his ears because hairdressers are all closed. I hadn't seen either of them for a while and Sam appeared to have a few pre-pubertal spots on his face. Or was that Zoom? I leant over and adjusted the camera which fell off.

'We might have to take it back to Mr Shabir,' I suggested.

'Oh Granny! Look, you fix the clip here and there's nothing wrong with it, just leave it alone!'

Sam and Sara had a conversation I found it hard to follow because of its speed and their use of incomprehensible teenage terms. I wondered if I could leave Sara to her own devices while I did a bit more Maud-ing or Ahmad-Wicks-ing.

'What are we having for supper, Granny?' Sara was a real foodie, a wise woman after my own heart. As soon as she'd finished one meal she wanted to know what the next one would consist of (of what the next one would consist).

'What would you like?'

She wrinkled her nose thoughtfully as bright pictures of various meals cantered through her mind. 'A stir-fry. With that Chinese cabbage. And cashew nuts. And those white worm-y things. And wholewheat noodles. Mum says they're more nutritious than the rice ones. And can we have chocolate mousse for dessert? I haven't had chocolate mousse for ages. We don't have desserts at home. Too much sugar, Mum says. I can help you make it, if you like.'

Such enthusiasm. So that was the evening taken care of. I explained that I had a bit of work to do and Sara acknowledged that she did too.

'I've got to write a book review for my English teacher. We can choose any book, but we have to have read it. Obviously. I think I'm going to do this amazing book I'm reading at the moment, it's called *Educated*. It's a true story about a girl who grows up in the middle of nowhere in America and she doesn't exist officially because she had these radical parents who didn't register her birth or send her to school. She never went to a doctor either. When she was my age she was bottling peaches. And then she decided she had to get an education so she left her family and ended up at Cambridge University.' Sara sighed expansively.

What thirteen-year-old wouldn't be imagining what it would be like to create a different and better world for herself? And what, I thought suddenly, would our world be like if everyone existed unofficially? If nobody knew which babies were born and when and to whom and where people lived and how many illnesses they had and their actual cause of death? It's awkward enough to get these questions answered now with all our officialdom. But if we didn't have it I would have been able to know even less about Maud Davies than I do, which isn't nearly enough.

Sara agreed to take her nascent book review into the bedroom so I could get my hands on all the official records my computer could locate. And it was then that I made a weird discovery. When Maud Davies had visited her family in Rutland, she'd been just a couple of miles from Elsa's cottage, up the hill in the next village. Imagine! I did. I thought about Maud there, walking across some of the same fields and down the same muddy dog-fouled paths as I had. I saw her look at the same trees, winter-black against a pink-streaked sky, loaded with fresh green leaves in the summer. Maud stayed in a house called The Pastures which is set back from a bend in the road and designed by a famous architect called C. A. Voysey. He built it for one of Maud's aunts, her mother's sister, a woman called Gertrude Catherine Conant. I found this out by doing a little exploration on Ancestry of Maud's maternal family history. The 1911 Census showed Gertrude Conant aged sixty-five with 'private means' living in The Pastures on her own with three servants. There were two housemaids, an Emma aged twenty-eight and a Susanna aged thirty-seven, to take care of her in the fifteen-roomed house, and a twenty-eight-year-old cook, another Gertrude. The descriptions of the house I uncovered were lyrically architectural. 'A charming composition on three sides of a quadrangle. A small but spreading house,' Nikolaus Pevsner called it in his *Leicestershire and Rutland*. There were stables, a coach house, and a tower with a clock and bell, and a saddleback roof. The extensive gardens had flagged paths, pergolas, yew hedges and a dovecote, now all gone. The website of the C. A. Voysey Society mentioned the removal of a sundial to another grand house only a mile or two away, Lyndon Hall. And lo and behold, when you look up Gertrude Catherine Conant in the 1891 Census, before The Pastures was built for her, there she is in Lyndon Hall on what was effectively a Conant family estate village, a tiny place called Lyndon tucked away in the midst of fields with its own little thirteenth-century church and a door leading directly to Lyndon Hall that the Conants could slip through to worship without anyone noticing. In 1891, Gertrude's father, Maud's maternal grandfather, was a widower of seventy living with Gertrude and two other adult children. The family was serviced by no fewer (not less) than fourteen servants, including two laundresses, a butler and two footmen.

All those servants: how overwhelming. What did they all do? The sense of connected history conveyed by these digital discoveries is somehow deeply moving. They make me feel close to Maud's life. Which is ridiculous, really. She's nothing to do with me, and if it weren't for the BV I'd be doing something more sensible than wandering about on websites for any remaining traces of Maud Davies. For a start, I would have finished this indigestible

113

treatise on female detectives which is riddled with unnecessary adjectives and mishandled prepositions, and got stuck into whatever grammatical challenge The Publisher has lined up for me next. I would have done a bit more housework and not suffered from the small dose of servant envy I caught just now. History is all about class. I knew that in theory, and Maud certainly discovered it when she used her own class position in Corsley, Wiltshire, to infiltrate and report on village life. The villagers didn't like it. They didn't admire the way she criticised their diets and leisure habits:

House bare, dirty and neglected.

Not very energetic man.

Wife very loose character.

Too lazy to do anything.

Had she chosen to study the communities round Lyndon Hall or The Pastures, I'm sure the moralisations would have been similar, so those villages don't realise how lucky they are.

Sara burst into the room with that guileless energy only children have and handed me some sheets of paper. 'It's my review,' she said. 'Please Granny can you read it? You're good at that sort of thing.'

'Hang on a minute,' I said, 'I've just got to send an email.' It was to Elsa about my Rutland discoveries. I wanted someone to share my excitement and she was the only possible candidate.

Sara's book review needed a bit of work. There were too many misplaced subordinate clauses and 'I think's, and the usual confusion between 'affect' and 'effect'. She took my editing quite well and was adamant that the teachers at the school she attended in Buckingham never went on about grammar and punctuation the way I did. They never mentioned them, in fact.

By now we were both hungry from our labours, and we cooked the stir-fry together. Sara cracked the eggs and then she stirred the melting chocolate for the mousse. When I poured myself a glass of Devil's Creek Merlot she asked if she could have one. I didn't know the protocol for just-teenage people and alcohol, but I remembered the way French families are relaxed about allowing their young a taste of the grape, so I gave her a little in diluted form.

Later, Stephen Dearlove rang in the middle of a *Dinnerladies* scene in which Victoria Wood's daft mother turns up with a teenage boy in tow. Stephen wanted to know whether we might go on a walk together, perhaps a little further afield than the local park. Had I, for example, ever been to Railway Fields in Harringay? Our conversation was rather stilted because Sara was sitting next to me oozing curiosity. I explained that he was someone I'd recently met, a poet.

'How exciting!' she said, clapping her beautiful young hands and swinging her shining copper hair. 'Oh Granny, do you think you might get married again? Have you told my mum and dad?'

I tried to calm her down and insisted that sitting with your feet in the mud and discussing potential walks weren't necessarily harbingers of wedding bells. As I reached for the remote to restart the episode of *Dinnerladies* we were watching, she said, with a sideways smile, 'Have you had sex with him yet? Do old people actually *have* sex? You can tell me, you know. I won't tell anyone else.'

When I didn't answer immediately, it didn't take one of Dr Ahmad-Wicks's detectives to work out that here was a trail I was quite possibly putting her off the scent of (I wrote the sentence like that as an excellent example of incorrectly placed prepositions). Children cut through all our pretensions and excuses and airs and graces with a blast of clean spring air or the force of a cleaning fluid that kills all known and unknown germs.

Elsa replied to my email about traces of Maud in Rutland in quite a technical non-excited way. She reminded me that I had actually walked past The Pastures on many occasions.

'It lies on the circular walk we often do when you come here,' she said. 'You can't see the house properly from the road but there's a magnificent tree where the road swings round to go down the hill. And that other grand mansion, Lyndon Hall, I have been there. It was open for one of those National Gardens days a few years ago. It's a splendid William and Mary house, but you can't normally go in the grounds.'

I felt deflated. 'You've missed the point,' I said. 'Isn't it exciting to find out that Maud and her family actually had roots in your area?'

'Well, they have to have roots somewhere. You're getting far too obsessed with this, Alice.'

I look forward to going to bed (by myself) these days because I'm reading a very whimsical novel about a ninety-five year old detective who lives in a Finnish care home full of bodies that really are on the brink of mortality.

They shuffle around rattling with pills and relying on zimmer frames and canes that get stuck in doorways, but their eyes and minds are razor sharp. They have this quality I'm aware of in myself and Elsa, a determination to speak the truth because there just isn't much time left. The book is the second in a series of three written by a journalist who investigated elderly care in an entirely non-fictional way and was appalled by what she found out. Her ninety-five-year-old detective Siiri Kettunen (whom Dr Ahmad-Wicks really should have included in her repertoire) is totally in control of her life, and when she's not investigating the untoward happenings in her care home, along with her two friends who are also well into their nineties, her favourite occupation is travelling round Helsinki on trams. She knows all the routes by heart. Number 4, which goes to and from Munkkiniemi, where the retirement home is located, is the one she enjoys most. Across the top of the front cover of *Death at Sunset Grove* is the line, 'You're never too old to solve a mystery'.

12 Drawing blood

My appointment was for 4.30 and the vaccination clinic was housed in a neglected basement area next to a Covid-closed flower stall. A person in the doorway, of a comfortable-looking size and uncertain gender, asked my name and various other BV-type questions, and held a thermometer to my forehead before handing me a ticket with a number 9 on it and directing me to the reception desk inside. This was walled in plastic and staffed by another not very identifiable person. Here I was given a form by a gloved hand to read and sign. It was, said the voice, my consent to receive a vaccination. My new lenses hadn't yet arrived at Mr Barrow and Son, and this font was far too small but I signed it anyway.

The next step was to sit in a waiting area with about ten other people on meticulously spaced chairs. Most of the waitees were assiduously studying their phones. I took mine out to keep them company and saw a muddled, totally unpunctuated text message from Alan: *alice can you come next week not Tuesday best would be am no lunch here*. Down the corridor, which I could see from my chair, was a set of cubicles with curtains. The curtains must surely be a contamination hazard. Every cubicle had a seat outside and there was someone sitting on it. As I watched, two of the cubicles ejected people who were busy rearranging their clothing and who then left the building. A PPE-protected nurse promptly arrived in the corridor to carry out vigorous sanitising actions (PPE stands for Personal Protective Equipment, an item in the nasty lexicon the BV has delivered to us). This nurse then called out the names of two of the waiting people to occupy the cleaned chairs. It was like a cattle market. I'd been watching farming programmes on telly recently, and this is what farmers do to their animals, though without asking them to sign anything.

When it was my turn to sit on the chair, I went gladly because I just wanted to get this over with so I could text Elsa and boast that I'd got mine before they got round to hers. We were told that vaccinations were being rolled out equally rapidly everywhere, but as usual the reality was somewhat different. Areas of over-supply alternated with vaccination deserts. I tuned in to the conversation inside the cubicle.

'I really don't like having needles stuck in me. It makes me feel very dizzy.'

'Best to look the other way, then. It'll only take a few seconds.'

'Owwww!'

It can't be that bad. I wonder how many needles I've had stuck in me over a lifetime, well, nearly a lifetime. Hopefully, this one will prolong it. The needle-averse person came out of the cubicle, a stick-insect of a woman pulling a worn tartan coat around her freshly punctured arm. I smiled at her behind my mask. She returned what was probably an anxious grimace. And then I was invited in.

The young man inside the cubicle looked tired. When

119

I asked him, he told me they were doing five hundred a day.

'Are you a doctor?' I asked, hopefully.

'No, I'm a volunteer vaccinator. We do a proper St John's Ambulance training, it doesn't take long to master the art,' he added consolingly. He said he normally worked in the Accounts Department of a supermarket, and his grandfather had died of the BV, although he had been ninety-six when it happened and he died in his bedroom, not a care home, and it was in fact possible that he hadn't died of the BV at all.

'Underlying health conditions,' he said.

'Old age,' I countered.

The sleeve of my jumper rolled up, we were ready. A segment of my upper arm was swabbed with alcohol (I could smell it), and in went the needle. I watched it go in most intently. There it was, the precious, much fought-over and scientifically debated substance that would spell the end of the BV. For such a significant moment, it was over far too quickly. There was a small trickle of blood before the volunteer vaccinator stuck on a plaster. Blood, the stuff of life, that joins families together despite the arguments and differences that divide them, that connects me to baby Ed, conceived instrumentally on a Dutch kitchen floor. Blood that flows out of women periodically throughout much of their lives and most explosively as new life emerges, a reminder that our lives are governed by biology and the phases of the moon. At the inquest into Maud Davies's death, it had been reported that spots of blood had been found on the lavatory and basin of the boat train that brought her from Liverpool to Euston that Saturday afternoon in February. Had she been practising stabbing herself with a hatpin in preparation for the later tunnel denouement?

I took the bus home, again turning over in my head all the possible explanations for Maud's demise, churning them round and round, just as the good gardener I am not tosses around ancient vegetables and fibrous cardboard (I'd resorted to watching gardening programmes as well) in the effort to create a nourishing compost heap. Then I remembered that Stephen Dearlove would want to know which brand of BV vaccine I'd consented to admit to my body, and I didn't know the answer to that.

13 Hot topics

Maud Davies may not have been married or lived with a man, but her social investigations gave her a fairly good idea of how such relationships fared among the poverty-stricken populations that she researched. Women were expected to be good wives and mothers as well as economically productive members of society. Men were berated for not being sober, secure providers:

No good. Was compositor and tailor. Would not work at either. Has deserted his wife time after time.

Husband killed in drunken brawl.

Maud was obsessed with drink. Alcohol was blamed for many evils and it went hand in hand with poverty as a method for ruining character. At Christmas time in 1905, she loitered outside the six pubs in Corsley, recording her observations in a notebook: *at 9.30 p.m. on Christmas day, 11 men, 4 strange women. Singing; on Boxing day at 8.30, 17 men with 5 wives or daughters, 4 strangers, male and female. Gramaphone.*

I wonder what they thought of her hanging around like that. Well, we know what they thought. They were recognised by her book. They recognised themselves in it, and so did their neighbours, even though she took the trouble to change their names. They lobbied the parish council to stop publication.

Maud's understanding of women, marriage and identity was incisive and well ahead of its time. When she died, she was in the process of writing a chapter about women in rural districts for a book called *Married Women's Work*. This was a hot topic in the early 1900s when the middle classes discovered that the working classes had been pursuing this habit for ages mainly because they had to. Should married women work? Was it good for their children or their husbands? Maud was still labouring to put right the middle-class view of women's work among the lower classes when she died, which was surely more evidence that she didn't intend to.

For her unfinished chapter, Maud talked to women in Worcestershire, Essex and Wiltshire and asked who in the household did what kind of work, who earned what kind of money, how the money was spent, and how families were fed. In old timbered cottages with whitewashed rooms and hams and strings of onions hanging from the kitchen beams, great open fireplaces, damp walls and peeling wallpaper, women told her that, as well as making meals and baking bread and growing vegetables in their gardens, they worked three or four ten-hour days a week for the farmers who owned the cottages in which they lived. The women laboured at ground-dressing – picking sticks and stones out of the fields – hop-tying, hay-making, potato-sorting, sack-mending, and gathering fruit, hops and vegetables. The little children went with their mothers to the fields and the farmers regarded that as perfectly acceptable.

Maud observed that this outside work and its income gave the women a healthy independence. She compared them with rural women who stayed at home. A stay-at-home woman was isolated and unhealthy, experiencing 'a depression of spirits and a morbid exaggeration of minor ailments that robs her of pleasure in living,' wrote Maud. I was especially impressed by her remark that in Essex women married to sailors had the housework and cooking taken off their hands by the men when they came home, so the women, as the main breadwinners, could get on with their work. Sadly, this tradition didn't last.

In the weeks following our muddy meeting in the Clissold Park café, Stephen Dearlove and I sauntered around a number of London's parks and gardens, not just Railway Fields (a disappointment), but Regent's Park, St James's Park, Holland Park, Victoria Park and a much less well-known medieval space, Coldfall Wood in Muswell Hill. We didn't ever discuss the sexual division of labour – a term that actually means the division of labour by sex. The use of the words *sex* and *gender* has become so vastly confused recently that it's easier not to talk about it at all. I discovered that Stephen was knowledgeable about an eclectic range of subjects – classical music, especially Haydn's early symphonies and Shostakovich's string quartets, the history of the London Underground (which came in handy with respect to Maud Davies), the technology of cheese-making (not very engaging), and poetry, of course. He introduced me to the work of the American poet Emily Dickinson which I'd never read. She was an extraordinarily morbid woman who called death 'sleeping the churchyard sleep' and wrote dozens of poems about it. She was also a most unconventional user of dashes and capital letters. I'm glad I didn't have to copy-edit her.

The only trouble with all this discussion was that Stephen seemed more interested in telling me about himself and his interests than in finding out about me and mine. I did point this out once and he said, 'Well, I assume that if you want me to know about you, you'll tell me'. I explained that the division of labour by sex doesn't normally work like that. He looked disbelieving.

One day we decided to do a proper tour of Abney Park Cemetery which is close to both our homes but which neither of us had examined properly. We went on a Friday when streets in the area are heavily patrolled by Hasidic Jewish families. It's a spectacle that's always fascinated me. The men and boys have hats and side locks and severe black-and-white costumes, their white stockings flashing like advertisements for washing powder in the grimy streets. The women are corralled in their wigs and cover-up clothes and surrounded by assemblies of small children.

The Cemetery itself is a theatre of neglect with its rampant ivy, headless angels, fallen tombs and unreadable epitaphs. While Stephen searched for the historic graves, I studied the way in which people's bodies had come to repose here. Many just 'fell to sleep', or 'passed peacefully to sleep'. Emily Dickinson would have approved. Some 'passed peacefully away' but only a few actually died. It's just the same as in the newspapers I sometimes peruse where death remains the great unmentionable, and everyone dies peacefully, never noisily. I was in the room when my mother died, and it was far from peaceful. She made a horrible rasping noise like a steam train drawing out of a station.

Eventually Stephen and I came to the rectangular ruined chapel in the middle of the Cemetery. A group of women and children were picnicking on rainbow rugs with animated chatter and small boys rampaging round the tombs wielding sticks. The seated figures were much huddled in coats which is how you have to do BV socialising in December. Life in the midst of death. On several of the larger tombs people sat communicating with their phones. Stephen and I sat down too. Instead of looking at our phones, he took my hand, which was resting on the vivid green moss that covers old tombstones. Rather absentmindedly, and while continuing to talk about the Northern Line extension that will connect the massive residential developments around Battersea Power Station to the rest of the City of London, he played with my fingers, stroking them one by one. I wondered whether he felt the arthritic nodes that disfigure several of them. I met a physiotherapist at a party once, in the days when one could go to parties, who told me they were called Heberden's nodes after an eighteenth-century English doctor and classical scholar who was renowned for listening to his patients – the only reliable way of collecting clinical evidence at the time. I didn't draw Stephen's attention to the state of my fingers, or what he was doing with them. I asked him whether he was getting fed up with all these walks. Would he perhaps like to know what happens next? He didn't get my meaning but I decided to invite him to dinner at the weekend anyway. Yes, he would be pleased to come.

I made fish pie. In my experience, British men like the concept of pie and they enjoy the creamy mashed potato which rests on top of the fairly unidentifiable marine objects floating beneath. Impressed by the food economies practiced by Maud Davies's wives, I used some fish I found in the freezer – two pieces of cod, two of smoked haddock, a few prawns. The cod was a bit greyish but I thought it was probably ok. A fish pie was quite a lot of work, bringing back doleful memories of moussaka in Crouch End, but it did have the advantage of clearing much-needed space in the freezer.

I thought he might bring a nice bottle of something and some flowers, like the robust ungrammatical young men on *Dinner Date,* another programme I'd been watching in order to pass the time. At the last moment I realised that the wheat in the small amount of flour I'd used to make the fish pie sauce might upset Stephen's gluten-sensitive digestive system: perhaps if I said nothing, neither he nor it would notice?

He stood there on the doorstep punctually at 7.30 with a transparent British Library bag containing books. I do like books, of course I do, but I must admit to a feeling of disappointment. Did it show in my face? 'You look worried, Alice,' he commented, as we moved inside and stood under the white glare of the kitchen lights where I'd led him because the fish pie was undergoing its delicate operation of browning under the grill. People have to know each other well before they can read with any degree of accuracy their expressions. He seemed pleased to show me the books he'd brought – a copy of his *Traffic Lights*, the volume penned in the aftermath of Diane's death, and two others, *Street Signs* and *Magic Roundabouts*. He had inscribed all three in careful black italic handwriting, 'For Alice Henry with fondest regards, Stephen Dearlove, December 2020'. 'Fondest regards' struck me as a tad old-fashioned, perhaps even a phrase Maud Davies would have used.

We ate the fish pie on the table in the bay window with its view of the street while Stephen waxed lyrical, like the music, about a Haydn concert he'd heard the other day on Radio 3, and then moved seamlessly on to the topic of various literary conferences he'd attended over the years. This made me think of Malcolm Bradbury's novel *Doctor Criminale*, about a young journalist's search for an elusive cultural hero of postmodernism, a journey that took in a number of pretentious literary events and some engagingly rampant sex with a young woman called Ildiko Hazy who had a predilection for shopping and never quite telling the truth.

Stephen and I didn't have sex after the fish pie as might have been expected had we been replicating the plots of Malcolm Bradbury novels. But he did kiss me fondly (with fond regards), and the whole thing was definitely better than a night spent with *Dinner Date* or roaming Netflix. I can't work in the evenings, my eyes get very inefficient in the dark at spotting those misplaced apostrophes and confusions of –ise and –ize. But they are still equal to the task of washing up. Stephen didn't offer to help. He exited promptly after the kiss, taking the empty British Library bag with him.

14 A Christmas to remember

Elsa phoned me on the Sunday morning after the Saturday night. 'I take it you've seen the news? That buffoon has done it again. I wonder who he's going to spend Christmas with.'

'He'll go in his helicopter to visit a mistress, I expect,' said I. 'It's probably what most men dream of doing at Christmas.'

Our non-esteemed PM, Boris Johnson, had just invented a further tier of BV restrictions with the result that nobody could really do anything any more. Elsa said that people would be downsizing their turkey orders in droves.

Christmas. What to do about it? When the boys were little, Alan went to the pub on Christmas day morning while I tried to cram the over-sized turkey he'd ordered into our under-sized oven. His parents always came, and my mother (my father was dead by then), who took a dim view of the way I treated Brussels sprouts – halved and fried with chestnuts. Until he was about ten, Nathan would have a tantrum during the meal because the food on his plate looked different from his non-Christmas food. Alan's parents were puritanical and didn't drink, causing me to have an extra swig of wine whenever I went into the kitchen, which was often. We watched the Queen's

Speech, or they did. Alan went to sleep and I did the washing up. Happy days.

This year, Jack, always the responsible one, had invited me to Steeple Claydon for Christmas but that was before they'd taken in Mila and Ed, and before the latest rules and regulations.

'Buckinghamshire,' pronounced Elsa, 'is in tier 2, and you're in tier 4, so you can't go there.'

'Well, I can't go to the Netherlands to see Nathan, can I? I would really like to find out what he's up to. Well, I would really like to find him.'

'You know what he's up to,' said Elsa smartly, 'and the result is that baby with the name that really isn't quite a name at all.'

I considered Nathan dreamily for a moment, my bipolar child with the amazing eyelashes, my baby of Christmases past. Motherhood is memories. The children come and the children go, leaving behind only mnemonic traces. Through torn snapshots and judiciously edited conversations we reconstruct our children as we want to remember them, which is selectively. The good moments hit star status, the bad ones drop into the abyss, and everything in between is just a massive blur. I'd told Stephen Dearlove he was lucky not to have any children. Diane had been hit by a premature menopause at thirty before the car got her on the Holloway Road. 'I miss fatherhood,' he'd said, mistily. 'Well, what I imagine fatherhood is like. It might have enriched my poetry, though judging from that new Plath biography I'm reading, it doesn't necessarily have the same effect on women.'

Elsa and I agreed that I would spend Christmas with her which was equally against the rules of between-tier travelling but it would triumph over the problematics of family life.

'They might have border patrols out,' I speculated. 'It would be quite exciting to be arrested at Christmas.'

She wanted me to go a few days early. 'We'll have oysters and champagne and walk in the woods and talk about Maud Davies.' Where would Elsa get oysters in Rutland, a deeply inland county, at Christmas?

Maud Davies spent the last Christmas of her life somewhere in Jamaica. It would have been warm, the temperature well into the twenties or early thirties. The island was just coming out of the hurricane season. Maud would have worn white linen. She might have bathed in the sea. In the early 1900s, Jamaica was vigorously promoting itself as a tourist resort, the Riviera of the Caribbean, and a plethora of new hotels were being built while government propaganda stressed the country's safety for solo-travelling white women such as Maud. It was possible, therefore, that she had actually gone there for a holiday. Not everything has to be a sinister plot, although, once you start thinking about sinister plots, it's remarkable how many you find.

I went by train to Elsa's for my own mini-holiday. I'd put another of Maud's publications in my bag to prevent me thinking about the state of my life and to allow me to continue the diversion of thinking about hers. This publication was a practical guide for members of a recently set up outfit called School Care Committees. When a law was passed in 1906 permitting local authorities to feed needy children, it was stipulated that such cases must first be investigated by home visitors, in other words someone had to go into homes and work out whether children were sufficiently malnourished. The visitors were usually philanthropic women from the local community. Maud did this work herself in three South London schools. Home visitors were untrained, and Maud's book was a how-to-do guide for them. Visitors were to listen sympathetically to the trials of impoverished motherhood before extracting information about household finances. A kind of quid pro quo. Remembering the sensitive intelligence of her face on the cover photo of her other book, I could easily imagine Maud stepping over the threshold of decrepit tenement buildings, holding up her skirts to avoid the damp and the filth, and extending a warmly compassionate upper-class hand to the undeniably harassed mother of indisputably underfed children.

Elsa's cottage had sprung a whole new display of fairy lights which were entwined in the ivy at the front, mingled with the weeds in the low wooden fence and balanced in circles of declining size on the round gateposts on either side. The lights were flashing wildly.

'I can't stop them,' she said, desperately.

In this England of rampaging mutated viruses, out-of-control politicians, and an insane and inept restructuring of national borders, a few badly behaving lights were surely neither here nor there, I thought.

Jack rang to find out where I was, and Stephen Dearlove phoned with a similar enquiry but because of the poor reception in Elsa's cottage I didn't get their calls. On Christmas day, a clear bright-sky day and a very welcome interlude in the monotonous deluging wetness, we left the cottage and my phone finally pinged to tell me what I'd missed.

'Aren't you supposed to talk to your children on

Christmas day?' Elsa asked bossily. 'And your grandchildren? I hope you've sent them presents.'

'You sound like Maud Davies. Very moralising,' I said.

I had, as it happened, done the present thing. Sam and Sara got fifty-pound book vouchers because I thought they ought to read more books as a change from social media. A propos of which, I was glad to read that David Attenborough had suspended his Instagram activities and would reply to actual letters if you sent him a stamped, addressed envelope. I'd picked out an amusing outfit for baby Ed from an online catalogue of ecological Scandinavian clothes and dispatched it with some more money to Mila. I sent Jack and Patti a copy of Maud's *Life in an English Village*, with a note explaining what an interesting person she was, and a suggestion that Jack might like to run a story on her in his newspaper to which I'd be happy to contribute. No-one would know I was the editor's mother because Jack and his brother had their father's surname, as did all children of their generation. Nathan would have opened his Christmas card from me on his houseboat in Leiden or wherever he was. In it I said how nice it had been to meet his sperm-receiver and her son. I mentioned Ed in my card to my sister Susie as well and told her I'd acquired another grandson. It was no competition with her family. They were a prolific lot, her girls – they'd already generated sixteen or seventeen grandchildren and possibly a great grandchild or two.

Elsa drove us to another village for our Christmas day walk. She said she was tired of saying good morning every day to the same people and their dogs. A great band of snowy mist lay on the fields out of which poked church steeples and a windmill with persil-white blades against the kind of blue sky that can only be described as radiant. Patches of ice on the road gleamed in the sun.

'We will walk for 3.83 miles,' announced Elsa. This was a calculation demanded by the number of steps she made herself do every day.

'If you say so.'

A few cars passed us, causing us to tuck ourselves into the frosty verge. The sun, in the process of dissolving the ice, faced us, extraordinarily low in the sky, a great golden face warming ours. We walked out of the village towards the local tourist attraction, a brick-built viaduct spanning the flood plain of the river valley, eighty-two arches, said Elsa, built in the 1870s by three thousand five hundred men and a hundred and twenty horses. A special encampment of wooden huts had been created at one end of the viaduct during its construction to house the families – seven men, two women, and three children in each one. A peculiar number, mused Elsa, always the anthropologist, thinking about who might be related to whom and what they all did with their bodies.

Some women walk next to each other chatting all the time and erupting into screechy laughter and scaring the birds. Elsa and I aren't like that. We talk when we've got something to say. I did quite want to offload on her the narrative of Stephen Dearlove with his self-absorbed manner and deranged intestinal system. 'But do you like him?' she queried. I had to reflect on this. Was I flattered that a man wanted to have whatever Stephen Dearlove might want to have with me, me at my age, the owner of a flabby body and a poorly-hidden disinclination to nurture other people's egos? Was it perhaps just a pleasant diversion at a time when diversions of any sort, particularly those requiring actual human contact, were governmentally outlawed? I thought of Stephen, his neat silver hair, the jowls round his jaw, those marine eyes, and his hands – he did have rather nice long-fingered hands – before answering.

'I don't really know him,' I confessed.

'Are you being sensible?' demanded Elsa fiercely. 'He could give you something.'

'He has actually,' I said.

'I don't mean objects,' she said. 'I mean a virus.'

'He seems very clean,' I observed.

'Oh Alice, how stupid can you get?' After a long pause, she said, inconsequentially, 'It's a long time since I had sex with anyone.'

'Exactly my point,' I said, not having made it. 'It's assumed that women of our age, on our own without men, have finished with all that.'

'Well, I definitely have,' she responded, pulling me sharply into a holly bush to avoid a roaring Range Rover with a male driver who waved magisterially at us. 'And I must say it's a relief.'

'Don't you miss it at all, then?'

'Not one bit.'

'Why not?'

'How can you know why you don't miss something? Surely you only know when you do?'

Elsa's phone rang as we turned the corner of the road and saw a steep hill ahead. She jabbered away in Croatian, which I've always found a most melodious language, like Italian, but more disciplined. She began to show signs of exasperation as the conversation went on and on. I stopped for a bit because of the hill. She finished the call and turned to see me panting and stationary (stationary is a

135

word I often have to correct in people's manuscripts).

'That was my mother in the care home. The staff go round on Christmas day trying to connect everyone to their loved ones even if they can't remember who they are. It's very good of them.' I tried to visualise Elsa's mother whom I had met a couple of times. 'She is ninety-nine, you know,' said Elsa, to help me. 'She's thin as a starving bird but completely with it, apart from being nearly blind, half deaf and almost toothless. She wanted to tell me that they made her a special vegan Christmas dinner.' Elsa's mother had given the care home staff a shock by converting to veganism a few years ago. 'Oh, and she wanted to remind me that millions of people round the world are dying of Covid because someone in China wanted to eat a dead animal for lunch.'

After doing 1.9 miles, Elsa and I turned to walk back to the car. Coming down the last hill, three church steeples started sounding off one after the other so that, as the first finished its twelve midday chimes, the second started, and so on. I pointed this out to Elsa. It was thirty-six o'clock and definitely time for lunch.

I could have eaten one of those horses they used to build the viaduct, but an obstacle awaited us when we got back to Elsa's village. A bevvy of police cars was surrounding a cottage just down the lane. (I don't know how many makes a bevvy – I must look it up.) Anyway, four of them were parked at angles in order to block any escapees. Two policemen in yellow jackets were standing in front of the house. Another was shouting into his radio. In the lane all the neighbours had gathered with their Christmas hats on and bits of turkey between their teeth, not a mask in sight. Small children were having to be restrained from climbing into the police cars. Above us a helicopter circled ostentatiously.

'Well I never!' exclaimed Elsa, who had a nice line in conventional English phrases picked up from a posh boyfriend she had before she gave up sex, who went to Winchester public school.

'It's quite an entertainment, isn't it?' exclaimed a woman with a fuzz of curly hair and red Christmas-y spectacles who was propping up the wall next to Elsa's cottage. 'Really a Christmas to remember!'

Elsa introduced me to Isobel and her husband Toby who was pulling one of their children out of the nearest police car while telling us that he'd noticed, well they all had now they came to think of it, a strange smell coming from that cottage recently. Drains, possibly. And the blinds were always down. And once, Toby had seen someone carrying sacks of potting compost into the house, which was distinctly odd.

As we watched, two of the shouting policemen pitted their might against the front door which gave in, while the other two shoo-ed us back so we were unable to see what was happening inside the house.

'Apparently,' said Isobel, who was acting as the spokesperson for the neighbourhood, being generally the kind of woman who kept an eye on other people's affairs, 'they sent a drone over the house last night and the roof was hot. Toby told the police about our suspicions. He definitely reported that there was something odd going on.'

I didn't understand what hot roofs had to do with it but Isobel was eager to explain. She told us that if you grow cannabis inside a house you have to turn the heating right up, the additional heating costs being more than offset by the profits to be made from the drug trade.

'Well, fancy that!' said Elsa, using another public-school phrase.

'I wish I'd known you lived next to a cannabis factory,' I said. 'I could have taken advantage of that.'

Elsa gave me a reproving look. 'Did Nathan introduce you to the habit?' she asked, after a bit.

'No, I took it up all by myself. When I was younger. With that boyfriend you didn't like, the one with the sports car.' Idly I wondered if there might be pickings to be had from 14 Marigold Lane, and whether I might share them with Stephen Dearlove, and what that might do to or for his gut, poetry and libido.

We continued watching for a bit, but there was a lull because the police were waiting for an interpreter, Isobel explained. She filled us in on the details after edging close to the scene of the crime and nosing around. The cannabis plants, growing hotly on a floor of plastic sheets and potting compost in every room in the house, had been attended by two young Vietnamese men who'd kept such a low profile that no-one in the village had spotted them.

What on earth might it feel like, I wondered, to be an illegal immigrant, paperless and stateless, transported to the monotonous English countryside by international drug barons and stuck in a hot cottage with only cannabis plants for company? Maud Davies knew very well that what seems bland and benign on the surface may turn out to be anything but. And the temptation to make money out of criminal activities can yield a wealth of material for sleuths of all dispositions.

My fascination with her story was now getting dangerously

mixed up with Dr Esmeralda Ahmad-Wicks's excursions into the possibilities of feminism among fictional female detectives. I'd reached the section on Scandi Noir, a genre Dr Ahmad-Wicks pointed out is quite devoid of female investigators which is curious when you consider the generally egalitarian tenor of that culture. Henning Mankell has the depressive borderline diabetic Kurt Wallander we all know and love from watching too much television, especially now; Camilla Lackberg has the equally masculine Patrik Hedström though with some nice domestically-involved-father scenes; and even that innovative 1960s duo Maj Sjöwall and Per Wahlöö, who achieved the difficult feat of creating crime stories together, have Detective Inspector Martin Beck as their hero. Dr Ahmad-Wicks makes a particular point about this subversion of a female crime writer's vision to a male one. She's quite as alert as the best of BV tests for any symptoms, here of sexism, but she's missed a few tricks in her scanning of the Scandi Noir literature. Detective Inspector Louise Rick in Sara Blaedel's *Blue Blood*, for example, who uses the word *fuck* a lot and who lives in Denmark with Peter who does the shopping and cooking and a bit of infidelity on the side.

I could hardly wait to get back to London and my personal detecting projects, but we had to have our delayed Christmas dinner first. Elsa had taken great pains to prepare a feast, although the promised oysters didn't turn up. She even treated the sprouts in a way my mother, the sprout expert, would have appreciated. We ate by candlelight. It was dark by then with the walk and our police-watching having taken the best part of the day. After dinner, we opened another bottle of champagne and watched the news, despite my intention not to. Thousands of irate East European lorry-drivers were stuck outside Dover toilet-less and turkey-less because France had closed its borders to our new 'mutant' version of the BV. Then Elsa and I ate a box of Belgian truffles and watched the carol service from King's College, Cambridge, a big disappointment with no congregation, socially distanced choirboys, and the adult ones replaced by men in suits because bits of the BV had been detected in one of the choir men. A suited voice has none of the allure of a ruffled choirboy's. It prompts an entirely different set of imagined possibilities.

15 The dangers of travelling

January 2021. The second January of the BV. This is always a desolate time of year, the celebrations over, and months of wintery darkness stretching ahead.

Just before the end of 2020, a magnitude 6.4 earthquake hit central Croatia. Its epicentre was a town called Petrinja where Elsa's family live. Her mother in the care home was ok, although she complained to Elsa that all the tiles in the bathroom had cracked. At her age, and as a survivor of the Croatian war of independence, she'd endured so many earthquakes and explosions that a few more really didn't have much of an impact (on her).

I was back in London when the earthquake happened but I could hear Elsa wringing her hands down the phone. In normal times she would have leapt on a plane for a personal visit, but border-crossing was vetoed. By the time our third national lockdown arrived, we had an array of confusing border and other rules which varied from country to country. In some you could still eat in restaurants, though only in daytime, while others had night-time curfews. In some you could still get haircuts and in France shops selling chocolate were kept open as an 'essential' service. It was easy to lapse into a state of lethargic confusion about what we could and couldn't do and why (especially why). EVERYTHING was closed (sometimes capital letters are called for, although not nearly as often as people think).

The news was replete with warnings about crackdowns on 'Covid law-breakers'. A human rights lawyer in South London who'd been keeping a keen eye on it all said that the law on what we were and weren't allowed to do had been changed sixty-five times in the last nine months, and most of it was in any case just 'advisory'. Two women in Derbyshire with bleached hair were stopped for taking a cup of tea to a reservoir a few minutes' drive from their home. The tea was renamed a picnic. The phenomenon of home-lightened hair was everywhere, with UK hairdressers closed and unable to pursue their normal practice of drenching female heads with hydrogen peroxide. The result was a highlighting (a technical term to them), or a general distortion of national hair colour. Dark roots spreading sideways and downwards were particularly noticeable among TV presenters, but you could also get a good view from the top of a bus (this wouldn't count as essential travel). I discussed this with Elsa in view of her academic interest in hair, and she observed that her previous book on the subject had an entire section devoted to peroxidation which she could easily amend in the next edition.

Swimming baths, appropriately full of bleach and thus obviously some of the safest places around, had shut in the first lockdown, reopened in the second and now had been shut again. Elsa moaned about this a lot, since she considered swimming important for keeping the ageing body flexible. Schools had been opened and shut like yo-yos and the rules about which children belonged to a key worker and so were allowed in had become a moveable feast. However, there were a few glimmers of light at the end of one or two tunnels. After an extensive campaign, VAT on sanitary products was abolished. It had never been fair that menstrual bleeding was a revenue-earner while beard growth was not.

Crackdowns in lockdowns – where will it all end? We're trapped in a so-called liberal democratic system that isn't either liberal or democratic. When I was younger, back in the 1960s, we had a sense of optimism that things would get better, and that we as citizens could help this to happen. I grew up believing that politicians would listen before they would dictate, that government was based on reason, judiciously applied, although not always fairly. It was evident to me, growing up on a council estate in Pinner, that material resources were very unevenly distributed. Dad had used this to imbue us with a sense of civic duty. Mum was more phlegmatic, concentrating on good manners, tidy bedrooms and modest ambition. She herself cherished the unattainable ambition of moving us all to one of the upmarket homes in old Pinner.

I was getting down to some serious work on the female sleuth manuscript and quite enjoying it. Dr Ahmad-Wicks indulged in a sufficiently large number of grammatical peccadillos to keep a copy-editor on her toes. I first read Ernest Groves' *Plain Words* when I was a student at EMU and Dr Ahmad-Wicks should have read him too, especially on 'The lure of abstract words'. The section on 'Common mis-arrangements' would also have been useful, for example, 'In accordance with your instructions I have given birth to twins in the enclosed envelope'. When I'd returned the indigestible Pluss to The Publisher, I'd added a note suggesting that in future all their authors might be supplied with a guide to the correct use of punctuation and related matters. I would be happy to write such a guide for them, if they paid me. I would include George Bernard Shaw's wonderful peroration on the use of the colon: 'The dash...is the great refuge of those who are too lazy to punctuate...I never use it when I can possibly substitute a colon; and I save up the colon jealously for certain effects that no other stop produces.' These tips were directed at the famous T. E. Lawrence and his *Seven Pillars of Wisdom*, whose pages Shaw found liberally sprinkled with incorrectly used colons, and almost totally bereft of semicolons. He called this a habit symptomatic of mental defectiveness. I wouldn't myself put it quite as strongly as that.

I decided to discuss my various predicaments with literary texts and domestic obligations and my future plans and Maud Davies with Stephen Dearlove at our next meeting. I had a Christmas/New Year present wrapped up for him, a blue cashmere jumper the colour of his eyes.

'Why don't you cook me a meal?' I suggested, recalling my altruistically indulgent fish pie.

'Alice,' he said with disarming firmness, 'we aren't allowed to do that.'

'We are if we're in a bubble,' I pointed out. Could that be a new lexicon for romantic love? I'll be your bubble. I'll bubble with you – no, I'm not sure it should be allowed as a verb. Too many nouns and verbs are changing places these days: for example we have 'ask' as a noun, and 'action' as a verb, which they aren't.

'You should be in a bubble with your family,' Stephen declared.

'Which bit of it? The bit purportedly on a houseboat in the Netherlands or the conglomerate in Steeple Claydon? Or maybe one or some of my nieces and great-nieces and great-nephews.'

'The grandchildren in Buckinghamshire would probably like to see more of you,' he observed, not knowing anything about grandparenthood. 'But haven't you just spent Christmas with someone who isn't in your bubble? In which case...'

The night after Boris was caught seven miles from home on a non-local cycle ride, I actually dreamt about him. It was an unnerving experience. He had very pink eyes and slimy suntanned skin à la Donald Trump, and he was sitting between two flunkeys. In the dream I commiserated with him for getting caught. I woke up wondering how on earth my subconscious had ever concocted such a ludicrous scenario. No-one should be held accountable for their dreams, but a lot of money has been made out of the opposing view.

While the prospect of a Stephen-Dearlove-cooked dinner was on hold – I left the decision to him – I hibernated with Maud Davies. I laid out all the books and notes on my dining room table. In the street outside, falling temperatures had spawned an epidemic of bobble hats that moved distractingly across my line of vision. Following my dialogue with Elsa about the white slave trade, I'd invested in some reprints from Amazon. *Fighting the Traffic in Young Girls, or War on the White Slave Trade*, had been published in 1910, around the time Maud would have started her own investigations. It was a hard-to-read hyperbolic volume in which missionaries, district attorneys, doctors and such like across America told enraged

145

judgemental stories about girls and young women who'd been disgracefully seduced by promises of love, marriage and employment into working in 'houses of disrepute'. All sorts of institutions had become haunts and procuring places for the white slave trader. Fifteen-year-old Margaret Smith from Michigan, for instance, was led astray by a man introduced to her by 'a gramaphone' agent. I thought this was a typo, but I looked it up and it wasn't, a gramaphone was an early form of gramophone, hence the way Maud Davies had spelt it in her public house observations. The agent called on the Smith family trying to interest them in his musical machines. He was accompanied by a friend who enticed Maggie to go to Chicago with the promise of an excellent job. Once there, she was sold to an Italian called Battista Pizza – yes, really – who ran one of the 'the lowest dives' above a saloon with a back alley entrance through which Italian men streamed for immoral purposes. Maggie was held there for more than a year, but the story had a happy end because her parents finally tracked her down with the help of the local vigilance association.

Elsa had retrieved from her attic a sheaf of notes about white slavery she'd once used for teaching students at the University of East Anglia. I searched for any connection with Maud Davies but there was no mention of her name in any of the long multi-national lists of attendees at the international white slave trade conferences. At the National Vigilance Association in London in the summer of 1899, for instance, there were loads of dukes, counts, judges, baronesses, lords, earls and reverends, but no Miss Maud Davies. This was clearly pretty high level stuff, with letters of support from the Queen of Sweden and the Empresses of Russia and Germany. The documents showed how the mission of saving female bodies from their misappropriation by evil slave-traders overlapped with the wider cause of emancipation, a term that means – and I wonder how many vigilantes then or indeed now were/are aware of this – 'to lead out of slavery'.

It was a soup of good causes that included emancipating women, feeding poor children (provided they were poor enough), abolishing sweated labour, cleaning up dreadful housing and removing drunks from the streets. A lot was about imposing middle-class standards on working-class life – the very problem Maud had met in Corsley when the villagers had objected to her unsympathetic descriptions of their habits. Bettering the lives of the people could also mean selective breeding and all the other unpleasant corollaries of eugenics. Dark motives cowered behind philanthropic ones.

The texts referred to in Elsa's notes were unpleasantly demonising and emotionally violent, a kind of international mass hysteria. I can't imagine Maud, the social-scientific investigator, being hysterical like that, except possibly about alcohol which she hated with a vengeance like many of her sisters in the temperance movement.

There were articles in Elsa's bundle about the National Vigilance Association, originally called the Travellers' Aid Society. It was a propaganda-generating machine, putting pamphlets, placards and warnings at ports and stations, on steamboats and railway trains, advising young women to think carefully about the purpose of their travel. Was it really essential? Was it proper and respectable? Were the women going to a real job, and not one entailing the misuse of their bodies? If they were going to join a man, was it a moral liaison? Stuck to the back of one of the articles was a photocopy of a newspaper item dated the year Maud died reporting a publicity campaign by the operators of London telephone exchanges to warn their female employees about these dangers. Girls must never speak to strangers in public and they should particularly avoid helping any woman who appeared to faint in the street. They must never go to Sunday schools or bible classes when invited by an unknown man. They must be suspicious of anyone dressed as a nurse who told them a relative was ill or had had an accident. Apparently these were all common kidnap strategies. And then there was the 'station visitor' who hung around waiting-rooms which were much more prevalent then than they are now, like the one at High Street Kensington Station wherein Maud was suspected of practising her stabbing operations. The station visitor's job was to greet young women and ensure that they reached safe destinations safely.

Women in the public world were the basic underlying problem here. Various papers in Elsa's collection made it clear that the campaign against white slavery coincided with a period when women started moving round the globe more freely, including from Europe and Russia to the Americas, South Africa and Asia. They were searching for work or marriage, and other forms of liberation or oppression. Their independence threatened the way Victorians saw women's sacred role in the family, and, by a far-fetched piece of emotional logic, this fear was extended to a general panic about a loss of national identity.

When I allowed my eyes a respite from these depressing narratives and glanced out of the window, I was surprised to see a covering of white lying over everything – the street, pavements, hedges, fences, trees, pavements and bobble hats. I didn't realise so much time had passed. I'd been planning to look at this material for an hour or so and then get back to Dr Ahmad-Wicks but it was now two o'clock. I really was enjoying this new role I'd invented for myself – of scurrier through the secrets of the past, uncoverer of reprehensible opinions, and constructor of tenuous hypotheses and improbable explanations. I was, perhaps, actually *becoming* Maud. Our problem – I was sure it was hers as well as mine – was to establish the facts behind the hyperbolic stories of white slavery. What was really going on? What kind of international networks enticed pure young women into what, in the language of the time, was called 'involuntary prostitution'?

I warmed up the remains of a nice earthy mushroom risotto, adding a fried yellow pepper and a tomato salad. A text from Stephen Dearlove arrived as I was grating parmesan to sprinkle over the top. *The Indian in Victoria Street is open for takeaways*, it said. *Tomorrow evening at my place?* An Indian takeaway hadn't been uppermost in my mind when I'd suggested he cook me dinner. I'd envisaged a nicely prepared meal, fresh linen, candles, a pleasing wine. I've never understood why men who live on their own are so reluctant to cook. It isn't that they don't enjoy food, because they palpably do and you can see the results about their persons. But they think of food as coming from somewhere else, and, if it doesn't, they eat cornflakes or microwave supermarket packages enriched with unhealthy Es.

While I ate my lunch I watched a little video on my phone of a goldfish with a condition called 'incurable swim bladder disorder'. After observing that it could only swim upside down, its thoughtful owner had taken it to an animal sanctuary in Wolverhampton where a goldfish-sized suit of polystyrene and plastic tubing had been constructed. Now it was swimming the right way up.

Do you think it's safe? I sent in reply to Stephen Dearlove's text about the Indian takeaway.

Curry powder kills all known germs, he told me. *I want to see you, Alice,* he added seductively.

In the plethora of material about white slaves spread out on my dining-room table, it was similarly hard to distinguish fact from fiction. Although I foraged with all the commitment to objectivity of social investigators like Maud Davies, I simply couldn't penetrate the haze of hysteria which enveloped the topic of white slavery. Western Europe was apparently a source of female workers for brothels, especially in Buenos Aires, reputedly the world centre for prostitution, its 6,413 registered prostitutes in 1889-1902 including 4,361 from Europe. Britain was cited as a prime conduit – a clearing-house, depot and dispatch centre, particularly the ports of Glasgow, Southampton, London and Liverpool, the last port being where Maud had landed from New York in the winter of 1913. There were two main routes – the Western route which led to South America, and the Eastern to East Africa and Asia.

Moral reformers who focused on these networks were frequent travellers themselves, and none more so than a religious fanatic called William Coote who headed the National Vigilance Association. Coote reported a Divine Vision in 1898 that directed him to visit every European capital in an effort to set up an international policing network. His success was limited because he couldn't speak any language other than his own. Maud probably knew him. It was deeply frustrating not to be able to discover the worlds of knowledge that lay behind these names and condensed internet biographies.

Thinking about the dangers of travel, something else occurred to me. When I'd made my little trip to the High Street Kensington tunnel, the orange-jacketed official at the ticket gate had referred to the railways' regular function of hosting death. I've watched both film versions of *Murder on the Orient Express* a dozen times but this is only one example of Agatha Christie's profound fascination with transportation as a context for unexplained fatal happenings. People are pushed out of trains or killed inside them. The transporting vehicle is a closed setting from which death is the only escape.

In real life Maud wasn't the only one. Searching for 'train deaths' and 'unsolved train murders' on my laptop uncovered a universe of malign transportational events. I was now worried that I might be developing a new disorder – googleitis, or an irresistible addiction to internet-searching. Like gamblers who believe that the next stake will be the lucky one, we googlers are powered by the conviction that a bit more looking, a few more keyword searches, more downloaded pdfs or orders for obscure secondhand books will take us to the Holy Grail of whatever it is that we want to know.

In 1897, sixteen years before Maud's demise, the still-warm body of Elizabeth Camp, a barmaid at the Good Intent Tavern in Walworth, was found stuffed under the seat on a train from Hounslow to Waterloo. She'd been visiting friends on her day off, and her fiancé, a fruit dealer, had arranged to meet the train at Waterloo Station, but instead he met the commotion of the police and an ambulance. Elizabeth Camp's head had been battered and lacerated by some sharp weapon whose user was never traced. Eight years later, the mutilated body of twenty-two-year-old Mary Sophia Money was discovered in Merstham tunnel, which today is traversed by all travellers going between London and Gatwick Airport. Mary was a book-keeper for a dairy in Lavender Hill, Clapham, and she'd left that establishment, where she also lodged, one evening in September to go for a stroll, or so she told a friend. She stopped to buy chocolate and then put herself on a train to Brighton. Hardly a stroll. In the tunnel where she died there were claw marks suggesting a struggle to survive. A man with a moustache and wearing a bowler hat was seen leaving a train that passed through Redhill at about the right time, but the police never found him. His description matched that of a man who left the train in which Elizabeth Camp died in 1897. And really even more improbably, in 1906, the eighteen-year-old daughter of a French count, Lillie Yolande Marie Rochard, was discovered dead in a tunnel on the London and North-Western Railway line between Northampton and Rugby. She'd just returned from a holiday in France. She was wearing a black skirt, a muslin blouse and jacket. Her hat, like Maud's, lay at the entrance to the tunnel some distance from her body. As befitted her status, Mlle Rochard had been bedecked with jewellery, none of which was found on her dead body. It was the fall, or push, from the train that had mutilated her and there were no other signs of attack. With Mary Money in Clapham, however, it was horribly evident that someone had wished to kill her because a white silk scarf was found stuffed down her throat. At the inquest it was reported that a woman in the next carriage had heard a scream just before the train entered the tunnel, and presumably before the white scarf arrived at its own destination.

The same questions were asked after these deaths as after Maud's: accident, murder or suicide? It seems clear that Mary Money, Elizabeth Camp and Lillie Rochard were murdered, the latter perhaps for her jewels. Mary Money's purse was missing and the investigation into her death exposed a nasty and possibly unrelated story concerning her brother, a key inquest witness, who went on to murder two women, three children and himself in Eastbourne seven years later.

The peculiar horror of train deaths, as the man at High Street Kensington Station had said, is what trains do to human bodies. This much was clear from Maud's own decapitated death. Another gruesome incident my googleitis uncovered would have been personally known to Agatha Christie. The semi-conscious body of a nurse called Florence Nightingale Shore was noticed by three workmen on a London-Hastings train in 1920. They thought she was asleep, but one of them observed blood trickling down her face from under her hat which was a bit of a give-away. Shards of bone had been driven into her brain by some blunt instrument. Her eyes flickered momentarily but she died in hospital four days later. The case got a lot of publicity. Shore really was a nurse. She'd served in the Boer War, perhaps nursing the wounded Byam Davies, Maud's brother, and then in the French Red Cross during the Second World War. And she really was called Florence Nightingale. The two Florence Nightingales were second cousins, the well-known one being the train-murdered

153

one's godmother. Truth really can be stranger than fiction.

At fifty-five, Nurse Shore was older than the other train fatalities but she had probably been attacked in the same tunnel as book-keeper Mary Money. None of the women displayed any inclination towards self-destruction. They weren't known to be unhappy or particularly nervous or mentally ill. They were just ordinary women going about their ordinary business, although Nurse Shore had received medals for her courageous war service, and Lillie Rochard enjoyed the privileges of a French aristocrat. By the time she ended up on the rails outside High Street Kensington Station, Maud Davies herself had lived a life of considerable intellectual renown.

All this was real – the women, their names, their ages, their costumes, their occupations, the exact positioning of their damaged bodies on the national rail network. It was all as real as I was sitting at my worn pine table in the bay window of my London flat with its untrammelled view of a January street. Out there the temperature was loitering around zero, rain alternating with snow; out there was a dangerous place compared with the safety of home.

Maud, Elizabeth, Lillie, Mary and Florence travelled alone on the railways in an era when a woman on her own was only just beginning to be respectable. What did you fear, and what real dangers did you fail to see? It was Stephen Dearlove, with his advanced knowledge of transport technology, who pointed out to me that the architecture of train carriages in the early twentieth century wasn't woman-friendly. Mainline trains were composed of separate compartments that opened directly to the outside with no linking corridor. It was well-accepted that

154

a train compartment was a place for unobserved canoodling, the moments of erotic exchange being as long or as short as the space between stations. If you substitute foul for sexual play you have the perfect circumstance for the foul-player to exit the scene of his deadly deed without anyone noticing. In the Mary Money case, indeed, a guard said he had noticed, as the train passed by, a struggle going on in the compartment she occupied, but he thought nothing of it, this entanglement of bodies in the separated compartments being quite commonplace.

The rain had turned to sleet, then snow again. The white flakes were falling thick and fast on the bobble hats passing my window, and the over-excited shrieks of small children unused to white stuff cut through the air. The unspoiled whiteness would be nice for a short while, and would give an altogether false impression of environmental quality before it melted and refroze, producing a hazardous alternation of lethal grey slush and black ice. This is the cynicism of the old who've seen it all and fallen down in it too many times before. Where were those crampon things I stick on my shoes in such perilous circumstances? After lengthy searching I found them in the back of the bathroom cupboard behind the professional limescale remover and an unprofessional empty mousetrap. The rubber on the crampons had perished so they were useless. How was I going to get out safely? I didn't want to slide down the street and career into someone's front gate or snow-covered car or hidden pile of dog shit.

I don't often feel sorry for myself, it's not an attractive trait. Have you noticed that it's generally not the old who give into self-pity because they know it won't make any difference and things will just go on getting worse anyway?

It's the young who feel sorry for themselves because they mistakenly feel they have a right to a thoroughly good life. My life was good enough.

I closed the curtains on the snow outside and roamed Netflix and BBC IPlayer for something to take my mind off my good-enough life. Everything on offer was about dismembered bodies in crime series, documentaries, wildlife programmes and the news. All of it. Then the house resonated with the weighty footfall of Mick from upstairs who banged on my door in great agitation and sunglasses with a towel wrapped untidily round the lower half of his face. Through its thick folds he said something that sounded like a question. He took a step back, unwound the towel, and asked me if I could spare some paracetamol because they had run out. The BV wasn't treating Angie well and she had a fever of 39.4.

'Is that bad?' I asked, being of the generation that deals only with numbers in the nineties and hundreds.

He regarded me glassily. 'You wouldn't perhaps maybe have a tin of soup or something to spare as well, might you?'

I think he wanted me to fuss over their predicament like the old mother some people mistook me for. My life was already pretty full of such people who were used to disappointment by now.

'I thought it was people of your generation who're supposed to be looking after people of mine, not the other way round,' I said, unspeakably primly. I gave him my emergency comfort ration of two tins of Campbell's Condensed Tomato soup and a packet of Boots' paracetamol. He looked grateful.

16 Teeth

I had hoped they'd cancel the appointment because of the BV. Going to the dentist seems a high price to pay for the preservation of discoloured rocks in your mouth. Why not have them all out and be done with it? My parents both had full sets of dentures, child-scaring marine objects in an overnight bedside glass of water. About once a year the objects had to be returned to the dentist for a general overhaul so on that one day neither parent spoke or ate much. I grew up believing that dentures were like voting – an inevitable accompaniment of adulthood.

The windows of the dentist's waiting room have an unforgiving view of the leaning gravestones in the cemetery. I didn't have to wait this time or flap through the tawdry copies of *Hello* magazine because of the military-style procedures introduced to keep the BV out of the surgery. There were no copies of any magazine. No-one could be admitted unless they had an appointment and a mask, the door was unlocked only when you phoned them from outside, your coat and bag had to be placed in a large lidded plastic bin, and your temperature was taken by a machine set at a height that was totally unable to capture mine. Then there was hand-sanitising, followed by compulsory hand-washing in a little bathroom at the end of the corridor, more hand-sanitising and the gift of a little plastic bag into which you inserted your mask and held onto tightly through the subsequent dental manoeuvres.

Virginia Woolf, that wonderful diarist of the Bloomsbury Group's saucy social life, once wrote that she must remember to pay a tribute to the humanity of dentists who do more for the soul than journalists. She didn't actually like either dentists or journalists. She absolutely wouldn't haven't paid any tribute to the staff of this dental surgery with its view of the cemetery in Stoke Newington. There were two of them that day – the hygienist and the nurse. I didn't recollect meeting either before, though it was hard to tell, given the paraphernalia covering their faces. The nurse handed me a cup of something which definitely wasn't tea and told me to keep it in my mouth for two minutes, which she would time exactly. I did as she asked. It felt terribly like bleach. Afterwards, spluttering, I asked her to confirm this, which she did. The hygienist, who had dark hair, dark eyes and dark glasses, then moved into the virus-free territory of a bleached mouth. She was a most savage operator, yanking my lips this way and that with absolutely no regard for the fact that they were part of me, and inserting metal instruments right, left and centre where they hurt the most. From time to time she said something, but whatever she said was muffled by the equipment on her face and by her accent, which I might have identified had I been able to hear it properly. Anyway, with a mouth full of her steel probes and giant cottonwool balls, speaking was out of the question. In all my years of dental experiences (a lot of them, as our mother had been very taken by the local dentist in Pinner, so she was constantly making dental appointments for us in order to get another view of him), I've never understood why dentists talk to you when you've got a mouthful. I once visited a dentist who took advantage of this enforced muteness by fixing earphones to my head and playing a tape about the dental advantages of consuming carrots. Brain-washing and mouth-washing at the same time.

What was the hygienist doing? I think she might have said something about a loose filling but she was supposed to be cleaning my teeth, removing all traces of the carrots I hadn't been eating and the chocolate I had. The light above the dental chair was extremely bright. The horrible corrugated plastic that encased it was smeared with something that shouldn't have been there, and the nurse kept yanking it closer in response to barked instructions from the hygienist. The room was windowless, small, a cabin of torture. They were getting the high-speed drill out now, and a new machine appeared in proximity to my face, some kind of fan which whirred wildly while the high-pitched shriek of the drill drove droplets of possibly contaminated water into the air. This was a high-risk operation, especially for me. My mouth felt like it was bleeding, as indeed it was. The hygienist put the drill away and commenced scraping my teeth and gums with an implement resembling a garden fork. Upside down, as you are in dental chairs, I began to feel distinctly faint. If I closed my eyes, might I be able transport myself somewhere more congenial, somewhere actually health-giving?

I lived in France for five years back in the 1990s with this French literary type, a man who liked to think of himself as an authentic European intellectual. He had an old stone house in a village in the valley between the Lot and Célé rivers, a paradisical place of precariously steep medieval villages and calmly sunlit water. He once took me to a field of sunflowers for a whole night because he wanted to see the sunflowers doing their nightly dance of closing, turning, and opening their yellow heads again as the morning light dawned. He cleared a space among the sunflowers and laid down a tarpaulin. Being French, he'd brought a sustaining pique-nique: a creamy quiche Lorraine, a salad with asparagus and a lemon Dijon dressing, tiny apple and cinnamon cakes and a bottle of something lightly sparkly from his cellar. Even with the thick sleeping bags he'd brought, the night was absolutely freezing: I don't know how the sunflowers survive it.

I was altogether more pliable then, bending like the sunflowers to masculine wishes. It was a time I remember fondly because the land was so beautiful, golden, fertile, unpolluted, dotted with incredible rock formations and sturdy ancient villages and tiny restaurants that served confit de canard and the dish of the day wordlessly without menus. I had a sense of immanence living there. That's the only word that describes it (immanence from the Latin immanere, 'remain within'). I'm probably romanticising the memory, of course. This is what happens as time separates us from the raw quality of experience and encourages it to assume another form. Why did I ever abandon Marcus with his endearing intellectual curiosity about sunflowers? The motives that inspire our actions are also buried by time, encrusted with layers of lies and simple forgetfulness.

The hygienist handed me another cup of something and asked me to rinse out my mouth. Blood streaked the basin. I thought of Maud Davies and the bloodstains in the boat train toilet. Were we finished? No, there was still polishing and fluoridising to do. And then there was the troubled business of payment. Did I have to pay? Was I an NHS or a private patient? What difference did it make? The hygienist didn't seem to know. She shrugged her shoulders and walked away. The nurse struggled with the computer screen behind the reception desk. Finally she said, 'you paid last time'. I could hear the words more clearly with her plastic shield removed. I had no memory of last time. Why would anyone want to remember dental experiences?

'Sixty-five pounds fifteen,' she pronounced decisively.

I got my credit card out.

'No,' she said, 'that was last time. You don't have to pay now.'

It was a complete mystery to me. And to her, I suspected. I really don't want to go to that place ever again, I thought, as she unbolted the door and let me out. A wilted old man, spattered with rain, was waiting to come in.

I told myself to ask Elsa about the anthropology of teeth. Perhaps she could do them next when she's finished with feet.

17 Stephen's takeaway

Stephen's house was pristine, minimalist and frighteningly empty of any personal touch. If you were to read his character off the interior you'd decide he was utterly bland. How has this undecorated space, with its plain wood floors, white walls, white sofas, glass tables, not a plant or a picture in sight, actually ever generated a line of poetry? There were books, yes, there would have to be, and what a cheering splash of colour they were, too, though I'm only talking about the outside. I knew without examining them that they were arranged in perfect alphabetical order. I had a go at that once in my own establishment but it required so much energy – all that lugging from one shelf to another as the Ps mysteriously multiplied and even a sizeable quantity of Qs materialised – that I decided to stick with an alphabetically random library.

So Stephen had ordained an Indian takeaway instead of home cooking. What would that do to all this impeccable whiteness? Immediately I was afflicted with visions of spattered salmon chilli machli and the spreading burnt orange of chicken korma and bits of brinjal bhaji on the sofa or caught in the beveled edges of the immaculate table. Takeaway pizza would have been better as more unitary and less orange, but what we really needed was something white like steamed chicken and mashed potatoes.

I searched the menu he handed me for pale unpolluting items. Rice, yes, perfect! Everything else was too highly coloured. 'Are we drinking white wine?' I asked nervously.

Forty-five minutes later, the food arrived in a blue plastic bag. The exchange between Stephen and the delivery man on the doorstep suggested that they knew each other quite well. Looking at me knowingly, Stephen said he would drink mineral water, it was better for his health.

I'd taken a little trouble with my appearance. It had been a long time since I'd had to decide between trousers or a dress and had to select a necklace from my vast and mostly unworn collection. After quite a lot of indecisive parading in front of the mirror, I chose a red and white jersey dress over grey leggings and a wooden necklace from Bhutan where Elsa and I had gone on a terrific trip to celebrate our sixtieth birthdays. We'd been drawn irresistibly by the Bhutanese habit of estimating national wealth in terms of happiness, not GNP. I mentioned this to Stephen when I saw him looking approvingly at my apparel. I didn't mention wanting to hide the extra pounds the BV had piled on.

I gave him the sky-blue cashmere jumper I'd bought him for Christmas from M&S online, together with the receipt so he could change it for something more useful like socks or underpants. And so he could see how much it had cost, a sign of the esteem in which I held him, both of us being inhabitants of a non-Bhutanese nation. Had he bought me a Christmas present? I hoped it wasn't another book. I had too many of those waiting to be read, about white slavery, train murders, Edwardian philanthropy, rural sociology and so forth. Jack, incidentally, had responded well to my Christmas gift of Maud Davies's *Life in an English Village* and said he was considering writing an editorial piece about studies of rural life to which I could contribute, but he might have said that because he thought it was what I wanted to hear. Children can be like that. Sometimes. The rest of the time they say things they know you definitely don't want to hear.

No, it wasn't a book, it was a subscription to the *London Review of Books*, which was, if anything, slightly worse, as it would encourage me to add to my alphabetically random library collection. The piece of paper announcing his gift was wrapped round a naked bar of Sustainable Citrus Burst Organic soap tied with a piece of string and a label saying that it had been made by impoverished village women in Northern India. For washing my hands after the Indian takeaway, I supposed.

'There's something else, Alice,' he said, getting up from the table when we were only half way through our hazardous repast, and returning with a sheet of paper which he held gingerly by the corners so as not to contaminate it with traces of Indian spices. 'It's a poem for you,' he said. The sheet of paper was indeed headed, 'For Alice Henry, February 2021'. The title of the poem was 'Humped Crossing'. 'It's for Volume 2 of my *Street Signs*,' Stephen explained.

I'd never had a poem written for me before, so I welcomed it as a novel experience. I read it quickly, definitely not in my slow, careful copy-editor mode. I couldn't wait to find out how I'd been represented poetically. But the sentiments turned out to be disappointingly conventional – the delight of making a new acquaintance, the jolting-out of depression prompting the possibility of spring eventually returning with all its attendant bloomings. The humps appeared to be figurative obstacles to a smooth journey from promising present to happy future. I began to feel horribly responsible for something that might not happen. I read the poem again carefully while Stephen watched me motionlessly, having put his knife and fork down on the remains of his chicken korma.

'Have you ever been to India?' I asked when I got to the end. The poem had, in conjunction with the food, suddenly made me see a moonlit Taj Mahal with Stephen and myself on a bench in front in a suitably socially distanced way. Perhaps my vacuum-cleaner mind had hoovered up that other indelible image of Princess Diana there alone.

'Thou art a soul in bliss, but I am bound upon a wheel of fire,' quoted Stephen abruptly. This remark bore as much relevance to his poem as my question about passages to India. 'Shakespeare, King Lear,' he said.

'Are you trying to tell me something?' I asked. 'Because, if you are, why don't you just come out and say it?'

Stephen placed his elbows on the table, dangerously close to the half-empty container of brinjal bhaji. Resting his head in his hands, he said, 'I don't know whether I can do this, Alice.'

'It? What is it?'

'I want to have a relationship,' he confessed, 'and you really are like the spring flowers in my poem, especially the miniature purple irises, iris reticulata, there's a wonderful display of them in the park just now, have you seen them? By the first lake. They're such a brilliant colour, and they have these very surprising yellow and black and white crests inside. A hidden jewel.' He opened his fingers slightly and looked at me earnestly, as though he'd just said something very important that required an equally weighty response from me.

'I'm not your hidden jewel, Stephen,' I told him, honestly. 'And I'm certainly not particularly miniature. Why can't we just be friends?' Even as I said it, I realised that this would be extremely difficult for him. He had too much emotional baggage he wanted to unload on me, I would become one of those luggage carousels at airports that jettison suitcases onto the concourse all the time. What's that phrase I'd heard young people use? 'Friends with favours?' 'Or even friends with favours,' I said daringly. 'I really think we should keep it simple.'

'That doesn't sound at all simple to me.' Stephen looked worried.

'Do you actually know what I mean?'

'I'm not sure,' he admitted.

'Where's your bedroom?' I said, surprising myself. 'We've finished with all this food, haven't we?' I took him by the hand that was on its desultory way back to collect the last few forkfuls on his plate. He stood up, not altogether reluctantly, and I saw again that he really was quite a handsome man, lean, well-dressed, an astute high-cheekboned face, abundant lockdown hair. A man's hair could be quite important in bed. Something to hold on to.

The bed was white, of course, white sheets in a white room with white curtains and very high up under the window so Stephen could have a view of the rooftops when he lay there composing his poems. He told me that was where he did most of his writing. There was no question of leaping into that bed because my arthritis had been playing up recently with all this precipitation we'd been having. I'd brought a large tube of KY jelly with me as a precaution, being mindful of the fact that a decade of non-use might have shrivelled things up somewhat. When I produced it from my bag, Stephen admitted to the prophylactic ingestion of a small blue pill for a matching malfunction. 'Actually, I took two. It might be a bit of an overdose.'

It was and it wasn't. Afterwards he cried. We were both affected by this renewal of an activity that had been ruinously removed from both our lives by the departure of old lovers and the consequential anxiety (him) and lethargy (me) in relation to finding new ones. The velcroness of bodies, the imaginatively improbable positioning of bones and limbs, and the long-forgotten scent of bodily secretions was poetry in motion. I wondered what the sequel to 'Humped Crossing' would be called. His body was quite admirable. Mine, I knew, was not. There was too much of it, and it was too old.

'Oh Alice,' Stephen said, 'do stop harping on about age. Age is nothing to me.'

'Please don't quote Shakespeare again,' I said, knowing the Bard had produced a poem especially about this.

Later I looked at my wizened skin in his bathroom mirror. It seemed less wizened, almost rosy and young-woman-like. Stephen, wearing a luxurious white towelling bathrobe, brought me a white cup of Earl Grey tea. I didn't really believe this was happening. It must be a dream or a film. I would wake up soon or the film would come to a sudden whirring end. He slipped a hand round my left breast, jacking it up a metre or two, and bent his head to kiss it, causing the tea, that was perched on the bathroom basin, to crash to the floor.

I remember the very first time I had sex back in the dark ages of unliberated youth. I remember how on the bus afterwards I was grinning like the Mona Lisa, except that modern experts say she was smiling because she was pregnant, and this couldn't conceivably (an apt word) have applied to me, as I was totally committed to preventing that occurrence. Nonetheless, I harboured a secret. I'd been admitted to that entire new world of people who were sexually consummated. My vagina was sore, which proved it, and I was relieved of that old-fashioned burden called virginity.

On my walk home from Stephen's, picking my way most vigilantly along the grey slushy pavements in order to avoid the perilously hidden patches of black ice, I found myself grinning once again.

18 The moon and I

I was reading the news, well just a few selected portions of it, on my phone, and was fairly captivated by a story about a woman in South Africa who went shopping without a mask, and who, when remonstrated with for this oversight, whipped her knickers off and stuck them on her face. Necessity is the mother of invention. My sister and I heard this a lot in Pinner when we were growing up, usually to justify one of my mother's less fortunate culinary concoctions. I particularly remember her use of beetroot to colour the icing on a birthday cake. So when the phone in my hand rang, my mind was elsewhere, where it usually is. I was expecting another one of those recorded American voices telling me a pack of lies about my Amazon account, which was doing very well, thank you, due to the BV, but instead it was an alarmingly professional-sounding English soprano voice.

'Is that Mrs Henry?'

I agreed, for the sake of argument. 'I'm ringing from Peterborough City Hospital, it's about your friend Mrs Elsa Posavac.'

'She isn't a Mrs,' I said, 'and neither am I.'

'She gave us your details,' the voice continued undeterred.

'Apparently she doesn't have any next of kin in this country.'

'No,' I agreed, wondering irrelevantly who my own next of kin were and whether they realised it. Then this great sinking feeling hit me – what could have happened to Elsa that necessitated this person calling me from a hospital?

'It isn't Covid,' I said very fast, 'is it? It can't be Covid, she's had both her jabs. And she's very healthy. She takes all this exercise.' Stop talking Alice and just listen.

'Mrs Henry,' said the voice officiously, 'Mrs Posavac' – there was always something unpleasantly levelling about the overuse of these titles – 'Mrs Posavac has experienced something called a transient ischaemic attack. That is a minor stroke. A temporary disruption in the flow of blood to the brain.'

'What? Are you sure? How did that happen?'

'We are doing tests,' said the voice unhelpfully.

'I need to come and see her.' It seemed urgent to visit Elsa as soon as possible to establish that she was still alive and/or that the officious voice wasn't mixing her up with someone else.

'Unfortunately because of Covid no visitors are allowed in the wards. But she needs some things to be brought in from her home. Would you be able to fetch them for her?'

'Why didn't she ring me herself?'

'We've given her a sedative. She was quite agitated when she came in. And her phone has run out of charge. That's one of the things she needs, her phone charger. Her phone is quite an old model and we can't find a charger here that will work.'

No, they wouldn't be able to. Elsa's phone was a small

170

orange Nokia, a revitalised version of the original tiny Nokia mobile that was popular in the 1990s. She was unreasonably fond of it. I found myself crying. It was the thought of Elsa on her little orange Nokia, her herself, my actual living friend, who had no right to have succumbed to whatever it was that had caused whatever it was she had got. Elsa is never ill. That's one reason why she always complains about me complaining about illness. 'Wittering on,' she calls it. I think she believes she's inviolable. Believed. Poor, poor Elsa. I'd always considered her stronger and healthier than me, but our bodies are such annoying repositories of all kinds of hidden faults and dysfunctions we can't do anything about because we don't know they exist.

So there was nothing for it but for me to get myself to Peterborough and then to the City Hospital, a journey of great complexity for someone without a car or any sense of (geographical) direction. The nurse who'd rung me – she could have been a doctor, I'm just as prone to stereotyping as the next person – had no idea I was ninety miles away.

I rang Jack for advice. Children like to be asked for advice, it makes them feel grown up, but it has the unwanted side effect of encouraging their view of us as afflicted by ever-encroaching feebleness.

'You can rent a car, Mum. Zipcar it's called, I'll send you a link. Ask for a four-by-four, the roads are lethal, well at least they are round here. Will you be alright? Do you want me to come with you? Or I could drive you, I suppose, but....' There was a tremendous crash in the background at this point. 'I'll ring you back.' When he did, he explained that Sara had been assembling an Ikea highchair for baby Ed and the whole thing had collapsed in the middle of the kitchen while Patti was stirring one of her potions. Meanwhile, Jack had told Patti what had happened to Elsa, and Patti had obligingly explained that TIAs – which is how transient ischaemic attacks are known in the trade – are blockages in arteries carrying blood to the brain and are generally caused by cholesterol and another substance called homocysteine which you pick up from eating meat. Thus Elsa must immediately give up eating meat, and she must adopt a diet high in anti-oxidant foods. B vitamins and potassium were particularly vital as in, for example, almonds, kale and bananas. Patti could provide a tea made with Danshen and Ginkgo which would be of value.

Zipcar delivered a small grey Fiat four-by-four that afternoon. I packed a suitcase with Dr Ahmad-Wicks, a bottle of brandy, some Maud Davies, and Agatha Christie's *The Mystery of the Blue Train*. 'Life is like a train,' intones Hercule Poirot in it, twiddling his moustache. I would rather have taken the train, but I drove very carefully up the A1 at speeds well below the radar of the speed cameras, thus probably causing a lot of the light-flashing and honking I observed en route. An old person going too slowly in the slow lane. I got out at Sainsbury's in Biggleswade and took a brief walk to stretch my legs along the banks of a turgid river. It was my intention to reach Elsa's cottage before the solar lights in her hanging baskets came on, which I just achieved. The spare key was in its usual place under the fake ivy.

She'd obviously left in a hurry. A saucepan of something very congealed sat on the cooker next to her favourite tea-stained Cath Kidston mug with a squashed tea-bag stuck to the bottom. Elsa's TIA had happened in the morning. The heating was on, the thermostat reading twenty-one degrees. I was glad of that because it had been freezing even in London and it was always colder here. I rubbed my hands together to warm them and stood in the kitchen wondering what to do first. I went to the toilet, which leads off the kitchen in a most insanitary fashion, and there I encountered in the bottom of the lavatory pan an awful dark green moving object. Like most women who live on their own, I'd given up screaming at spiders and suchlike a long time ago because it achieves nothing useful and only gives you a sore throat and afterwards the spider or whatever is still there. But this was something else. I put my new glasses on and fetched a torch from where I knew Elsa kept one underneath the electricity meter between the boxes of wine and the bag of baking soda, and had a good look. The thing was still moving. It seemed to have arms and legs. I flushed the toilet and it disappeared for a few seconds then back it came victoriously waving its little limbs. My excellent detective work – looking out of the window – revealed that the toilet was against an outside wall and the thing was a frog that had mistaken the outside pipe for a river. I got a soup ladle and a plastic bag from the kitchen and after a few slippery manoeuvres I managed to re-home it in the garden.

Quite pleased with myself for overcoming one of life's little hurdles (while failing at all the big ones) I went upstairs. Elsa's bed was unmade, and, judging from the pile of clothes on the chair, she'd been borne off to hospital in her night clothes. It was too late to drive there that night, so I went back down to the kitchen, sorted out the congealed saucepan and made myself an omelette. Then I went back upstairs and packed Elsa's things: a set of clothes, pyjamas, a couple of towels, soap, a bar of chocolate, a book about the Clarks shoe industry that was lying on her bedside table, and the phone charger, of course. I thought I would stop on the way to the hospital in the morning and buy her some provisions. I took Agatha Christie's train murder out of my suitcase and put it in hers. She needed it more than me.

The next day I drove to the hospital, which was a frightening experience because I got lost in a system of roundabouts that kept returning me to where I'd come from. Eventually I spotted the hospital and managed to reach it by doing a U-turn. Trying to park was also a nightmare because I needed a parking app on my phone which I didn't have in order to donate an overwhelming amount of money to the private company that ran the parking system. After sorting that out, I felt quite weak, but I suspected the hospital café was closed so I ate one of the bananas I'd bought for Elsa. I wheeled the suitcase containing everything else up to the main entrance where I almost fell over on a broken paving stone and the security guard watched impassively rather than helping me. The reception desk had no record of an Elsa Posavac but that's because they'd misspelt her name as POFFASICK. Anyway, as the nurse/doctor had said on the phone, I wasn't allowed to deliver the suitcase to her personally. They gave me a label for the suitcase and I wrote her name, spelt both ways, on it, together with the ward number.

'Is it possible to speak to someone on the staff about her?' I inquired.

'No, not at the moment, we're all much too busy,' said

the bleached-hair-and-masked schoolgirl behind the desk.

So this is the new normal – your friends get taken into hospital and hidden there, out of sight, thoroughly unreachable in a saga stripped of all identifying details such as who they really are and what's being done in the way of treatment and for how long and what might transpire next.

I handed over the suitcase, returned to the Zipcar, and renegotiated the troublesome roundabouts. I felt quite desolate and disoriented. Were they lying to me? What had really happened to Elsa? It was obvious that I would have to stay in Elsa's cottage for a few days in the hope that some of these questions would get answered, hopefully when Elsa and her orange Nokia had been reunited and she'd recovered sufficiently to reconnect with me. I had Dr Ahmad-Wicks to amuse myself with meanwhile. We were presently in the midst of a dense chapter about 'Gender Binarism and the Detective Project'. Dr Ahmad-Wicks and Professor Pluss shared an affinity for losing their plots in deadening theoretical places.

On day two, Elsa rang me and we had a reasonable chat, although her speech was a bit slurred. They were doing scans, she said. The food was terrible. So was the Agatha Christie I'd taken in. Too much schoolgirl French and that American heiress was just not credible. The woman in the next bed had a brain tumour and the one on the other side vomited all night. Elsa would like to come home. Had I found the prosciutto in the fridge that needed eating? I told her what Patti had decreed about meat and cholesterol. Elsa made a non-committal noise. 'I'd do the same for you, Alice,' she said, meaning that if something went wrong with my brain she'd pack me a suitcase and give me a lecture about my lifestyle habits.

On day three the sun was shining and I took my morning coffee into Elsa's garden which seemed quite full of things that looked like non-plastic weeds. Some amazing pink and white orchids had appeared on the back wall, but, naturally, when I went to examine them, they revealed themselves to be man-made products. On the way, I stepped over a bird that had plonked its dead body on the path. This is life in an English village, I thought, the very same life that Maud had written about. A copy of the village newsletter had arrived that morning containing some valuable hints about how to survive the pandemic: *Meditate for two minutes on your garden bulbs, bake a cake for a shepherd, love a churchwarden, rejoice in your body because God made it beautiful. Unfortunately we can't meet liturgically to celebrate The Imposition of the Ashes but remember you are dust and to dust you will return. Zoom compline is on Sunday at 11 o'clock.*

On day four Alan rang me. 'That woman you found to come in and clean, she's no good,' he shouted. 'She brings her dog with her, an awful fluffy thing, and fusses over it all the time. I even caught her opening my spare tin of spam for it. I can't abide dogs, Alice, you know that. And the cat has gone somewhere else because it doesn't like dogs either. When are you coming back to live with me again?'

Is there no end to all these calls upon my time and attention? Why am I the answer to other people's problems but never to my own?

One afternoon I took the grey four-by-four to the next village where I'd spotted on a walk with Elsa, before all this happened, a large Ministry of Defence notice advising of great potential danger to all who walked on the land it fronted. The land was a disused airfield. Elsa had said all the local dog-owners went there. It had a reputation for growing the most marvellous selection of wildflowers, although these wouldn't be in evidence now with temperatures dropping below freezing at night and a limited supply of sunshine in the daytime. The snow had gone, but all that lives in the earth was holding its breath wondering if a second coming was planned.

I walked up the track behind the threatening notice thinking about poor Elsa in her hospital bed away from all this countryside she loves so much – although I've always felt she loves it for her own purposes rather than for itself. I had to squeeze past a coterie of rusty oil drums to get onto the airfield proper. Judging from the crumpled bits of paper and dented beer-cans on the ground, other people did the same. Pleasure perhaps, not always of a savoury nature, was to be had there, and happiness can always be found in unexpected places. But now, in this one silent moment, the only person here was me, plodding in Elsa's oversized wellingtons across the furrowed field at the edge of the old aerodrome, and then over the patchy winter-tired grass and the acres of fractured concrete laced with weeds and the roots of the legendary wildflowers. Behind and ahead of me everything was flat and colourless, animated only by a slight wind and the blue velvet of a late afternoon sky. Above the horizon hovered the golden globe of the sun. The flatness was odd in a hilly county like this. It was an engineered landscape, devoid of any memorable features apart from the abandoned runways, empty fuel pits, and weed-strewn hardstandings for heavy bombers.

Elsa had told me that ballistic missiles had been housed

here in the 1950s and 60s, those nasty American devices of mass destruction that featured as main characters in the Cuban missile crisis of 1962. I was fifteen then, enclosed in my school uniform at Pinner Girls' School, bored and querulous, but childish still, and I remember being really frightened at the news on the square wooden black-and-white television in our sitting-room. Those missiles, named Thor after the Norse God of thunder, carried thermonuclear warheads, and dozens of them had been placed all over England and kept in a state of readiness for that ultimate pressing of the button or issue of the final command. Much was made at the time of the fact that it would take only fifteen minutes to get the missiles airborne, the last fifteen minutes before an all-out nuclear catastrophe killed or maimed most of us. In 1962 I was seized by a total incomprehension, which has never really left me, that adults had somehow managed to create a world in which boys' playground squabbles had metamorphosed into political disputes threatening mass annihilation.

It's not surprising that this whole place had a creepy feel to it. The air was heavy with history, packed full of atoms recording the journeys, collisions and decay of aircraft, the staccato instructions of airmen, the shattering sound of guns, the lives and the laughter left behind in family homes. You could feel it – the sense of desolation and despair that comes when the events shaping your life completely escape your control. We do what we have to do, not what we choose. The past walks with us, holding our hand if we let it. But too much intimacy between past and present is not a good thing. The Germans have one of their shockingly long words for it:

178

'vergangenheitsbewältigung'. It means 'overcoming the past'.

As the air cooled and the blue of the sky deepened and the sun dropped down behind the black winter trees, I realised that I had been fighting my past just as persistently and vainly as the bombers whose ghosts sprint across the runways here. I've weltered in the past, got re-entangled in its plots, developed a kind of metaphysical confusion about it. I've spent my life searching for the meaning of life and I'm still doing it now, trying to understand what my life means, to create some sort of grand plan. But it's all rubbish. Every grand plan is sabotaged by some random event. What self-conceit to think that the future can be laid out like an airfield in arithmetically determined patterns to become the launching pad of dreams and desires! You just have to live as best you can, put one foot in front of the other, even in wellingtons a size too large. And I absolutely had to find my way off this bloody airfield with all its unkempt ghosts before the sun had completely gone.

A cluster of strange buildings loomed in the distance, squat, red-walled and asymmetrically windowed. There, on my left, were the remains of a runway with potholes and faded arrows. And then I came upon a corrugated iron building, about ten metres long and three metres wide, with an oxidised and corroded door swinging on its hinges. I peered inside at the darkness, at stacks of objects that looked like giant old paint pots with labels that would be indecipherable even in the full light of day. My face caught the dangling threads of a spider's web. It was getting cold. I turned round and something moved in the undergrowth. A fox, or a dead airman? I looked up and there was the sky, its diminishing blue lit on one side by the blanching rays of the sun, and on the other by a most striking moon, huge, silver-white, utterly full, its famous face benignly watching as I continued to struggle over the blemished ground. It must have been what's called a super moon, so much closer to earth than usual, right next to us in the sky, close enough, a small child would think, actually to touch. But that elegant, knowing, white face was disfigured by the dark artwork of tall trees. I wanted the trees to move out of the way so the moon and I could see one another more clearly, without impediment.

An enormous feeling of solidarity flowed through me from my head to my fingertips and my toes. The moon and I were alone on this sad confused sick earth, riven by malignant viruses, the corrosions of old bodies, ridiculous conflicts of both intimate and public kinds, and fragile attempts at human connection. The obsequious and psychopathic inhabitants of planet earth are unable to grasp the truth, that we are all lost and have no choice except to walk blindly and lovingly towards that great white face in the sky.

Then it rose higher, well above the trees, floating in a navy blue sea. The stars were pinhole points of light, some more scintillating than others, but none of them made any impression on the dense white flooding light of the moon.

19 Mystery man

'What are you doing all the time up there?' asked Stephen rather crossly on the phone, perhaps breeding designs on my person that couldn't be satisfied by its continued sojourn in Rutland.

'Working,' I said. That was one advantage of the digital BV age – you could do it anywhere, or claim you were doing it anywhere, and because 'work' means so many things, it provides a good one-word answer. Especially for women, who engage in so many forms of work.

I was still in Elsa's cottage. They were still doing tests. Basically, they couldn't understand why the stroke had happened because she was doing all the right things – she was thin, she walked a lot, she ate salads, though she did eat meat. Her voice, on the phone to me, had rapidly returned to its usual self, and it delivered meticulous descriptions of the strategies the doctors were using to suss out what was going on inside the hidden tunnels of her arteries and her heart. 'It is such a problem,' she declared, with what I considered misplaced sympathy, 'that the human body is opaque.' Being Elsa, she was taking notes which would doubtless emerge as a riveting article with a long subtitle about the alienating and transforming experience of being a stroke patient. She sent me a photo of a notice board in a department where she'd been pushed in her wheelchair which actually said 'National *Impatient* Centre for Psychological Medicine' in bold white letters on bright oceanic blue. At least they got that right.

To fill the time, and because I'd eaten everything in Elsa's fridge, I went shopping. The nearest Sainsbury's was eight miles away. There was reputed to be one remaining village shop the other side of the A47 but I guessed it wouldn't have everything I wanted and I find the cloned orange of Sainsbury's oddly comforting; this may have something to do with my childhood fondness for Terry's Chocolate Orange.

I'd tidied Elsa's hastily exited bedroom but I drew the line at deep cleaning, and there was no chance of my touching the garden because I found it particularly hard to spot non-plastic weeds.

'What do you mean, working?' barked Stephen.

I explained. 'And of course I'm also getting on with my research into Maud Davies's tragic end.'

'You should give up this Maud malarkey. It's going nowhere,' he pointed out. 'There's nowhere it *can* go because it's impossible to find out what happened.'

'Is that what you say to yourself when you start a poem?' I asked him. 'Do you always know the end when you're at the beginning?'

'That's different,' he argued.

'Why is it different? Because poetry is fiction and Maud Davies's life was real? Anyway, poetry isn't fiction, is it? Look at your own poems, like how you felt when Diane lost her life on the Holloway Road. Look at Wordsworth and his daffodils, or Sylvia Plath in that enormous book you bought, and hers. Everything is written from the writer's own experience. Everything is ultimately subjective, horribly or wonderfully so.'

'I think I love you, Alice,' he said. 'You're so obstinate, so determined, and so independent, in your thought as well as your action.' He sounded a bit hopeless as he said this.

'Every man loves an independent woman, Stephen,' I answered. 'But it's all a bit theoretical, isn't it? Independent women are like distant stars in the night sky, best looked at through a telescope rather than close up.'

I didn't take him seriously, mainly because it would have been inconvenient to do so. There were too many loose ends in my life and, in any case, love in the time of a pandemic felt like high fiction. It was safer to think about Maud. Maud and men. The person Maud had dinner with, a few days before she took off on her world travels, was James Joseph, alias Jimmy, Mallon, a social reformer and campaigner against exploitative working conditions. He was a little older than her, thirty-eight, and unmarried, the popular, well-liked son of Irish Roman Catholic parents in Manchester. Like Maud, Jimmy was active in the Fabian Society. He was a force behind the National Anti-Sweating League, set up in 1906 to argue for a national minimum wage and better working conditions for the millions of men, women and children who laboured long hours for pitiful rates of pay. In 1906, a Sweated Industries Exhibition was opened in a London concert hall by one of Queen Victoria's daughters and ran for six weeks, attracting 30,000 visitors. Among the exhibits were forty-five exploited workers themselves – trousers-makers, button-carders, boot-makers, glove-stitchers, shirt-finishers, sunshade-coverers and shawl-fringers. The 'poverty tourism' of the Exhibition helped to bring about the first national wage legislation and regulation of industrial working conditions in the UK.

Maud would almost certainly have visited the Exhibition. Apart from its high-profile publicity, several of her friends, such as Clementina Black and Bessie Hutchins, were involved in organising and writing about it. Maud would have walked from her London County Council flat by Euston Station to Langham Place W1, a distance of only a couple of miles. The Queen's Hall was the eccentrically designed musical centre of the British Empire. Stephen Dearlove probably knew all about its history. Musicians loved its excellent acoustics and put up with the eccentricity which included a painting on the ceiling of the Paris Opera with gesturing cupids, and a fountain full of pebbles, goldfish and waterlilies into which young women regularly fell. Fortunately the fountain wasn't in operation during the Sweated Industries Exhibition or falling into it would have added to the hazards already experienced by the attending workers.

Jimmy Mallon must have been an engaging dinner companion. His contemporaries described him as full of Irish wit and humour, a fluent conversationalist who enjoyed entertaining an audience more than writing serious socialist propaganda. He did start an autobiography but it was destroyed, like the Queen's Hall, in the London Blitz. Eight years after Maud died Jimmy Mallon married Stella Gardiner, the daughter of a prominent newspaper editor. She was thirty-one when they married but they had no children.

That much I can find out. The rest has to be imagined. Was Jimmy Mallon the rejected suitor Maud's brother mentioned at the inquest into her death? Or a new one? Or was this just an innocent appointment, an opportunity for two socially conscious and politically active colleagues to meet and talk about topics of common interest? What do you think?

Perhaps Jimmy Mallon said something about loving an independent woman to Maud Davies, but the reason she didn't take it on board was because she was just about to board a ship. She was at the start of a journey not just around the world but across a landscape of questions about the shape and direction of her life. That's what her travels were all about. I felt sure that Maud was, like me, hovering on the brink of earth-shattering, or at least mildly significant, decisions about what to do with the rest of her life. She needed time away to consider what she, a thirty-seven-year-old unmarried woman at the close of the Victorian age and the opening of whole new vistas of opportunity for women, should do next. Might she follow her *Life in an English Village* with some other raw exposé of social secrets? As had been suggested at the inquest into her death, perhaps she had begun a study of the scandalous social and economic system that lured young white maidens into selling their bodies for cash and bread. Or might Maud have chosen work alongside the likes of the charming Jimmy Mallon in order to help exploited workers rise above their debilitating oppression? Or maybe she would join the network of women investigators who were establishing the tools of a new social science with which to greet the dawn of a new and exciting age? It's even possible that somewhere out there in the world was a man who would become Mr Maud Davies, perhaps a radical lawyer or a philanthropic businessman. At any rate, it would be someone who admired independent women and who, like her, would look askance at the habits of a socially divisive society and would apply his intelligence to investigative and remedial acts.

As the people who knew her, and who were forced to examine her life in order to determine the cause of her death, must have endlessly wondered, what really was the identity of this person, Maud Frances Davies, this authoress of independent means? In fact, when you consider her busy history, other mystery men can be glimpsed flitting across the stage of Maud's life. Edward Pease, for example, co-founder and Secretary of the Fabian Society, a finely-moustached man to whom Maud would have left money had she made a Will, or so she said in a note found among her papers after she died. On the other hand, Edward Pease was married to a schoolteacher and he was twenty years older than Maud. Sidney Webb, Pease's friend, a man of many talents, described by his wife Beatrice as 'an ugly little man', would also have been left money in Maud's non-existent Will. She clearly considered herself intellectually indebted to both Webbs, as she acknowledged in the Preface to *Life in an English Village*: 'Everything that may be of value in the book is due to some suggestion of Mr. or Mrs. Sidney Webb.'

Another possibility was John McKillop, the LSE librarian, whom she also thanked. And then there was Hubert Hall, an economic historian and archivist, who counted Maud among his most promising postgraduate students at LSE. But he was in his fifties and married too. Not that marriage prevented inappropriate lust, of course.

It's as though, I begin to feel, Maud *wanted* her existence to be ambiguous because ambiguity was a quality she cultivated. Her place of habitation, for example, at times in Corsley, the Wiltshire village where her parents had settled, at times in her little LCC flat in Euston, interspersed with visits to The Pastures and other nearly-stately homes. She also spent a lot of time at the Whitehall Residential Hotel in London's Coram Street, for which I can't find a website entry. And her postal address was something apart from all of these: the Writers' Club, a social and work centre for women writers and journalists in Norfolk Street off the Strand, close to the heart of London's newspaper world, so women journalists could drop off their copy on their way home. Maud was said in some of the newspaper reports to have been almost a daily visitor there throughout the last year of her life.

My googling showed me that clubs of all kinds, but especially for women, flourished around this time. Women's clubs were invented because women were barred from men's clubs, and they needed somewhere to meet, eat, talk, smoke and, most urgently of all, to use the toilet. Public toilets for women were extremely thin on the ground. They were regarded as promoting immorality. Maybe they still are, since there are never enough of them and the queues are abominable. Poor Maud, struggling with an overloaded bladder. The toileted Writers' Club was a shabby, rather austere, place, where the food was dismal but the literary culture was unmatched. Strong tea was served on white damask tablecloths at the Friday house teas that were attended by many well-known personages and were acclaimed as among London's star literary attractions.

So Maud thought of herself as a writer. And the clientele

who came through the doors of the Writers' Club could well have included other eligible men who found Maud an affable companion. We will never know.

20 Not making much progress with anything

Elsa's encounter with the frailties of the human body derailed her rather badly for a while. She said it had been a life-changing experience. It had totally dispatched her belief in personal invulnerability. 'It's all about cognitive restructuring,' she had told me when I brought her home from the misspelt confines of Peterborough City Hospital. Whatever had happened to her brain didn't get in the way of her ability to navigate all those roundabouts far better than I could, and she managed to explain cognitive restructuring at the same time. I think she'd been missing intelligent conversation. 'When something bad happens we have to reorganise the way we think, Alice,' she said. 'In relation to bodies, the theoretical knowledge that we're not immortal is suddenly activated and for a time we live under its shadow. Then we realise life has to go on and we lock mortality up in the cupboard again.'

Thank you for explaining, Elsa. Apparently, she had eventually told her mother in the Croatian care home about her TIA, and her mother had said she'd been having them for years. The first one had happened when she was fifty-one and attending as a proud mother in a large magenta hat

– Elsa never forgave the hat – a lecture her daughter was giving at the inaugural meeting of the Croatian Anthropological Society in Zagreb. Elsa had been discussing her doctoral research on the understanding of reproductive genetics by Hvar islanders. Hvar today is a tourist trap, but back then it was an isolated, inbred place full of forensically excited scientists who were measuring everything they could: the size of Hvar islanders' bodies, the performance of their hearts, the dimensions of their bones, the constitution of their blood. The project was about the heritability of traits. As one of the scientists, Elsa wanted to know how the islanders themselves saw things. How much did they engage with the language and logic of genetics? Her mother had been so absurdly delighted to see her daughter up there on the rostrum with her box of slides and her slide pointer delineating the important words in her interviewees' accounts, that she succumbed to a weakness in an artery in her brain and lost the last ten minutes of the lecture. 'It's genetic,' she had told Elsa. 'Nothing to worry about. They come and go.' Both Elsa and her mother were now on a medication called Warfarin which thinned their blood so any incipient clots would be neatly dissolved before they could do any harm.

Elsa was very happy to be home, back with her flashing lights and improbable garden. I made balsamic-glazed salmon fillets the first evening, the fish being full of Omega-3 and thus good for her arteries. Insisting that she was quite well enough to stand in the kitchen and operate machinery, she opened a tin of artichoke hearts for our first course, and cut her thumb on the lid. Blood went everywhere. It was pink, not red, because of the medicine, she pointed out.

After a week of my hovering over her, making annoying recommendations about valuable life-enhancing strategies such as more oily fish like mackerel which she hated and no alcohol, especially not the lethal purple Croatian plum brandy she favoured as a nightcap, Elsa released me from my duties and sent me home. 'It is time,' she pronounced, 'for me to work through the emotional impact of my thromboembolic event. I have important psychological work to do.' Aided by the National Impatient Centre perhaps, and following the guidelines for submitted articles provided on its website by the erudite journal *Medical Anthropology*.

Back in London, I ordered another package from Amazon which was summarily dumped on the doorstep as usual. In it were four packets of dental floss (post-dental-appointment guilt), two containers of Vim for my unlikely lockdown cleaning project, and a book on the train murder of Florence Nightingale Shore. Naturally I fell on this with indecent excitement. This murder took place, remember, seven years before the murder of Maud Davies. Both murders were equally brutal and equally unsolved, but in Nurse Shore's case there was a suspect, a man in a brown suit who was seen getting into her compartment before the train left Victoria Station and who was probably spotted again jumping from the train an hour and a half later at Lewes Station.

The Nightingale Shore Murder contained graphic descriptions of the injury to Nurse Shore's brain that occurred in the sealed compartment of the train between Victoria and Lewes. Three separate wounds inflicted with enormous force had driven pieces of bone inwards and provoked a massive and unsurvivable haemorrhage. There was blood on her face, her clothes, a newspaper on the floor and traces on a one pound note that turned up in a hotel near Lewes Station. This was a red herring, as it belonged to a local butcher.

All this material about railways as sites of death was probably itself a red herring, but one thing leads to another in the jerky world of BV-driven research. An innocent-sounding book about life in the English countryside takes you to an ambiguous Edwardian life and an even more mysterious death whose possible causes would fire up even the dullest imagination, and I don't have one of those.

The schools went back and children with their rucksacks, lunch boxes and over-excited voices streamed past my window again. For two days the sun shone and the police were out in force fining people for breaking the BV rules. People sat in their droves on Primrose Hill and London Fields and Hampstead Heath and in Clissold Park with their cans of drinks and MacDonald's bags or sushi containers (depending on social class) and when they got up you could see exactly where they'd been because of what they'd left behind. They motored to the Peak District and the Lake District and the Cornish beaches and camped dangerously on cliffs that were about to fall into the sea. A few early daffodils came out. Elsa, now cautiously walking again in Rutland, although only at the new low total of five thousand steps or 2.08 miles a day, said nothing was out there yet except for dog-owners with exceptionally long leads she's afraid of getting tangled up in (in which she is afraid of getting tangled up). The long leads are necessary because of leaping lambs in the fields which make dogs hyperventilate (I could have written 'get excited' but 'hyperventilate' is much less pedestrian).

It was rumoured that England might come out of lockdown soon. Naturally, I wanted to be liberated – who wouldn't – but would I remember how to be liberated, and what about all my lockdown projects?

I forced myself back to Dr Ahmad-Wicks. She was writing about Fredrika Bergman, the young, straight-backed female detective in Kristina Ohlsson's *Unwanted*. What was thought at first to be an ordinary custody battle turned out to be much more when a lost child was discovered somewhere in Northern Sweden with the word 'unwanted' stamped on her forehead. Fredrika tried to be a new brand of female investigator, Dr Ahmad-Wicks decreed, one who prioritised objective detecting over the emotional involvement usually ascribed to women detectives. Moreover, Fredrika Bergman was an academic, having studied criminality at university. Dr Ahmad-Wicks puzzled over the prevalence of high-achieving academic backgrounds among fictional female sleuths. Although none can match the combined legal and medical degrees of Patricia Cornwell's Kay Scarpetta, it does seem that fictional detecting mirrors real life in its demand that female practitioners should have higher educational qualifications than male ones. There are also differences in fitness. Hercule Poirot is obese and Kurt Wallander has diabetes. The men can be ignorant, sleazy and unhealthy and still be admired for their excellence at the job.

I thought Dr Ahmad-Wicks read too much into it, but then that's what academics do. My task was to make sure that her meaning was clear and not too camouflaged by errors of grammar and punctuation. Like most academics, she suffered from the delusion that a long sentence, preferably in the format of a whole dragging paragraph, is better than a short one. And that long words are superior to short ones. I can be blamed for the same thing but I get bored with short words and feel a professional responsibility to exploit the full glory of the English language. Please forgive me. That's a nice short sentence. The footnotes in Dr Ahmad-Wicks's text were a complete hornet's nest. Chapter 6, for example, had two footnote 36s, neither of which referred to anything relevant in the text, and footnote 105 was missing entirely. In any case 105 footnotes per chapter are far too many – although they were fewer (not less) than in Chapter 10, which had 404.

The week of my return to London was also the week of my niece Crystal's fortieth birthday. My laptop pinged with an email from her. *Dear Auntie Alice, I hope you're doing ok. Have you had your jabs yet? Isn't it all so grim!!! Can you meet me at St Pancras Station on Monday at 11.30 for a coffee? You can give me your birthday present then!!! Love and kisses, Crystal.* I can't be the only person who's noticed how exclamation marks have proliferated in modern forms of communication. The cumulative effect is to dull the senses completely. Crystal was an exclamation mark person before all this anyway.

She was waiting for me in a black-and-white striped bobble hat, dark glasses and an immense padded white coat on a bench hung with an 'out of use' sign near the Eurostar section of the station. She was on her mobile, of course, as I approached, but she did look up from it to welcome me with metaphorically open arms. We took the escalator to the upper floor, purchased takeaway coffees from a small hidden-away Greggs, and repaired to another bench by the barriers to several waiting trains.

'It's well ventilated here,' noted Crystal happily.

That was certainly true: the arched iron and glass roof enclosed air that was almost the same temperature as the cold outside. An amazing number of people were embarking on essential and non-essential journeys and getting their enormous suitcases stuck in the ticket gates. I couldn't hear much of what Crystal was saying due to the commotion and her thick face mask. 'Drink your coffee,' I said, in order to get the mask relocated under her chin. I gave her her birthday present – a book about Kumihimo wirework jewellery. I knew that jewellery-making was her latest craft enthusiasm, replacing flower-painted furniture and pickled vegetables. She seemed to like the book, although what she said was drowned out by an announcement about the departure of the 12.31 to Derby.

I asked Crystal for all her news. She lived in a cooperative housing project by Ravenscourt Park in West London which never seemed very cooperative as they were always having rows, about which she naturally had to update me. Barrie, a dyslexic transwoman, was upset with Johanna, an out-of-work opera singer, for the politically unfriendly notices the latter had posted in the communal laundry room suggesting that men were genetically deficient in laundry skills.

'What upsets me more,' explained Crystal, as a woman with a huge scarlet suitcase created a total blockage in the ticket gates, 'is that neither of them ever cleans out the powder compartment. It's full of slimy mould. And they're also always leaving odd socks or unexplained items of underwear scrunched up inside it. I don't like handling other people's smalls. But, Auntie Alice,' said Crystal, anticipating my complaint that other people's domestic trivia are so much less engaging than one's own, 'what I really wanted to tell you is that Melissa and Candida have had the most awful row and they won't speak to each other at all. Mum's quite beside herself.'

Crystal is the most peaceable and charitable person I know and she never has rows with anybody, because she can always see their point of view, which can be a disability and may help to account for her never having made a lot of progress, professionally speaking, in her life. She's just not selfish enough. These two older sisters of hers ought to have stopped squabbling long ago, but they enjoy it too much. 'It was about Covid,' went on Crystal. 'Melissa found out that Candida had been having supper with a friend indoors all through this lockdown and the last. And then Candida went to Melissa's house and even though she didn't move off the doorstep she could have given it to her. Melissa can be quite unforgiving,' said Crystal reflectively as though she'd only just realised this.

'I must call Susie,' I said, 'how is she?'

'Well, you know Mum, she copes. Never complains.' This wasn't my experience of my sister, but that's family dynamics for you. 'She's thinking of moving into a retirement home in Eastbourne.'

'Isn't she a bit young for that?'

'She's eight years older than you,' reprimanded Crystal, 'and she's not fit like you are.'

I liked this perception of me as fit. I wondered whether to tell Crystal about Stephen Dearlove. She might find it amusing. But there again she might be shocked, which I wouldn't want. And she might tell Susie. If Susie were to know, I'd tell her myself. 'Why Eastbourne?'

'Mum says she went there as a child. She has nice memories of the place.'

Yes, I think we did. We stayed in a B & B which had the same menu every week and a particularly revolting onion soup on Wednesdays. In order to get to the beach, we had to walk past the splendid white palm-treed Grand Hotel where I thought we ought to stay instead. We went there once for a cream tea, but it wasn't a success as Dad complained about cost and the scones were stale. 'It's not very easy to get to Eastbourne,' I pointed out, thinking it possible that long years of duty visits might be required.

'I heard the news about your extra grandchild,' said Crystal, moving onto a more bracing subject. 'It's sooooo exciting!!!' She clapped her hands and a traveller walking by looked round in alarm. 'But what I don't understand,' she continued, 'is why Nathan didn't tell you about the baby. It must have come as such a surprise.'

'Yes it was, and I don't know why he didn't.' Nathan and Crystal are almost the same age; Susie and I had been pregnant at the same time, her with her fifth and me with my second. She and Johnny lived in London then, they had a pet shop in Mill Hill, so Crystal and Nathan played together quite a lot. 'Have you heard from him?' I asked tentatively, conscious that an affirmative answer would both please and upset me. I wanted to know he was okay, but I'd prefer to know that from him directly.

'I had an email,' said Crystal, 'a while ago. Before Christmas sometime. Probably October actually.'

'What did it say?'

'Oh, it was just a one-liner,' she said offhandedly. 'You know, "Hiya Crystal how are you, hope to see you soon" sort of thing.'

On the other side of the concourse, a waiting Eurostar emitted a deafening pneumatic noise. Crystal looked at her watch. 'Must go in a minute, Auntie. Thank you so much for the book. It looks really interesting.'

She scrumpled up the wrapping paper and looked around the bin-less platform for somewhere to put it. 'Give it to me, I'll take it home. Where are you off to now?'

'Blood,' she said. 'I'm going to give blood. It's my third time. My birthday present to the NHS. That's why I've come into Central London today, the centre's in Margaret Street. They're short of donors at the moment, with the pandemic, you know.'

'That's a very good thing to do.'

'More people ought to do it. It's so easy and they give you tea and biscuits afterwards. But not you, Auntie, you're too old.'

'That's not a very nice thing to say.'

'No, I mean they won't let you give blood if you're over sixty.'

'Why on earth not? My blood is as good as yours.'

'Yes, but you need it more.'

We got up from our cold seats and walked past the deserted champagne bar. 'Wouldn't it be nice,' said Crystal wistfully, 'if we could just go and grab a glass of Pol Roger and sit on those high-up stools and imagine all the journeys we could be making.'

'When this is over,' I said to her, 'you and I will go away somewhere nice and hot together and drink champagne every day. We won't tell anyone, we'll just do it.'

Oh, it is nice seeing these young people, it does make me feel better. Crystal had lockdown hair like the rest of us and her face was pale and undeniably in need of sunshine. She was wearing a lot of home-made jewellery: dangly white earrings, several chains round her neck, and a congregation of bracelets on both wrists. They jangled as we said goodbye to one another, me returning to Stoke Newington and my fascination with train murders, and her to Margaret Street for her next episode of venesection, a most admirable word. 'Phlebotomy' is another one. I could be a phlebotomist in another life. That would look good on a passport.

On the bus home I think of Crystal lying on a couch in the blood donation centre offering a pint of her valuable life-giving fluid altruistically, unlike the comedian Tony Hancock in that famous sixties' episode about blood donation. 'It's either this or joining the young Conservatives,' says Hancock as he stumbles in, then mistaking the tiny preliminary sample they take for the whole donation. A pint is nearly an armful, he complains, and therefore far too much. When he gets home he cuts himself with a kitchen knife and has to go to hospital where he needs a blood transfusion. We never know when altruistic acts might suddenly reconfigure themselves as selfish ones.

21 Not being a seductress any more

The magnolia two houses down is thrusting its white and pink buds hopefully into the atmosphere. We are surrounded by signs of spring but spring itself is nowhere to be seen. The news is full of vaccine wars and advice about summer holidays but where is summer, if spring never comes? We are all infected with the virus of lockdown pessimism. Discarded face masks disfigure not only our streets but the virgin coral at the bottom of the sea in the Philippines. Tidal waves of refugees choose the riskiest forms of travelling to pursue their dream and their human right to live in a place where they won't be randomly killed, persecuted or die of starvation. The newsreaders with half-bleached hair go on mispronouncing 'economics' – it should be 'eeconomics' not 'ekonomics'. Complaining is the province of the elderly for the simple reason that you require experience to do it well.

My granddaughter, Sara, at home with her locked-down family, emailed me the completed version of the review she's compiled of that unhappy memoir, *Educated*, for her online schoolwork. I dutifully edited it and sent it back. Another Sarah flooded our TV screens with her open, expressive face. Sarah Everard's death was evidently an extra-horrible murder because dental records were needed for identification (dentists can be useful for some things). The nation realised anew two things that were quite well-known before: that violence against women and girls is endemic and mostly male, and that the forces of law and order, also mostly male, can do more harm than good. I sighed as I watched the news, and the temptation to reach for the solace of crisps or dairy milk chocolate or another glass of wine was huge. My clothes were getting tight. I even needed new bras which I don't understand because how do the crisps and chocolates and wine end up there? But fortunately, I was nothing like the absolutely gargantuan bodies, torsos and limbs so enormous that cranes are needed to get them out of bed, that I had caught glimpses of in a dreadful programme called *My 600lb Life*.

The dreams that have taken over my nights were deep and thick. I woke sweating in a deluge of alarm, panicking about nothing in particular, merely everything. The light of dawn crept round the curtain edges, sinister and uninviting. Who could walk out into that dawn and greet another day with any sense of joy? I hid under a pillow to shut out the light, but then I couldn't breathe which didn't seem to matter much as I was under there thinking about euthanasia anyway. One solution to the problem about what to do with the rest of one's life was to end it. Why hadn't I thought of that before? Feverishly, I chucked the pillow on the floor and rushed to the computer. I typed in 'assisted suicide' as I thought that was what it was called, and I was immediately directed to lots of stuff about the terminally ill and campaigns to help them on their way. That wasn't what I wanted. What I was looking for it, and found after some more digging, is called 'rational' suicide. This presumes that the other sort is always irrational which surely can't be the case because a wish to die is a wish to die for whatever reason.

'Meet the woman campaigning for the right to die just for being old,' says the video clip above the elegant honey-blonde face of Jacqueline Jencquel aged seventy-six, a French woman who's been talking about this for at least ten years. There she sits in her smart casual cream clothes – only the French know how to do casual – on a plush cream-coloured sofa in the 7th arrondissement in Paris talking matter-of-factly about why she would rather not go on living. She can't digest anything any more. She can only drink vodka, wine is too sour and the bubbles in champagne hurt her stomach. Yes, she knows half the world is starving and these are trivial complaints but that's the way it is. She mourns, also in a very French manner, the loss of her role as a seductress. She fell in love with her young fitness coach four years ago. She couldn't possibly fall in love with an old man. Anyway, it's impossible to fall in love properly at her age. Yes, the grandchildren are cute, she's full of ecstasy when she looks at them, but she's not really in their lives or they in hers. She doesn't have a job, there's nothing going on in her life, therefore it has no meaning. She will die in January 2020. But once this date arrives, she decides she'd like to see another spring. In the summer she postpones again. And again in December.

The media mocked Jacqueline Jencquel for her indecision. The wish to die isn't constant, she responded, rationally. I got up and looked at myself in the mirror above the fireplace. I felt it was a long time since I'd faced myself squarely like this. You know your own face very well, but you know it through all its transformations from that very first moment when you saw yourself in a mirror but you thought it was another baby, not you. When you smiled, the other baby smiled back. This history inhabits the image you see today. Mine was sleepy, world-weary, furrowed, and chubbier than I'd like. The chocolates ended up there as well. But this absolutely wasn't the face of someone who wanted to die. There was residual light and a trickle of energy in the eyes, traces of flexibility and laughter in the lines around the mouth. These seemed more important than the silver hair or the fading of whiteness in the teeth and eyes. Maybe it was because I'm not French and never cared about my appearance as a seductress like Mme Jencquel who, according to Wikipedia, is still alive and is sensibly declining to give any further updates on the timing of her exit from this world.

Perhaps, all the same, I'd better join one of those organisations that does help you should the time come. 'Exit International' charges a hundred Australian dollars for annual membership and a thousand for a lifetime one. The latter must be a good deal for them financially since most of their members join precisely because they don't want their lifetimes any more. Exit International also sells copies of books about the choice to die with titles like *Killing Me Softly*, and *An Act of Love,* and actual kits called *Barbiturate Test Kit* and *Nembutal Sampler Kit,* although these don't contain actual drugs so what is the point? Membership brings you free copies of *The Peaceful Pill Handbook* available in six languages and with constantly updated R & D results, and the *Deliverance Newsletter* which is published quarterly. And probably lots of unsolicited emails to add to the ones I already get from Amazon, Facebook, Travelzoo, Homebase, LinkedIn,

Lands End, Booking.com, Uber, Paypal, Railbookers, Royce Lingerie and many more. I delete them in huge chunks every now and then, with great spurious satisfaction since there's no real achievement involved.

'What do you think about rational suicide?' I asked Elsa in an email, suspecting she, the body expert, will know all about it.

'I hope you're not considering any other sort of suicide, Alice,' she answered. 'I take it that you're still harping on about what happened to that Maud of yours?'

That reminded me that I had yet to inspect the two places near Elsa's cottage that I'd recently discovered to be haunts of Maud and her family. Elsa claimed she was well enough to go out on little jaunts now, especially since the local pub was open for freezing outdoor meals. She'd sent me a picture of giraffes black against the skyline of a colourful Tanzanian sunset, part of an article about how female giraffes who bond together live longer than others. One reason is that they share the best food spots.

When I returned to her cottage we had a lot to talk about: her illness, and the new insights hospitalisation has given her into the theology of the medical profession, my ruminations concerning Stephen Dearlove, Maud Davies's stubborn reluctance to let me know the causal antecedents of her decapitation, how well those boys/men of mine are doing – and the little one with eyelashes – that splendidly stupid Oprah Winfrey interview with two spoilt royals and whether Elsa should trade in her orange Nokia for something better equipped to meet the challenges of modern life. She talked about the progress of her shoe research and the saga of the Clarks shoe family which goes back hundreds of years and features another woman called Alice who was a student at LSE. Having established that the dates match, more or less, I realised that this Alice would have known my Maud who was at LSE doing her rural sociology research around the same time that Alice was reading the archival records of women's work in the seventeenth century. And they were both suffragists. Perhaps they met at suffrage demonstrations as well as in the cramped teaching rooms of LSE. So quite coincidentally Elsa and I were immersed in the probing of two historically intertwined lives.

'It's a folie à deux,' meditated Elsa.

I thought, irrelevantly, of all the manuscripts I've copy-edited in which the accent on the 'a' has gone the wrong way.

'A shared psychotic delusion,' Elsa continued, referring to our curious obsession with other women's lives. 'You have transferred to me the mistaken belief that getting inside someone else's life will solve the problem of what to do with your own.'

'I don't mind what you call it,' I said, 'but can we please go and look at those houses I told you about?'

She agreed because it'd help her get back on track for her daily walking target.

The Pastures, up the hill from Elsa's village, looked sadly ramshackle, a house no longer loved, and suffering from an earlier unhappy Art Nouveau marriage of styles. We scrunched timorously up the wide gravel path between two old stone walls fringed by tiny clusters of white starry flowers. As we passed a raised area of grass covered in snowdrops, our steps on the gravel unfortunately sounded a warning to any current inhabitants. It was a spread-out house with various wings. Some of the outhouse doors were open, revealing spaces inside crammed with rusty farm machinery, all looking very neglected. Three cars were parked by the house's main entrance.

'It's flats now,' said Elsa in altogether too loud a voice, I thought.

If there were ghosts here they were hiding. I sniffed, ridiculously, trying to pick up any enduring historical atoms.

'Have you got a cold, Alice?' shouted Elsa.

We crunched over the gravel back to the road.

We had more luck with Lyndon Hall, a fine building whose every stone proclaimed history, and which could be seen clearly in all its glory from the tiny thirteenth-century church. The evening sun came out, gilding the moss on the old graves in the churchyard and backlighting the elegant symmetry of the Hall. Elsa poked around among the gravestones and kept calling me over to examine unreadable names.

After these excursions, it felt strange to re-enter Elsa's twenty-first century garden which had sprouted yet more artificial adornments since I was last there.

'They don't look real, you know,' I observed. I'd been dying to say that for ages. (Why does one *die* to say things?)

'Artificial flowers are an art form,' insisted Elsa fiercely. 'I picked them up at the local recycling centre when I gave them my red hoover which is so clogged up that I can't unclog it any more.'

'I expect there's a YouTube video that would have helped with that,' I said.

'I haven't got time for that sort of nonsense,' she replied sharply.

I looked concerned. 'Please don't bark at me. Remember the giraffes and the enhanced mortality that comes with female bonding, we don't want to lose that, do we?'

'Alice,' she said, 'do you appreciate how horribly critical you can be sometimes? Be charitable for a change.'

We did go to the pub, but we confined ourselves to one course called Rutland trout which rested on a few stems of dehydrated broccoli. Afterwards we bonded over three repeats of that BBC comedy *One Foot in the Grave* that starred the bumbling, accident-prone Victor Meldrew and his irritated wife who works in a flower shop to get away from him. Something I hadn't noticed when the series was first on was that Victor was only sixty-one. One foot in the grave at sixty-one? 'I don't believe it,' was Victor's constant refrain. He said it, for example, when his local garden centre delivered a Yucca plant and he asked them to put it temporarily in the downstairs bathroom and he found they'd actually planted it in the toilet.

I didn't believe it either when Elsa showed me a book she'd recently ordered about the sociology and anthropology of ageing. Newly sensitised to her status in life, Elsa was doing what she always did, treating her life as a topic of academic study. She said she was thinking of doing ageing next, after shoes, and not teeth, as I'd suggested. *Autobiography of an Elderly Woman* by Anonymous was a slim American book, a reissue in 1995 of a text originally published in 1911. It had an elegant typeface and an admirably neat line under all the page headings. I scanned a few pages and didn't identify any grammatical or typographical errors. They knew how to write and print in those days.

'It's a marvellous book, so unsentimental and plain-speaking,' enthused Elsa. 'The narrator is fussed over by her adult children, in particular her over-protective daughter, Margaret, who wants her to sit quietly in a shady room without moving and eat tapioca. The whole thing is a diatribe against the social conventions of ageing and the idea that for old people life is essentially over and all we can do is wait patiently for death.' Elsa had underlined a number of passages in the book:

I have lived so long in this world that I feel free to express my opinions without being afraid of being misunderstood.

I hope that I shall keep my family alert over my misdeeds until my end.

I know a valiant old lady of seventy...One day she arose, saying, 'Before another of those granddaughters of mine gets the croup, I'm going round the world!

'Would you like to jump on a boat, Elsa, and go round the world? We'd make a valiant pair of giraffes.'

'How can we?' she said in the same quietly despairing voice she used to criticise her erratically flashing garden lights. 'Only essential travel is allowed. We are completely trapped.'

It was true. The BV was far from gone, on the contrary it was having a whale of a time changing its appearance continually in order to avoid detection.

'When you read it,' said Elsa, returning to the subject of her newly discovered book, 'start at the end.'

I immediately turned to the end, an Afterword by the American writer, Doris Grumbach. Here I learnt that the

Anonymous author wasn't the elderly woman everyone supposed but a thirty-seven-year-old journalist, a radical socialist and feminist called Mary Heaton Vorse. *Autobiography* was a novel, fiction not fact, exactly like the Finnish novel I was reading in bed, *Escape from Sunset Grove*. Why is it, I wonder out loud to Elsa, that the condition of old age is so unpalatable that it must be dressed up as a story?

This name, Mary Heaton Vorse, was one I recognised from my own wanderings through the world of early twentieth-century feminist political agitation, the world Maud Davies was on the verge of embracing. It was so extraordinarily annoying that she went to America just before she died leaving no clue about what she did there. Perhaps she glimpsed the amazing Mary Heaton Vorse down a side-street in Greenwich Village, or perhaps she took a train somewhere for a pre-arranged meeting with a group of transatlantic social investigators with Mary Heaton Vorse among them because of her interest in the labour movement, or even the white slave trade.

On the Saturday morning, Elsa and I drove to Waitrose to buy ourselves some treats. A new BV sign had appeared on the side of the store recommending the use of something called 'SmartShop' that would help us to 'Shop safer and more quickly', a truly awful fate, grammatically speaking. Everyone was very polite and a marshal at the entrance checked our face coverings and passed us a heavily sanitised trolley, the odour of which quite drowned out the scent of roses and lilies from the flower display at the front of the store. There were easter eggs and bunnies in different formats everywhere and bottles of pink champagne with untempting bows. On the way back to the cottage we went for yet another walk (you're probably getting just as tired of reading about these walks as I am of doing them) in a village that cowers in the shadow of a cement works. We parked the car by the church and found ourselves in the midst of some really rather lovely old stone houses arranged at peculiar angles to one another, some of them with lawns sloping down to a little river fringed with sprightly daffodils.

'I think I'll avoid rational suicide like the plague for the time being,' I remarked to Elsa.

'But we are in the middle of a plague and most people don't appear to be doing very well at avoiding it,' said she.

'I've got my second vaccination next week,' I boasted. That's something to look forward to (to which to look forward) (I agree it doesn't flow as well).

22 Alice has a birthday

And so Philippos, born in a villa called Mon Repos on the island of Corfu, nearly a century ago, to a mother also called Alice, dies in an English castle after being married to Queen Elizabeth the Second of the United Kingdom of Great Britain and Northern Ireland for an extremely long time. Even republicans like me are adhered to our TV sets or other convenient broadcasting devices as the curtailed funeral unfolds. There is an assembly of royals, grave in black, with the secrets of their misbehaving lives tightly and temporarily buttoned up. Then Elizabeth the Second herself, concealed beneath a large black hat and behind her virus mask, a little old lady who has, like millions of others, lost her husband, not in a car park or a shopping centre or even in the grounds of a historic castle, but to death.

Like these millions of others, Elizabeth the Second will just have to engage in what Elsa would call cognitive restructuring. She'll have to learn to live without her Philippos. He will no longer look at her over the Tupperware boxes of their morning cornflakes, or share with her his incredulity, disappointment, anger or other emotion in response to their miscreant offspring. He will not express a mutual despair at the self-serving antics of

211

her government. His footsteps will never again pound the grand halls and corridors of their many state-subsidised homes. He will never again make a politically embarrassing joke or drive into someone's car because the sun blinded him and he was too old to drive any more.

Philippos dies, but Alice Henry doesn't. Indeed, she's about to be called on to celebrate seventy-five years of living, of bumbling on, conceiving plans and children and then abandoning them or being abandoned by them, making mistakes and wondering why, growing in size and certain forms of wisdom while giving up on others. I don't want to understand how iPhones or self-driving cars work, nor how ekonomists calculate the GNP. I can't be bothered following the machinations of politicians or being polite to doctors. But I still want to know what to do with the rest of my life. A fugue of hurdles erected by others has got in the way of that straight path to happiness that stretches into the distance in my dreams.

In preparation for the event of my achieving seventy-five years on this earth I did what I'd been meaning to do for months and bagged up an entire wardrobe of clothes for charity. Then I located my Will, after hours of searching, at the bottom of the airing cupboard. The legal sheets were quite crispy. I didn't know what to do about Mila and Ed Kuiper who, being recently arrived on my genealogical landscape, weren't in it. Writing a Will is an immensely tricky exercise, almost as bad as planning a birthday party. You need to predict what will happen over a long period which involves the whole mind-bending issue of plan-making. Eventually I attached to the Will a note expressing my desire for an equal division of all my (limited) worldly goods between my children and grandchildren. I got Angie from upstairs to act as witness. I noted she gave 'Feng Shui Consultant' as her occupation, not that there was much room for that trade in their tiny two-room flat. When I said that, Angie agreed. There's more space in New Zealand, she told me, so they're going back there as soon as the BV allows.

'What are you going to do for your birthday?' asked Elsa at the end of an email reporting on the cataclysmic events happening in her village: the birth of two foals, and fourteen ducklings spotted swimming behind their mum on the stagnant village pond. The cottage that housed the cannabis factory has now finally been sold. Its rooms will struggle to relinquish the mouldy scents of the plants that once flourished there, and the neighbours will go on peering through the windows, wondering if this sort of weed will ever grow again.

'I don't want a fuss,' I replied, not entirely truthfully, about the birthday celebration. A fuss would be lovely so long as I didn't have to make it myself.

Events took a different turn when Jack rang to say that he'd booked the entire outside of a smart Italian restaurant in Barnsbury for lunch on my birthday, which would happen on a Saturday. Very well-arranged that, I thought, although it meant that my eightieth would be on a Friday and my ninetieth, not that there's any possibility of my making it that far, would occur on a Thursday, which wouldn't be a good idea at all.

'It might be a bit cold,' said Jack, 'but they've got patio heaters and a kind of marquee thing and we can bring rugs.'

On the Saturday of my birthday the BV rules changed yet again to allow both inside restaurant eating and

213

hugging everywhere. With respect to the latter, the government had felt it necessary to tell us how to do it safely – only hug low-risk people, keep it short, turn your face away and wear a mask. I don't think I'll bother.

Jack and I had of course been plunged into the agony of who should be invited to this celebration. I mentioned Elsa, as I knew she would invite me to stay with her on my birthday and would offer to cook me one of her Croatian specialties. Skradinski risotto and a Zagreb schnitzel had been mentioned.

'Of course she must come, she's your oldest friend,' Jack said. And most of the others are dead, though he didn't say that.

'What about your father?' I asked. 'I'm not sure he'd be able to make it from Dagenham.'

'I'll send an Uber for him,' replied Jack magnanimously.

Patti's business must be doing well, I thought, to pay for all of this because I doubt whether Jack earns all that much as the editor of *The Buckingham Mercury*. And then there was Nathan.

'Where is Nathan?' I asked.

'I'm on the case, Mum,' said Jack mysteriously.

And what about Susie and all her lot, especially Crystal, my eccentric niece? 'There are just too many of them,' I said, anticipating his question. 'We'd need the most enormous marquee and anyway I can't remember all their names.'

'I think you must invite Aunt Susie.'

I knew she wouldn't come. She never leaves Sheffield, her obsession with burglars had been hopelessly inflated by the abduction of next door's Norwegian Forest cat.

'Anyone else? If Crystal comes and Susie doesn't that's

ten of us including baby Kuiper who'll need a high chair, and not counting Nathan which we can't until we know where he is.'

'Sara did mention,' began Jack hesitantly, 'that you might have a new, well, special friend.'

'Oh, did she? Yes, I might.'

'Well, you might like to bring him.'

'Yes, I might.'

My new special friend had declared that he wished to take me out for my birthday for a romantic dinner in another cold garden. He still didn't want to cook. I said fine, but it can't be on the Saturday because we're having a family party then. This prompted a gigantic sulk; Stephen Dearlove lay, metaphorically, on the ground, kicking his legs and bawling and saying this isn't fair, and that he felt very excluded and this was no way to treat someone who'd given you three books of his poetry and access to his body.

Men, as they prove time and time again, are the hysterical sex. They deposit their emotions freely on other people (women) because they believe that what they feel is a matter of fact which must be acted on, whereas other people's emotions (women's) are just plain annoying.

'Do I have to come?' asked Elsa petulantly. 'There are never any parking spaces outside your house, and I don't intend to take the train.'

'If you don't come to my seventy-fifth birthday party, I won't come to yours.'

Then she wanted to know if all the people had been vaccinated. Jack and the staff of *The Buckingham Mercury* had all been done, and apparently Patti had inveigled her way into a vaccine queue by claiming she was a key worker. Alan was so old he must have been vaccinated

215

by now, though he wouldn't remember if he had or not. I thought Crystal might have been given the vaccine in return for the blood she'd given the NHS, but Elsa said those two systems were insufficiently connected up for that to happen.

'We will be sitting outside,' I pointed out.

'Oh, alright then. I've got to meet my publisher anyway.' Elsa had finished her feet/shoe book: *Footprints: An anthropology and cultural history of human feet*, and was gearing up for the painful process of its production and launch. I hoped she wasn't going to ask me to copy-edit it.

I studied the weather forecast in order to decide on my birthday apparel. Because I'd given most of my dresses away I had an excuse to buy a new one. I was constantly being invited by my phone or my laptop to desire frocks with flappy arms and frilly hems costing hundreds of pounds and quite unsuited to my figure. But I bought one anyway. It was covered in green carnations, and was called a 'tiered midi-dress'.

The actual day began quite unpropitiously with another hailstorm. I would have turned the heating up if we hadn't been going out. Elsa, who'd arrived the previous evening (I'd given her a whole pack of visitors' parking permits which I'd managed to extract from Hackney Council after a humungous amount of trouble) stood next to me watching the hailstones dance on the pavements and saying how stupid it was that we were expected to sit outside in this.

Jack had ordered Ubers for everyone. Crystal refused on climate grounds and Jack's 'everyone' didn't include Stephen Dearlove.

When Elsa and I were in our Uber in transit from Stoke

Newington to Barnsbury, the hailstones stopped and the sun came out. This improved my mood because it meant I could off take my coat and reveal my tiered midi-dress. Elsa was completely muffled up in layers of jerseys, coats and shawls and even a fur hat.

When we arrived at Bono Bottega Nostrana Jack was at the head of the table looking very personable in a crisp white shirt and a dark grey jacket. Patti had newly spiked hair and what I considered a slightly resentful look, but she was very animated in her communications with baby Ed who gave me a knowing luxuriously-lashed look. Mila, an altogether calmer and better groomed person than when she'd originally appeared on my doorstep, stood up to greet me. She looked quite beautiful with her long shiny hair streaming down the front of a turquoise quilted coat. Sara threw herself at me energetically, contravening the government hugging guidelines, and Sam said, 'Happy birthday, Granny,' most politely and with reasonable conviction. After Elsa and I had sat down, there were, I noticed, four empty spaces at the table which occupied the whole of the restaurant's outside marquee space. Four?

A car drew up on the double yellow line and out of it, very slowly, emerged Alan with his cane in one hand and a Sainsbury's plastic bag in the other. His head was more bent than ever, quite like Elizabeth the Second's at her husband's funeral, but without any black hat. He remembered Jack, his son, and me, but everyone else was a mystery to him, even though we patiently explained several times who they were.

'Come and sit next to me, Grandpa,' invited Sam sympathetically.

Alan settled himself down, resting his cane on the uneven ground beneath the table from where it would probably advance towards the gutter. He handed the Sainsbury's bag to me.

'I've got you a present, Alice,' he said proudly, raising his bowed head just enough to make fleeting eye contact with me. 'You thought I'd forget, didn't you?' He chuckled to himself while Sara took the bag and decreed that all the presents should be put in the middle of the table and only opened when everyone was there.

Patti asked me how I was. 'She's not bad for seventy-five,' replied Elsa on my behalf. I have a British mother-in-law relationship with Patti. Elsa will tell you that mother-in-law jokes are a cultural effluent. They don't have them in Croatia or anywhere else that respects old women. I wouldn't want to know what Patti Henry says about me to Jack and her friends. But one might as well give her something to talk about.

'What do you think of my birthday dress?' I asked, stripping off my coat and revealing the acreage of chest exposed by the top half of my green-carnationed tiered midi-dress. 'Goodness,' said Patti, 'you're brave, aren't you?'

To wear this dress? To take my coat off? To have a family like this?

The masked and visored waiter plonked bottles of wine and plates of colourful antipasti all down the middle of the table, judiciously avoiding Alan's Sainsbury's bag which he eyed with some disdain.

'We'll start with some champagne,' pronounced Jack masterfully. He waved to someone behind me who turned out to be Crystal perspiring in a coat with a furry hood.

She'd walked, she told us, all the way from Ravenscourt Park.

'I could do with some of that,' she said, spotting the champagne which fizzed into our glasses while she disentangled herself from the over-heated hood.

I gave her a slight, well-managed hug. 'Dear Crystal, it's splendid that you could come. I don't think you know everyone, do you?'

'Well I've always thought that I probably don't know you very well, Auntie Alice, but her' (pointing at Elsa) 'yes, I remember her, she's your old friend from the University, isn't she, the one you went island-hopping with? And that' (pointing at Ed) 'must be your new grandbaby, what a lovely boy, and his mother, I do like your coat, whatever your name is!'

'Who is this?' asked Alan loudly. 'Why is she talking so much? She should go away.'

Crystal lowered her voice. 'I met a friend of yours round the corner,' she said to me. 'We were both staring at our phones trying to find this place. Google maps says it's on the other side of the road. I left him there trying to work it out. He said he'd follow in a minute.'

Stepping forward from the kerb, having successfully crossed the road, Stephen Dearlove smiled urbanely (that's a word I've been longing to use, but it doesn't apply to many people in my life). I was quite proud of how he looked in a tailored navy wool coat and a discretely patterned grey scarf with a glimpse underneath of my pale blue Christmas jumper. A very coherent outfit.

Everyone round the table gave him the once-over, except for Alan who raised his head a few millimetres and barked, again, 'Who are you?' in a very hostile manner. 'Why are all these strangers having dinner with us? Is he from the council? I don't like those fellows.'

'He's Granny's friend,' explained Sam with impressive gentleness.

'Alice lives with me, you know,' declared Alan, in return. 'She made me a nice apple turnover for dinner last night. Or maybe it was last week. Wednesday, perhaps. I don't know. Where am I anyway?'

'Don't give him any more champagne, Jack,' ordered Patti.

'I hope when I've got dementia I'll drown in the stuff. I can't think of a better way to go.' Unfortunately I say this out loud.

Patti looks disapproving and Jack says, 'Mum that's not a nice thing to say on your birthday.'

Birthdays, deathdays, what's the difference? We all have them.

'What does everyone think about Harry beetling off back to California and missing his own granny's ninety-fifth birthday?' I asked cheerily, trying for a change of subject. All of us, royals and commoners alike, are mired in the psychodramas of family life. They besiege our working hours, invade our dreams, and give us something to argue and write books about.

There's still one empty place at the table. Well, it's obvious, isn't it? I can see Jack looking at me looking at it. Mila, who's been feeding baby Ed morsels of mozzarella to keep him quiet, suddenly leaps up and dumps the cheesy baby on Patti's knee and disappears through the open doors of the restaurant. Elsa sees what's happening behind me before I do because she's sitting opposite me. I feel a hand alighting on my shoulder, and I turn round and see this person standing there. Like Alan, I want to say, why are all these strangers having lunch with us? But I don't have dementia (yet) and therefore I know there must be some rational explanation.

'Hello, Mum,' says a voice, considerably higher in tone than I remember. My brain cells fire wildly, creating an entirely new set of neural connections. Here he is, my Nathan, except that he isn't he any more. The person standing before me is a fully grown and attired woman, a woman in an elegant dark green coat, a colour that always went well with the burnt sienna of his hair, which is now curling a good few inches below his ears and around the mini-chandeliers of two delicately refracting glass earrings. I don't know what to do or say which is very unusual for me. A great silence falls round the table, except for Ed babbling away with his cheese.

Alan says, 'It's Kerry, isn't it? Are you coming back to me, or have you just come to fetch the cat? He's not a bad animal really, I'd rather you didn't take him, we watch the re-runs of *Yes Minister* together. Or perhaps it's the news. It's all so awful, isn't it? I think I'd like to go home now.' He starts crying, great snotty sobs.

Sam pats him on the back and gives him one of the restaurant's napkins to mop his nose. Patti gets up, saying, 'It's difficult for her,' and follows Mila into the restaurant. The new Nathan sits down. From the other side of the table Jack watches keenly. He pours and hands over an extra glass of champagne.

'So you knew, did you?' I say accusingly to Jack. 'You knew, and you didn't tell me? And you,' I turn to Crystal, 'you knew as well, didn't you? And what about the children, did they know? This table is full of spies.' It's a line from Maud Davies's life, not mine. 'All this time I've been asking where Nathan is and none of you was willing to tell me the truth.'

'I'm here, Mum,' says Nathan sitting next to me. 'I'm here now.' He takes my hand in his, and his are decorated with immaculate pink nails, the stigmata of a fully finished female. 'I'm so sorry to spring such a surprise on you. I really am. And about having not responded to any of the messages you left me. It hasn't been easy for me. I've been a bad boy.' He smiles, a smile I remember, even though the contours of his face seem strangely different. 'You just have to think of me from now on as a bad girl.'

'I certainly think you've got some explaining to do.'

Elsa, I notice, looks extremely interested in this new development in Alice Henry's mundane life. She would do: Nathan's transformation must have involved considerable bodily adaptations in which she would have a professional academic interest.

Mila comes out of the restaurant looking a bit washed out. She grabs Ed from Patti and sits down, avoiding eye contact with Ed's now-female inseminator. The waiter bristles at all these interruptions in the smooth progress of our meal and hands us all sheets of paper on which are printed a thankfully small number of options from which we are to select our main courses.

'You choose for me,' I say, handing my sheet to Elsa. It seems completely absurd to spend any time in trivial deliberations about food with this momentous revelation going on,

'Let me, Mum,' says my new daughter. I've never had one of those before. 'I'll decide for you. I may have been

222

away for a while but I can still remember most of your fads and fancies.'

'I haven't got my glasses,' complains Alan. 'Why have I got to read this? Is it some kind of official letter?'

'Granny,' says young Sara with amazing maturity, 'I realise this must be a shock for you, but lots of people change their gender these days because they're unhappy, that's the way the modern world works. You should be pleased that Uncle Nathan is much happier now he's become Auntie Norah.'

'Nora? Is that Norah with an H?' It *is* better with an H, I think. Though Nora in Ibsen's *A Doll's House* didn't have one. This Nora(h) hasn't come out of the Doll's House because he/she was never in it.

My pedantic observation about spelling drags another memory into the discombobulated space of my head: Jane Fonda, in the 1970s film version of Ibsen's play when she's about to leave the irritating Torvald, declaring that the most sacred duty any human being has is to oneself ('oneself' being easier for me at the moment than 'himself' or 'herself'). We must know who we are. We must be clear about ourselves as people separate from other people. We must hold onto this sense of being agents of our own destinies and negotiate as best we can the possibility of happiness. That's what my Nathan has done. That's all he's done.

'Happy birthday, Mum,' says Jack, raising his glass. 'Let's all wish Alice Henry many happy returns.'

23 Post-natalem

A post-natalem is a happier event than a post-mortem and, theoretically, a more straightforward one since it lacks the diagnostic drama of an interrogation into causes of death. However, the cause of a birthday is living, and that's a far from simple matter.

'Don't you dare mention cognitive restructuring,' I warned Elsa as we left the Bono Bottega Nostrana steeped in alcohol, fish bones and a very fine tiramisu. 'Norah Henry is a new concept for me, and it'll take me a while to get used to it. But I am glad that Nathan has been found, albeit in what appears to be a foreign body.'

'He went to that famous clinic in Casablanca,' remarked Elsa, who had conducted what looked like an academic interview with Nathan/Norah between the main course and the dessert. We all changed places several times to increase the conversational options, except that Sam stayed next to Alan because he seemed to have hit on a good system for managing him. At the end of the meal Alan still didn't know who Sam was.

'That's where the original technique for male to female sex reassignment surgery was pioneered,' Elsa continued academically. 'In Casablanca. They take the skin of the penis and invert it to make a vagina, and then use the head of the penis to make a clitoris. Nathan also had chondrolaryngoplasty and rhinoplasty, operations on his Adam's apple and his nose. I expect you're wondering why an Adam's apple is called an Adam's apple, aren't you, Alice?'

'No. I was thinking that I don't want the details of how Nathan became Norah. To us mothers, the purity and wholeness of our babies' bodies are sacred. Then and forever. And an Adam's apple is something to do with forbidden fruit, I expect.'

Both Elsa and I were fairly inebriated still as we conducted our review of the day. She had given me a new pair of wellingtons for a birthday present, and Alan's supermarket bag had proved to contain three tins of Spam and a Mars Bar. The other presents were much more upmarket, and they included a proof copy of Jack's novel that he'd been working on for fifteen years and that none of us had been allowed to mention. It's a story about a white witch who lived in a village near Steeple Claydon in the late 1700s. She was called Amelia Brimstone and so is the book.

'Patti has actually tried out some of her remedies,' Jack had commented, 'and they work.'

'So the novel isn't really a novel?'

'Well, it's based on a true story.'

'How deeply unusual,' I'd said, drunkenly.

'I wonder what you're going to do about your special friend,' mused Elsa as we sat in my flat trying to sober up. 'It's obvious that he really has the hots for you.' This was another one of those curious English phrases Elsa had picked up from her Winchester boyfriend before she gave up sex.

'It's nice to be admired.' Well, it is. Very flattering and at the age of three-quarters of a century, totally unexpected.

Stephen Dearlove had caused me to think fondly about my body again. Instead of being only the troublesome conveyor of senescent signs and occasions for annoying medical encounters, it had reasserted itself as it once was, a source of delight. I was quite keen to hang onto this, but I was less sure about the return to heterosexist gender politics. I had come out of the Doll's House and I didn't want to go back into it again.

'We'll see,' I replied, realising as I did that the unknowingness of this – what *will* happen to Stephen Dearlove and Alice Henry – is actually something to be embraced, fully hugged, face to face, and without a mask. Lockdown thinking had possessed us all. We'd become so used to rules and regulations and warnings of doom that we'd lost the art of thinking freely about the future. Now our futures were being returned to us – well, within those limits imposed by Machiavellian world-harming national and international politics.

'Alright,' acknowledged Elsa, 'so you're not going to let me in on the future you have planned for your special friend.'

'I've given up all future planning.'

Elsa laughed. As the light drained from the sky, it started raining again, and we couldn't think of an excuse to stay awake any longer.

But not before she asked another question. 'So tell me instead, whatever happened to Maud Davies?'

'Oh, her. I think after all that research I've finally worked out what happened to her. I've written it all down for you. I've had to use my imagination at some points, but I've stuck closely to all the facts. You can even add footnotes if you like.'

24 What Alice thinks happened to Maud

1 Crossing the ocean

Jamaica had been her friend Christian Mactaggart's idea. Maud had been working too hard, writing up her research on rural women, and volunteering in an East End Settlement, using this as a base from which to deepen her understanding of how working-class women struggle to maintain themselves and their families. It would be good for her to take a break from this exhausting work. In addition, counselled Christian astutely from her office at the London School of Economics, the cause of the white slave trade which so interested Maud, might be further illuminated by making some international connections. Some days on a ship, some weeks in a different clime, would give Maud a chance to consider different angles on the position of women and decide where her own contribution would best fit in.

And so a trip to Jamaica was planned, calling at the USA on the return leg. Jamaica itself wasn't known to be on any established white slave route, but the Jamaica Tourist Association had bribed the big steamship companies to promote the island as a tropical winter resort. Their free and enticing guidebook, over which Maud pored, was replete with languid white-sand beaches, waving palm trees, and brightly dressed islanders.

On the ship she boarded from Liverpool in early December, *The Arcadian*, Maud met others who'd fallen for this promise of a tourist paradise. She kept herself to herself on the journey, reading a selection of books by and about women that she'd brought with her. The first was a thick volume published a few years previously called *Women's Work and Wages*, an astonishingly comprehensive study of six thousand working women in Birmingham, just the sort of social science Maud thought ought to be done. She knew one of the study's authors, a woman called Marie Cécile Matheson, slightly, since their paths had crossed in suffrage circles. She also had tucked away in her trunk accounts of social research by American women, and a batch of novels that gave fictional form to the problems faced by poor women, and which, Maud felt, deserved to be studied as social documents in their own right: *In Darkest London*, for example, by Margaret Harkness, a radical writer and a cousin of Maud's mentor Beatrice Webb.

It was odd to be reading such literature in the middle of the Atlantic Ocean, and odder still, once checked into a relaxing hotel in Kingston, Jamaica, to have one's nose in perceptive observations concerning the impossible circumstances faced by women in the unclean alleys of Birmingham. Yes, the sun was certainly shining in Kingston, and one had to be careful not to get too much of it. The water was the very turquoise of the tourist propaganda, and the poinsettia trees exactly matched their pictures. A bad hurricane in November had brought down bridges, railway lines and many buildings, ruining a good portion of the island's banana crop. Beggars were everywhere on the streets, especially by the gates to the famous Castleton Gardens where even little children pestered tourists for a few pennies or tried to sell them liquorice seeds and postcards. Poverty seemed to follow Maud everywhere she went. Yet inside the Gardens, all was peace amidst the huge palm trees, the birdsong, and the calming waters of the quaintly named Wag Water River.

She hated to admit it, but after a stay of some days in this contradictory place, it came as a relief to board *The SS Prinz August Wilhelm* in Kingston Harbour on the sixteenth of January for the next stage of her travels to New York. Was this because she was best suited to a nomadic life, Maud wondered? In England she did seem to be forever moving between different habitations – the handsome Corsley House in Wiltshire, her mother's family home in Maidenhead, Aunt Gertrude's irregularly designed house in Rutland, her own little top floor flat in Willesden Buildings at the back of Euston Station, and the hotel in Coram Street nearby, where she'd been spending increasing amounts of time recently. Before she went away, Maud had told the hotel staff, who by now knew her quite well, that she was going to the seaside. It was true, in a way. A cruise ship was surrounded by the sea. And it was akin to a hotel for anyone averse to housekeeping, as Maud was, because everything was provided. So long as one's fellow travellers were congenial, there was really nothing to worry about.

Maud sat on the deck on the second steamship of her travels wrapped in a rug staring at the endless blue sea day after day. It looked so benign, this sleek blue water, but naval travelling was replete with hazards on which it was better not to dwell. In Kingston, a woman in the hotel, a real gossip-monger, had warmed to the subject of the sinking of a pleasure cruiser called *The SS Prinzessin Victoria Luise* at the entrance to Kingston Harbour in 1906 – a place that was itself riddled with corruption, intrigue and various forms of skullduggery, or so the woman claimed. The Captain of *The Prinzessin Victoria Luise* had got his lighthouses mixed up, she said. The ship crashed on the rocks and was a write-off, but everyone survived except the Captain himself who was so mortified by his mistake that he killed himself. And then they would soon reach the anniversary of the cataclysmic *Titanic* disaster that had killed so many, and so many more, so Maud had noticed at the time, steerage than first-class passengers.

On the deck of her own steamship, Maud finished *Women's Work and Wages* with its stirring final condemnation of an industrial system based on the profit motive. How can the fortunate ones among us be content to enjoy a comfort and luxury that rests on the hard and monotonous work of millions of people? it asked. Well, there was no answer to that. Maud passed hurriedly to another tome whose moral message would be, she hoped, further from home. The American reformer, Jane Addams, had recently published a book called *A New Conscience and an Ancient Evil*. Maud wanted to read it for two reasons. The first was because its subject was white slavery, 'the sexual commerce…wherein the chastity of women is bought and sold'. Miss Addams wrote stirringly of the cases that had brought the White Slave

Traffic Act in the USA successfully before Congress in 1910; cases such as that of Marie, the daughter of a Breton stonemason, who had worked as a drudge in a Parisian household from the age of twelve, and who was lured away to America by the promise of a theatrical career, ending up instead as a resident in a Chicago brothel. The second reason for Maud's interest in the book was the author herself. Jane Addams had founded a world-famous Settlement in Chicago called Hull-House, a centre for community action, research and reform. Maud was going to visit Hull-House.

From time to time she turned over Jane Addams' book on prostitution and rested it on her lap, allowing her own gaze to fall again on the calming surface of the ocean. Miss Addams, she knew, was in Egypt now, with her friend Mary Rozet Smith. They might at this very moment be watching processions of Egyptian women filling their vases from the waters of the Nile and bearing them back to the parched fields they relied on to feed their children. Maud knew of Jane Addams' whereabouts because she'd exchanged letters with a colleague of Miss Addams, a woman called Edith Abbott, an economist, who lived in Hull-House. Maud had already met Edith at LSE when both women had been studying methods of social investigation with Beatrice and Sidney Webb. Maud had written to Edith to say that she planned to spend a few days in America on her way back to England from Jamaica. 'You must come and visit us in Hull-House,' Edith had replied immediately. 'There are so many remarkable and interesting people in Chicago just now that you must meet. It is a pity that Miss Addams won't be here, but the rest of us will do our best to entertain you. And you will have a chance to see our great experiment in community living as it really is.'

Beatrice Webb had thoroughly approved of Maud's plan to see Hull-House for herself, although she'd warned Maud that a visit there might not be a wholly pleasurable experience. She and Sidney had been to Hull-House fourteen years earlier when it had still been in its infancy. 'The smell, my dear, the smell!' Beatrice had exclaimed, reaching for one of her cigarettes, as if to erase by smoking out any abiding scents of Hull-House. 'The refuse on the streets is really an excellent advertisement for the advantages of effective municipal government,' Beatrice had mused. 'I told Miss Addams as much. She had to take the official position of refuse collector for the Ward, you know, just in order to get something done about it. And the food at her establishment – well, I shall leave you to discover that for yourself.' Beatrice had allowed herself a slight smile, drawing heavily on her cigarette. Maud told Beatrice that she wasn't going for the food – she imagined there would be quite enough of that on her ocean travels – and she thought the smell of what Americans call 'garbage' was quite survivable, and indeed a small price to pay for the privilege of meeting an assembly of such impressive and spirited reformers as were rumoured to be associated with Hull-House.

It had been arranged that Maud would be met at the port-side in New York by someone from another Settlement House run by a friend of Hull-House, a Miss Lillian Wald. Miss Wald and Miss Addams were part of a core group of reformers bent on overturning the refusal of both federal and state governments to pay any attention to the problems of the poor, especially in large, congested cities such as

New York and Chicago. Maud found all this breathtakingly exciting. It seemed that America was completely populated with Settlement Houses set up by campaigning women who were determined to change their worlds for the better on the basis of gathering facts about what was wrong and why. She really identified with this emphasis on facts. It was what had driven her own modest investigation into what actually lay behind the saccharine image of rural life. But, while Maud had the Webbs to rely on, and the members of the Fabian Women's Group, and other cognate souls circulating in the buzzing spaces of the LSE and the silent ones of the British Museum Reading Room, it seemed that these American women possessed a whole enormous network spread out right across the country. The members of the network shared the conviction, voiced by Marie Cécile Matheson and her co-authors, that the motive of private profit would never guarantee the right standard of living for all. There needed to be legislation, and a government concern with the state of the people's welfare. Maud had read Karl Marx's *Capital* and she'd met his daughter, Eleanor, a wild-haired socialist herself, in the British Museum Reading Room, but she wasn't entirely comfortable with the language of class warfare. She felt that a gentler and more conciliatory approach would be more productive.

Life on board *The SS Prinz August Wilhelm* was regulated with military-style precision with much attention given to the ritual of mealtimes. Maud made sure she walked around the decks for at least half an hour a day in order to draw off the superfluity of food. During these ambulations she noticed a small coterie of young women who had boarded the ship when it had docked briefly in

Santiago. Most of them looked well under twenty, and, while they weren't fashionably dressed, they were markedly becoming with rich dark hair and eager eyes, and an excited, nervous way of moving. Twice a day, before luncheon and again before dinner, they paraded round the ship. At intervals they would be goaded on by a rotund fellow in an expensive well-cut suit who sported a small, groomed beard. He addressed them, not especially kindly, Maud thought, in another language, with remonstrations that induced physical clustering, a clutching of arms, like a band of frightened kittens. Maud watched, and wondered, and the girls watched and possibly wondered back, and none of this escaped the attention of the man who seemed to be in charge of them. His eyes, deep-set and very dark, alighted on Maud as she sat on her deckchair with her book on her lap.

As the ship approached the end of its voyage, there came an announcement over the loudspeaker system – so loud that you had to block your ears – of their impending arrival at the port-side in New York. Maud, infused with anticipation of the socially improving wonders that awaited her in the New World, unwrapped herself from her blanket and rose to walk round the deck nearer to the front of the ship from where she could examine the famous skyline emerging through the chilly mist of this January day. It was quite in tune with her thoughts that her eyes would fasten on the immense Lady with the torch and the crown of spikes, the Statue of Liberty, she who had promised to care for the huddled masses yearning to breathe free. The Lady was bigger and greener than Maud had expected, and she seemed unaware of her broken promise. If what Maud had heard about America was true, many of those masses were still yearning, and some were actually finding themselves locked in new forms of bondage.

She watched keenly as the passengers disembarked at the East River Pier and were either processed directly through Customs, or were borne off on ferries to the notorious Ellis Island where, she suspected, they would be subjected to an altogether lengthier and crueller process of interrogation. Maud located her trunk and experienced a brief and quite satisfactory interview with the Customs Officer. There were a couple of women in plain grey dresses and coats and sombre hats waiting the other side of the Customs barrier with a placard that said, 'Here to help keep women and girls safe, please come and speak to us'. As Maud scanned the crowd for a placard bearing her name, she saw the man with the girls from the boat again. He had one foot on a large cabin trunk, an elegant piece of equipment with leather straps, while the girls, chattering excitedly, shared between them an array of brightly coloured cloth bags. A large family with a straggling band of children then obscured her view and, once they had passed, her attention was instantly taken by the driver from Miss Wald's Settlement who had come to take her there for the few hours that separated the arrival of the boat and the train she would take to Chicago.

It was only a five-minute car ride along the wide grey Hudson River. Maud felt suddenly very weary and anxious about the next few days. She'd spent so much time on her own since she'd left England, at first recuperating from overwork, then quietly reading her various books, and considering her future. It was really a question of deciding either to work with Jimmy Mallon and others like him on helping poorly paid workers to unionise and so improve their lot in life, or pursuing this question of the trafficking of women and girls. One thing she was sure of – she'd finished with studies of rural life. The reception the villagers of Corsley had afforded her book could still, five years on, ignite fires of anger and distress within her. For she had done nothing but report the truth. What right had the villagers, albeit as the living beings behind her statistics, to dispute the veracity of hard-gleaned sociological evidence? Maud would undoubtedly have chosen a full blown career as a social investigator, but such a career was not yet in existence, if it ever would be. To become a doctor or a lawyer or a teacher or follow a military career – hardly an option for women – was one thing. To dabble in this new science of society was another. Maud's family disapproved both of its newness and of her audacity in wishing to take it up. She ought to be a wife and mother. She should live, pleasantly and uncomplainingly, in that station of life appropriate to the history and means she'd inherited from her fortunate family.

Maud grasped the brooch at the neck of her dress nervously as the worn-looking Benz car driven by a polite Italian took an abrupt left turn away from the river towards Henry Street and Miss Wald's Settlement House. 'Here we are, Miss,' he announced a few minutes later, drawing up outside a handsome terrace of redbrick houses with steps leading up to bright white doors. Her trunk and her cabin bag were unloaded. She had bought some packets of Blue Mountain coffee and bars of goat's milk soap in the gay Jubilee market in Kingston as presents for her American hosts, both here and later in Chicago. Miss Wald, a woman of comfortable proportions with sympathetic brown eyes and a welcoming smile, emerged from the back of the Henry Street house and proved to be kindness itself, offering Maud the tea she thought would immediately be needed by an English visitor. She'd arranged a light early lunch so Maud would be able to meet some of the other enterprising women associated with the work of her Settlement. The meal was plain – cold cuts and salad – but it was served round a grand oval mahogany table laid with fine silverware and small vases of flowers. Maud was too overcome to eat much.

The conversation, oh the conversation! It was such that she had never heard before. They talked of Associations for the Advancement of Colored People and Public Health, of the new government Children's Bureau, about a trade union league for women, about children's playgrounds, about summer camps for children, about plans for a neighbourhood theatre. Miss Wald told Maud that she had raised money for the Settlement by asking rich community leaders the simple question, 'Have you ever seen a starving child cry?' Her own chief interest lay in public health nursing. She had many stories to relay of the Settlement's work, especially among the Italian immigrants who lived in the streets nearby. Maud listened attentively. 'We older Americans have a great deal to learn from our new neighbours,' explained Miss Wald. 'Their traditions and values can only enrich our country and expand the meaning of our democracy.'

Maud nodded at these moving words, thinking sadly of the Lady with the torch's broken promise.

Miss Mabel Kittredge was there, a specialist in household management, sitting next to Miss Wald, and Miss Dock, who had mobilised women of all nationalities in the community – Russians, Italians, Irish and American – for the female suffrage campaign. Miss Wald's special friend, Miss Helen Arthur, a theatre manager and lawyer, was seated next to Maud. Miss Wald called them all her 'family'. They talked of Miss Addams, away journeying in Egypt, and of how there was a great friendship between her and Miss Wald, and how Miss Addams had accomplished such magnificent feats in the dreadful district of the Chicago stockyards, much more dreadful than the ordinarily littered streets surrounding the Henry Street Settlement.

'But you will see it all for yourself tomorrow,' said Miss Wald to Maud.

Maud asked her delicately about the problem of prostitution among young women. Miss Wald replied that the circumstances of family life in places like the Lower East Side were often such that it took little to persuade some young women to fall for the exaggerated promises of those who sought to profit from the use of women's bodies. 'But we have never known a case among the young women whose families are associated with the Settlement,' she declared proudly.

Maud mentioned the group she had observed on the boat. 'I didn't like the look of that fellow at all. But I did nothing,' she reflected, as much to herself as to Miss Wald. 'Perhaps I should have asked the young women where they were going? I should have offered to help.' Now she thought back on the scenes she'd witnessed it seemed to her that, as much as she had been observing them, the man, in particular, had been observing her, scrutinising her appearance all the better to remember it.

She tried to push the feeling of unease away and focus

instead on the tremendous warmth and courage of these Settlement women in combating the dreadful conditions that faced all too many people in this land of liberty. She felt almost more at home here than she did with her friends in England. Perhaps her future lay here? Perhaps this was just what was needed to make her feel more optimistic and settled about the future.

25 What Alice thinks happened to Maud

2 To Hull-House

Her hours in New York were over all too soon, and the Italian driver, together with Miss Wald, took Maud and her luggage to Grand Central Station for the Chicago train. The journey would be a long one. Maud had been able to reserve what was called a 'roomette'; it housed a berth on which she could lie down, so she rested for most of the journey. Once, when she travelled down the corridor in search of a toilet, she passed a compartment in which a man sitting by the window reading a newspaper resembled the well-suited and bearded one she'd seen on the boat and in the Customs Hall. There was no sign of the chattering young women, however, so perhaps she was mistaken. And there were three other similar-looking men in the same compartment. Maud hurried on, and the next time she needed a toilet she walked the other way down the corridor.

In her roomette, Maud also made notes about her visit to Henry Street and wrote a letter to Miss Wald thanking her for her hospitality and for the loan of two chapters of her book about the Settlement on Henry Street. These chapters were carbon copies, and so rather faint. One chapter was called 'Children who work' and it contained many heart-rending stories: Sammie, for instance, a white-faced little boy who sold papers in front of a big hotel every night and who caught a cold and died.

LaSalle Street Station in Chicago was a very modern spacious building topped by twelve stories of offices. The station itself was absolutely magnificent. Maud stood on its streamlined concourse marvelling and quite forgetting her purpose in travelling there. Fortunately, the woman who'd come to meet her was assiduous in her scrutiny of all incoming passengers. 'Maud, my dear, how wonderful to see you again!' Maud remembered Edith Abbott as reserved and given to brusqueness and so was a little taken aback by this effusive greeting. It was a nice contrast with the weather outside: frozen banks of snow on what Maud had already learnt to call 'sidewalks', and then, as she and Miss Abbott drove down them in Miss Abbott's old Ford to Hull-House on Halsted Street, a fresh fall of snow that caused large crystals to dance before their eyes.

In the car Maud and Edith reminisced about their time at LSE and their shared admiration for the Webbs, particularly for Beatrice, with her attention to the principles of systematic scientific study and her dedication to a professional life. But not all their meetings had been serious. With Maud, Edith had explored the green reaches of Hampstead Heath and enjoyed views of London from the deck of a steamboat careering down the Thames. Today she was serious about the plans for the days ahead. Tonight there would be a suffrage meeting. Tomorrow there would be a luncheon with members of the Women's Trade Union

League, and, after that, a visit to the Chicago fruit market and other famous sights. The next day Maud was invited to spend some time at the School of Civics and Philanthropy, where Edith taught with Dr Sophonisba Breckinridge, one of the first American women to train as a lawyer. Edith wondered whether Maud might like to talk to the School's students about her studies of rural life?

Hull-House stood in the midst of a busy immigrant thoroughfare crowded with tenements and shops, and small trades and businesses of all kinds where the air was nothing like the currents that circulated freely over the cottages and gardens of Wiltshire. The poor families in the Wiltshire village who subsisted on potatoes and onions from the ground they dug by hand, and bacon from the family pig, were better off than those who struggled here to raise enough money for basic necessities. The children in Wiltshire played in the open air contaminated only by ordinary mud and the water from free-flowing streams. Here they played among mounds of decaying garbage, horse manure and the human effluent from non-existent drains, all overlaid by the raw stink of the stockyards where thousands of animals were killed every day in sheds running with blood. As Beatrice Webb had warned, Maud's nose was violently assaulted by the stench. 'People ask how we bear these odours,' remarked Edith, 'and we say it is a free choice for us, but the people who live here have no choice in the matter at all.'

Hull-House was an empire of bustle. People, mostly women, hurried in and out, going to and from meetings and clubs, carrying small children or taking them by the hand, bearing books and piles of papers, or containers of food, and filling the big rooms with animated conversation, exclamation and much laughter. It was a hive of activity, although the Queen Bee herself, Saint Jane as she was sometimes called, was absent. To make up for that, Maud was introduced to a number of women whose names she already knew from her conversations in New York and from her reading. Most were residents at Hull-House, while others had been summoned especially to greet the English visitor.

Shortly after Maud arrived, Edith's sister, Grace, came down from Miss Addams' office where she'd been dealing with the mountains of mail that flooded Hull-House every day. The two sisters were versions of one another, Grace somewhat more practical and serene-looking, with a heavier face, Edith more delicate in appearance and scholarly in outlook. Maud had read of Grace's particular interest in the welfare of immigrant women and girls, and so was anxious to take her on one side and talk to her about the problem of sexual exploitation. And here was Dr Cornelia DeBey dressed in a shirt and tie and a fitted jacket like a man, an austere apparition behind steel-rimmed glasses. Predictably her handshake was forceful. After it, Dr DeBey begged Maud's forgiveness since she must hurry off to visit a family of sick children. Edith told Maud that another doctor, Dr Alice Hamilton, would be joining them later for dinner and the suffrage meeting. Maud knew all about Dr Hamilton's work exposing the medical hazards of industrial processes. Among the stream of casualties that regularly turned up at Hull-House were men, women and children directly injured bv the appalling work they had to do. Dr Hamilton had made a particular study of white lead, a substance used to make enamelled sanitary ware that caused poisoning and paralysis in many of those who worked with it. The men who ran these businesses naturally denied that the work was harmful and that they might be personally liable for the disfigurements it caused.

That first day, Grace Abbott took Maud on a tour of Hull-House showing her the theatre and the nursery for the children of working mothers, with rows of little cots and baths and bright pictures on the walls. The women of Hull-House staunchly believed that children's souls, as well as their bodies, needed to be nourished. Through a long tunnel-like passage Maud was brought to the Labor Museum, a place that demonstrated to visitors the real people behind the manufacture of pottery, linen and furniture. Here were men and women actually working. Maud watched an Irish woman spin, a German potter fashion clay. It reminded her of the workers at the Sweated Industries Exhibition in London. The noise was deafening and not conducive to the conversation Maud wanted to have with Grace.

It was easier once they moved on to the auditorium, a grand place with seats for some three hundred and fifty people who gathered for meetings and lectures on all kinds of social subjects. But they were the only people there now. Outside, the light was fading and the snow was still falling and Maud could see that it was settling on the grimy stench-ridden surfaces. A few children tumbled about, very thinly dressed and shouting to one another. Maud shivered sympathetically. The two women sat down for a few moments at the back of the auditorium.

'Miss Abbott,' Maud began, 'I am so glad to have the opportunity to see all this...all the wonderful work that's being done here at Hull-House. It is in quite a different realm from the Settlement work we have in England. Your sister may have told you about this after the time she spent at our St Hilda's Settlement in the East End of London.' Grace nodded. 'In England,' Maud continued, 'we are giving attention to a topic I know you have much experience of here, and that's the trade in what are called white slaves. I am thinking of making this the subject of my next research.' Now she was sitting here talking about it, Maud realised that she had quite made up her mind to do this.

Grace Abbott thought Maud's idea an excellent one. She said that they badly needed international work on what was clearly an international problem. 'We know that this trade in young girls and women is conducted by networks of men and, sadly, some women. In Chicago we have the notorious club run by the Everleigh sisters. The club made them millionaires, but thankfully it has now been closed down.'

Grace had been working on the subject of the white trade industry for a long time. She paused and tried to breathe slowly and evenly in order to slow the speed at which she was delivering all the information she so much wanted to share with Maud. She told Maud about the Immigrants' Protective League, which had been started in 1908. The League had arranged for the names of girls and women coming on their own from Europe to be passed on by the immigration authorities so that League staff could provide them with welfare services. As Grace spoke, Maud remembered the women with the placard in the arrivals hall at the port. Grace Abbott told Maud that these altruistic ladies were fluent in Greek, Italian, Croatian, Magyar, Norwegian, Polish, Russian, Slovak and

245

Yiddish. They were particularly on the lookout for the baggage handlers who hustled newly arrived young women into expensive cabs and sent them to mixed-sex boarding houses where their downfall would begin. She mentioned the report issued two years previously by a committee that carried out a most detailed investigation of prostitution in the city, an investigation to which she and others associated with Hull-House had submitted evidence. Grace had several copies of the report in her room: Maud might like to take one back to England with her. 'I can't say you will enjoy reading it. None of us find such a distasteful and demoralising subject in any way entertaining, but it is a most valuable study, and you also might learn something from the investigative methods the Commission used that would be useful in any work you plan to do in England.'

Maud asked Grace more questions about research into the transnational aspects of the problem – how the procurers of female bodies in different countries worked together, how they communicated with one another, and how they effected the transport of innocent young women to houses of prostitution. By now the two women had been talking for so long that the only light outside came from the snow. Dinner at Hull-House was at six, and the suffrage meeting would follow at eight. Maud might like to rest for a while or she could accompany Grace to her room and look at various papers and notes about this great social evil. There was some material, Grace thought, that related to a particular group of Jewish men originally from Eastern Europe who operated both in England and the United States. Organised crime syndicates working out of South America, especially the cities of Buenos Aires,

Rosario, Rio de Janeiro, Sao Paulo, Valparaiso and Montevideo, guaranteed a steady supply of young women for the brothels, and the life of a woman in such places was never long, five to ten years at the most. Then they were worn out, dying of venereal disease or a clumsy abortion or typhoid.

By dinner time Maud had transferred to her cabin bag for the steamship journey home quite a bundle of material from Grace Abbott's store. There would be plenty of reading time on the ship. There was none to be had here, as introductions to new faces and extraordinary stories of campaign and reform followed fast on one another. The elegant long panelled dining room with its white marble mantelpiece, elaborate cornices and Spanish wrought-iron chandeliers was a surprise to Maud, just as the grand mahogany table in Henry Street had been, for she had thought of Settlements as sparely furnished places, and had failed to appreciate the emphasis American Settlement women placed on aesthetic nourishment.

She was placed at dinner between Dr Alice Hamilton and Dr Sophonisba Breckinridge, the lawyer and professor of social economy who was a specially intimate friend of Grace Abbott's. Dr Breckinridge had very unruly hair – a thick mop of it was piled dangerously on top of her head – and sparkling, energetic eyes, and she was ready to tell Maud all about the social research department she ran with Edith Abbott at the Chicago School of Civics and Philanthropy. Dr Hamilton, altogether quieter, with a composed face and a distinctive motherly air, had a well-developed sense of humour which she displayed excellently in her story about the typhoid epidemic that had hit Chicago a few years earlier. The area round Hull-House had been the centre of the epidemic, and Dr Hamilton had determined to find out why. She had prowled around the ramshackle tenement houses, noting overflowing outdoor privies and indoor ones with broken plumbing and swarms of flies, and had decided that flies must be the culprits. They were feeding on typhoid-infected excreta and then alighting on food and milk. With others from Hull-House, Dr Hamilton had engaged in the delightful work of collecting flies from filthy privies and kitchens and taking them back to the laboratory for typhoid-testing. The entire episode proved, thought Maud, how wonderfully determined the Hull-House women were to get their hands dirty, both physically and metaphorically, in the cause of scientific research. Dr Hamilton's results – that flies caused the epidemic – were received with great acclaim by the Chicago Medical Society. It was only some time later that Dr Hamilton realised she'd got it all wrong. The true cause was an escape of raw sewage into the water pipes at the local pumping station in West Harrison Street.

'You see,' she remarked, when the friendly laughter around the table had subsided, 'one can become famous for the most nonsensical things. We none of us have any control over how we are remembered.'

Maud took this piece of wisdom with her to the suffrage meeting, which was a most uplifting event. It was chaired by Dr DeBey and several women spoke, including someone called Mrs Margaret Dreier Robins who was head of the Women's Trade Union League. Grace Abbott told her that Mrs Robins was married to the Progressive politician Raymond Robins, whose sister, Elizabeth, had spent much time in England, and had written many 'New Woman' plays and also a book about the white slave trade. Mrs

Robins' subject tonight, addressed in the most self-assured of tones, was the suffrage and women's place in the labour force. In the audience for the event were women from the neighbourhood around Hull-House who sat together in little clusters and were sometimes audibly puzzled by the foreign terms that Mrs Robins used. All the same, they were determined to take in and agree with the whole of the speaker's message.

The hall was crowded and it grew quite warm. Maud felt a flush coming over her as she turned to look at the audience seated behind. Right at the back of the hall, standing close to the last row of seats, was a group of men. There were men scattered throughout the audience, but mostly they were accompanying women. These men were not. The man at their centre seemed more rotund in appearance and overbearing in manner than when she'd last seen him but then her brain was probably suffering from a surfeit of the stories, theories, suspicions and allegations she'd heard since arriving in America. She shook her head to clear it. Seated next to her, Ellen Gates Starr, the gentle artistic woman who had helped Jane Addams found Hull-House, asked her if she was alright, and Maud said yes, but it had been a long day and perhaps she ought to go to bed.

The next day the sun shone, returning Halsted Street and the Nineteenth Ward to their usual griminess. Edith Abbott drove Maud in her rattling old car to the School of Civics and Philanthropy at the University. Miss Abbott wore a hat because 'it was essential to wear hats in front of students'. The journey was terrifying. The other traffic consisted mostly of horses and wagons carrying loads of foodstuffs which added to the compacted layers of filth on the streets. The ground floors of the houses were given over to shops: grocery stores; barber shops with their red and white striped poles; drugstores advertising their wares with coloured glass globes; kosher butcher shops; Chinese laundries; Italian bakeries. This was truly a mixed district that the ladies of Hull-House served so faithfully and so scientifically. Edith pointed out to Maud other establishments called 'saloons' where men went to talk and drink. These, she said, were the main centres of prostitution. Beer and liquor were sold at the front, and women in the back rooms. Maud thought of the public houses at home, in Corsley, that she herself had loitered outside in the interests of social investigation some years before. Perhaps these also harboured such ignoble activities. She chastised herself for not being assiduous enough in her enquiries to discover this.

By now, she was beginning to feel distinctly unwell. She had a headache and her throat hurt. The flush of last night could have been the start of a fever. When her visit to the University was over and Maud had met many interesting students and heard Dr Breckinridge give a lecture on the social and economic position of women, they returned to the Settlement and Maud asked if Dr DeBey might please examine her because she feared she might be sickening with something. Dr DeBey was very professional, taking her pulse and her temperature with a clinical thermometer and applying a stethoscope to her chest. She thought it was nothing more than an ordinary cold that would probably pass in a few days. The stress of travelling had compromised Maud's resistance to infection, Dr DeBey opined.

Unfortunately there was yet more travelling to be done.

That evening, Maud was due to take the long train journey back to New York and from Grand Central Station go directly to the pier where the White Star Line's vessel *The SS Baltic* would be waiting to fill with some two thousand nine hundred passengers for the Atlantic crossing back to England. In her current weakened condition and rather over-excited state – a consequence of her exposure to the fascinating inhabitants and activities of both Henry Street and Hull-House – Maud worried about this journey. Both Edith and Grace now knew about her sightings of the suspicious man in the well-cut suit. It was Grace who came up with the solution for the train ride back to New York. Mrs Lizzie Solomon, who housekept for the Robins family, was due to return to their New York home that very night and so could accompany Maud on the train and ensure that nothing untoward befell her. They would happily pay extra for Mrs Solomon to share a compartment with Maud. Maud offered to pay herself, but the Abbott sisters would have none of it. 'You would do the same for us,' they said.

And so Maud boarded her last American train in the company of a comfortable matron with a large carpet bag and a steady flow of anecdotes about the famous souls she'd had occasion to set her considerate grey eyes on during her many years of service to Mrs Robins and her family. Maud listened for a while, then pleaded tiredness. Her throat was more painful, her eyes hurt and her limbs ached. She slept most of the way. Mrs Solomon was knitting something complicated for her latest grandchild. Before she slept, Maud felt fleetingly glad that they were equipped with knitting needles.

26 What Alice thinks
happened to Maud

3 Final journeys

The Captain of *The SS Baltic*, Joseph Barlow Ranson, greeted the first- and second-class passengers as they stepped aboard. The ship he captained was large and very modern. In her cabin, Maud read the brochure which described its ample ventilation and light, its all-electric cooking and refrigerating apparatus, its electrical device for preventing collisions with other vessels, and its commodious public rooms furnished in dark wood and leather in the manner of the best men's club. It was nothing like the Writers' Club back in London, Maud reflected, but then, as Miss Breckinridge had lectured to her students, women everywhere were treated as second-class citizens.

Maud dosed herself with the tincture Dr DeBey had provided and slept fairly well that night, having arranged with the stewardess to take a warm bath in one of the public bathrooms first. She stayed in bed much of the following day. *The SS Baltic* had a world reputation for its steadiness at sea so in the evening she managed to make it to the dining room. She was pleased to secure a table to herself and took a small meal of grilled plaice and new potatoes. Into the dining-room with her went the copy Grace Abbott had given her of the Chicago Vice Commission's Report on *The Social Evil in Chicago* – four hundred pages of scrupulous facts and hard-hitting recommendations concerning kept women, ice-cream parlours, doubtful hotels, degrading saloons and immoral literature. Most telling in Maud's view was the Commission's computation that the average young woman working in a department store on a wage of six dollars a week couldn't possibly support herself on that amount, hence the temptation of brothels paying twenty-five dollars a week. Of its investigative methods, the Commission wrote: 'Trained expert investigators, both men and women, highly recommended for their efficiency and reliability, were placed in the field. The full results of their findings it is impossible to publish; first, because of their volume, and second, because of their unprintable character.'

The solicitous waiter who served her section of the dining-room asked Maud if she would care for a glass of wine. Might he perhaps suggest a light German Riesling? Maud didn't drink alcohol, knowing it to be the proximate, if not the actual, cause of many undesirable fates, but the conjunction of the present circumstances – the stimulating encounters with the American women reformers, whatever affliction might be coursing through her body, and her underlying nervousness about how she might have unwittingly attracted the attentions of a man or men involved in the very subject she planned to study – made the moment worth marking in some way.

The wine, pale amber and refreshingly cool, was delicious. It passed her lips very easily and had the added advantage of appearing to sooth her raw throat. She raised her eyes from *The Social Evil in Chicago* and surveyed the room more confidently. Almost everyone was with someone. The electric lights glowed and the waiters circulated gracefully between the tables, almost like dancers, she thought. The advertised steadiness of *The SS Baltic* was holding true, giving the impression of a smart hotel. Maud felt surprisingly and momentarily content. This entire trip had been a good notion. It had refreshed her spiritually. It had re-energised her. She reached for her wineglass and returned to the book, coming upon a passage about the 'professional male exploiters' who ran the white slave trade, an enterprise worth fifteen million dollars a year. 'The enemy of woman is man,' declared the Report. 'It is a man and not a woman problem which we face today – commercialised by man – supported by man – the supply of fresh victims furnished by men.'

A group of men passed close by her table on their way out of the room. They were laughing and talking rapidly in a foreign language. Hastily Maud pulled her napkin over the book to hide its title. The one with a beard who was leading the group smiled and shook his head almost imperceptibly from side to side. Maud gave the men a few minutes to get to wherever it was they were going and then rose, feeling distinctly giddy, and retired to her cabin.

She wrote two letters, one to her brother in England and one to Jane Addams. To her brother Maud stressed the value of her few days spent in the United States and the splendid spirit of those philanthropic women, although she knew Martin would be more engaged with descriptions of architecture in which she herself had little interest. She asked him to tell their father that she would be in Corsley after she had attempted to see her Kensington friends who were themselves due to go abroad shortly. To Jane Addams, Maud wrote an altogether different kind of missive. She had found her life's work, she told Miss Addams. She could not bear to allow this horrible exploitation of female bodies to continue undocumented and unchallenged for a moment longer.

The next day Maud felt distinctly worse. She avoided the dining-room and took herself out onto the deck where chairs were arranged facing the ocean, as on *The SS Prinz August Wilhelm*, and attentive stewards danced around with tartan blankets. She lay back and tried to relax. A woman, stout in a green gabardine coat and a hat with curling feathers that Maud thought quite unsuited to life on board, settled herself down in the next chair. She had a friendly face, although a little too heavily made up. The woman introduced herself in an American accent. Her name was Margaret Davies. Of course they exclaimed at the accident of sharing a surname. Mrs Davies was travelling with her husband and son. They'd been visiting her family in Minneapolis and were now returning to their home in Palmers Green in North London. Mrs Davies was ready to converse on any subject: the weather, naturally (fine so far); the service on *The SS Baltic* (very fair, considering the prices they had paid); the political situation in America (most exciting, with the recent election move to the left and the general rise of Progressivist politics); and in Britain (the engagingly alarming militancy of the suffragettes). What did Miss Davies think about the rumour that the British Government was about to throw out the woman suffrage bill yet again? Did Miss

Davies know there was to be a talk on the franchise for women on board tonight? This was quite forward for a ship of the respectable White Star Line, but apparently the Captain's wife was a supporter of the female suffrage movement. The two women on board who were organising the meeting, one a distant cousin of the Captain's wife, were joining Mrs Davies later, so Maud would have an opportunity to meet them.

Mrs Davies then brought forth from her bag a novel she was reading called *The Woman Who Did* by a writer called Grant Allen. Maud knew the book's reputation as somewhat scandalous, but she hadn't read it, and now she didn't need to because Mrs Davies treated her to a summary of the entire plot. Under the influence of her fever, Maud fell into a light sleep, which was interrupted just before luncheon by the two suffrage organisers. Mrs Davies introduced Maud and told them how she had just been visiting women reformers in America. The women were very pleased to meet her and asked if she would speak at their meeting that evening, perhaps about her American trip and about the necessity for social research to inform people about the true condition of women?

'I will if I can,' Maud replied, wanting to be helpful. 'But I am not feeling well.'

On hearing this the women and Mrs Davies fussed over her and insisted she see the ship's doctor. Maud resisted, it was just a cold, she said.

'Do you not agree, dear,' said Mrs Davies, 'that a doctor is in a better position to make that judgement than you are?'

Despite Maud's protests that she had already been examined by a highly competent woman doctor, they led her by the hand to Dr Rosenwald's office on the upper promenade deck. He was a lanky young German physician with, Maud fancied, not much of an interest in the health problems of ageing English spinsters. Mrs Davies stayed with Maud as a chaperone while Dr Rosenwald carried out a cursory examination.

'Pneumonia,' he said. 'You must rest.'

The only treatment was serum therapy but that was expensive and only done in hospitals. Dr Rosenwald looked almost pleased that there was nothing more he could usefully do for her.

Maud managed to shake off the attentions of Mrs Davies and her suffrage friends and she made her way a little unsteadily to the Purser's office to inquire about getting a copy of the passenger list. She wanted to know the names of the men she'd seen the previous night. Was there a seating plan with names for the second-class dining room? she asked. Armed with these sheets of paper Maud was only a little nearer to knowing the truth. She saw her own name on the list, or, rather, the one she had supplied when she boarded the ship, 'Muriel Davies', 'Domestic'. It had seemed prudent to conceal her identity.

Back in the cabin, Maud could now feel the ship moving, lurching from side to side. She held onto the white steel rails of her bed and registered a sickening sensation in her stomach. She lay down, but that was no better. Sweat trickled into the starched bedlinen despite her hands and feet being icy cold. Suddenly she could bear the confinement in the small lurching cabin no longer. She gathered up her shawl and the papers Grace Abbott had given her and made her way up to the lounge which extended the whole width of the ship and was filled with tapestry sofas and oak panelling. At one end was a compact library, and here Maud went to sit at a small table where she could spread the papers out. They contained the raw observations made by the Hull-House women who had aided the Chicago Vice Commission in its investigation. The women had provided detailed notes of interviews with men who ran houses of prostitution, and who were responsible for staffing them with innocent deceived young women.

Maud held firmly onto the sheaf of notes in case the ship resumed its unsteady movements. She felt very much encapsulated in danger, both from the accounts she was reading, which were meticulous and vivid, as the best research observations should be, but also quite horrifying, and from her vulnerable position on an eight-deck liner in the middle of a vast ocean. It might be best to avoid the open deck from now on, she decided, and certainly not go there on her own. She pulled her shawl more tightly around her shoulders. After an hour or so, she thought she had better try to sleep again, as the unhelpful Dr Rosenwald had suggested. Near her exit from the lounge, hidden behind one of the pillars and under the full light of a yellow electric lamp, the men were sitting playing cards. They had glasses of whisky at their elbows and they looked up momentarily as she passed.

After another restless night, Maud complained to Mrs Davies outside on the deck that the ship was full of spies. She reported feeling no better. Mrs Davies said her face had a distinct blue pallor, and Maud could feel her teeth chattering. Mrs Davies summoned a steward and asked for another blanket and a cup of hot tea.

They docked at Queenstown in Ireland for a few hours to offload and take on mail and exchange some passengers for others. Maud was entirely uninterested in admiring the picturesque harbour although other passengers were excitedly exclaiming at the view. She had taken to following Mrs Davies about like a dog, carrying her bag full of professional material about professional male exploiters of women, anxious to keep it about her person lest it should fall into the wrong hands. She asked Mrs Davies for her address in London, telling her that she might need it, that Mrs Davies might be called on as a witness if anything happened to her. Then, thinking about the next and final stage of her journey home, Maud asked if she might go on the boat train from Liverpool to London in the company of Mrs Davies and, if possible, for extra protection, in the same compartment as her husband and son.

This plan was agreed and once on the platform at Liverpool with all their luggage about their feet, Maud gave a porter a shilling to reserve a compartment for them. Mrs Davies chatted away. Where was Maud going? To friends, perhaps? Maud said she had many friends in the city, but she wished now to be quiet and on her own for a while. She felt it was inadvisable to tell anyone of her exact plans. Mrs Davies urged her to stay in a hotel and offered to help her find one but Maud was adamant – she would be fine on her own once Mrs Davies and her family had departed for Palmers Green.

'I hope it won't bring you any trouble,' said Maud anxiously, 'your having been seen travelling with me.'

On the train Mrs Davies resumed her reading of *The Woman Who Did*. Maud was burning hot now, and thought she could still sense the ship moving, but of course it was the motion of the train which was entirely different.

Mrs Davies was sitting by the window in order to get the light fully on the pages of her absorbing book with its tale of one woman's stoical, and ultimately fatal, addiction to independence. Between the two women were their bags, and Maud was next to the door into the corridor. She watched, half-mesmerised, all the people passing up and down the corridor looking for the refreshment car or for the toilet or for their friends or just whiling away the time with gentle exercise. She began to feel that her grip on what was happening around her had loosened, almost to the point where it would be difficult for her to produce any reliable record of it. The comings and goings outside the compartment blended in her mind with those she had witnessed on the American trains. It was all very menacing.

The pain in her chest was quite agonising and the heaviness in her limbs melted them into the upholstery of the railway carriage. She heard the men before she saw them, and when they walked past the compartment they looked in. Others had glanced in but not at all in the same way. Maud turned her head to the side, towards Mrs Davies and *The Woman Who Did* in an effort to become anonymous. When she dared to look back, the men had vanished. A few minutes later, when the train passed Pinner Station, she decided it was time to make her escape. Slipping off her coat, she left it on the seat and hurried to the nearest toilet where she locked the door and stayed for a good few minutes after the train had pulled up at Euston Station and everyone else had disembarked. In her haste to lock the door she caught her finger in the lock, and blood dripped onto the floor and the basin. She bandaged it with a handkerchief from her bag to stop the blood.

Maud's trunk was waiting for her on the platform. She told the nearest porter that she was ill and was going to hospital. There was no time to do anything about her luggage now. It would go to Lost Property probably but it was labelled with her name and address and 'Room 173, SS Baltic', and she would be able to reclaim it later. It would not be sensible to go to her own flat, despite the fact that it was so near the station. She needed really to lose herself in London so that anyone who wanted to claim her for any purpose would find his task impossible.

At Euston Square Underground Station she bought a ticket to High Street Kensington. The friends she wanted to visit lived near there but they had written to say they would most likely have left for their own travels to Scotland. At least High Street Kensington was in a different part of London, and perhaps her friends had decided to delay their departure so she would be able to see them after all. Outside it was cold and raining quite heavily, but the coolness and the wetness was most welcome. Maud's fevered cheeks had acquired a brilliant red hue that other people might notice, just as they might remark how odd it was that she lacked a coat. She still had her hat, though, but the pin had broken so the slightest wind would be liable to remove it from her head.

It was a short journey from Euston Square to High Street Kensington but Maud felt she'd been travelling for practically her whole life. She seated herself close to the doors in a carriage occupied by several peaceful-looking people and one boisterous family. The carriage included a conductor whose responsibility it was to supervise the opening and the closing of the doors. It was four o'clock on a Saturday afternoon in February: the scene was hardly a sinister one. Maud Davies, still clutching close to her chest the observations of keen American investigators into the phenomenon of the white slave trade, fell into a delirium that flawlessly merged fact and fiction. Through her mind travelled the narratives of man-made horror and of women's purity compromised, the habits of men stalking the earth for yet more victims, the shining examples of the new social science in action, the kind, intelligent faces of Miss Wald and the Abbott sisters, Drs Hamilton and DeBey and all the others in that silent movie of sisterhood.

It hurt even more to breathe now and with every breath came a painful tightening right across her chest. When the train stopped at High Street Kensington, she got up and waited for the conductor to move the handle that opened the doors. The family in her carriage stepped off the train just before her and Maud tried to insert herself in their midst so that she wouldn't appear to be what she was, a woman travelling on her own. But when the family left the station, talking loudly about what they would have for tea, sausages or a pork pie perhaps, no further disguise was possible. The rain had slackened. Outside the station was a commotion of considerable proportions. People were striding up and down in the street with placards, and others thronged around shouting loudly and waving their hands in the air. On the pavements, parents clasped their children's hands tightly, urging them to stay back. Guards from the station platform had come up to see what was going on, and to establish whether they might help to calm down the crowd.

Maud returned to the station and purchased a second ticket on the District Line to Notting Hill Gate, just one stop away. She had no special plan now, other than, it seemed, to continue travelling. Matters had been taken out of her hands. Clasping the new ticket, she turned to go back down to the platform, passing underneath the large London Transport sign. The stairs were slippery and her boots didn't have the right soles for this kind of surface. She put her left hand out for the rail to steady herself, and, as she did so, another hand landed on hers, a large one with black hairs on its back and nails that were not so clean. She looked round in terror and a heavily accented voice said, 'I beg your pardon, lady, you dropped your hat'. He held it out to her. She grabbed it from him and went as fast as she could down into the waiting room, slamming the door behind her. The platform was deserted because everyone who might have been on it was occupied with events on the street above. The man pushed in behind her. As he drove something sharp into her, not just once but repeatedly, Maud cried out in terror and pain. Her cries were drowned by the slow rumble of the advancing train playing like a requiem in her ears. She pleaded with him to stop. She shoved in his horrible face her bag that was full of remarks about men just like him who were impervious to women's rights to decide what happens to their bodies. Gathering all her remaining strength, she kicked his legs hard against the wall with the steel toes of her boots. While he was bent over and groaning, she squeezed past him, out onto the grey platform. There was no other form of escape now other than to hold up her skirts, jump down onto the railway line and scuttle, weak and bleeding, away into the dark sanctuary of the tunnel.

Acknowledgements

This is a work of fiction but it contains a true story – the life and death of the early twentieth-century sociologist, Maud Davies. So far as I'm aware everything relating to this story up to Chapter 24, together with much of the detail in the last three chapters, is based on reliable research. For that I have been enormously helped by several people: first and foremost, Robin Oakley, who diligently accompanied me on my geographical travels in Maud-land, and who carried out further research of his own, including into the architecture of country houses, the nomenclature of London streets, train timetables, and the design of stations and trains. For the latter, the London Transport Museum was also most helpful. It was a great pleasure to be shown round Maud's family home in Corsley, Wiltshire, by its current owner.

For the publication of *The Strange Lockdown Life of Alice Henry* I have to thank Alison Shaw of Policy Press who first pointed me in the direction of Linen Press who were brave enough to take on the challenge of bringing it into the light of day. The Director of Linen Press, Lynn Michell, and I, met on Zoom, and rapidly established an entertaining working relationship in which different versions of the text were batted back and forth between rural England, France, and the Outer Hebrides. It was a triumph of communication in troubled times. I owe a great debt of thanks to Lynn for her wisdom, insight, and intolerance of brackets and superfluous punctuation of all kinds.

To my friends, Catherine Cullen, Karen Dunnell, Anne Ingold and Joy Schaverien, who read the manuscript, many thanks for encouraging me to plough on. My granddaughter, Tabitha Oakley-Brown, convinced me that young people as well as old ones might find something of value in the book. And to Robin Oakley, as always, thank you for supporting me and believing in my lockdown project.

Ann Oakley
Rutland, September 2021

9 781919 624846